"You can't write convincingly about any profession without a thorough understanding of its down side, and Marianne Macdonald surely knows the pitfalls of being an antiquarian bookseller. That's what makes her Dido Hoare series so enjoyable . . . Not only will Dido and her young son Ben win you over, but so will her delightful father Barnabas and her young assistant and computer wizard Ernie. Then there are all the details of buying, moving, storing, pricing, and selling a great book collection, which Macdonald describes with authority and humor, making hers the only series of bibliomysteries we've seen, other than Denver author John Dunning's, which truly capture the essence of antiquarian bookselling."

Denver Post

"Atmospheric . . . Macdonald is as good on the antiquarian book trade as Jonathan Gash's Lovejoy is in the antique trade, and her plotting is complex and imaginative."

The Times, London

And the Previous Antiquarian Book Mysteries Featuring DIDO HOARE

GHOST WALK

DEATH'S AUTOGRAPH

"A solid, satisfying mix of amateur and police investigation . . . Highly recommended."
Library Journal

"[A] deftly plotted, cleverly resolved debut . . . Dido proves to be engagingly resilient and resourceful . . . Readers will eagerly anticipate the return of both Dido and her dad."
Publishers Weekly

"Macdonald is dandy at creating a sense of menace from the daily routine gone askew, and Dido and her father are an extremely appealing and affectionate duo. Fine writing done with style and energy."
Booklist

"Dido is fun and Barnabas surprisingly quickwitted . . . [A] clever hot-potato plot."
Alfred Hitchcock Mystery Magazine

"One of the most enjoyable mysteries we've read this year."
Denver Post

Also by Marianne Macdonald

DEATH'S AUTOGRAPH
GHOST WALK

SMOKE SCREEN

MARIANNE MACDONALD

AVON BOOKS
An Imprint of HarperCollins*Publishers*

AVON BOOKS
An Imprint of HarperCollins*Publishers*
10 East 53rd Street
New York, New York 10022-5299

First Avon Books paperback printing: September 2001

A hardcover edition of this book was published in 1999 by Thomas Dunne Books, an imprint of St. Martin's Press, and was first published in Great Britain by Holdder and Stoughton, a division of Hodder Headline PLC.

This book is for my sister, of course.

Acknowledgments

The Templeton house described here is modeled on one which still stands in a certain street in North Oxford, though it has changed ownership and been rebuilt since the years when I used to visit it. On the other hand, the people who live on Campion Road—like all the characters in my books—are purely autobiographical (or, as they usually say, "imaginary").

As always, I would like to thank Eric Korn (ME Korn Books) for advice on book-selling practices generally and current prices in particular. I would like to thank Andrew Korn for his Internet tuition; my sister Sandra for her fierce PR activity; and the people who read the manuscript for me: Eric, Alex Wagstaff, the lady who e-mails me to say, "I do not want to see my name in print anywhere, that is, if you want to taste my apple pie or lasagna," and most especially Andrew, whose editorial skills are exceptional. And last, but not least, thanks to all the readers who have taken the trouble to tell me how much they like Dido and Barnabas, not to mention Mr. Spock.

Contents

SMOKE SCREEN

Her Majesty

In my experience, trouble rarely arrives with a big placard reading "BEWARE!" It usually saunters in through some unexpectedly open door, looking casual, while your thoughts are on something else: minding your own business, making a living, being lectured to by a friend . . .

With most of my attention, I was listening to Jeff saying, "I happen to know that the 1895 American edition of *The Time Machine* takes precedence over the English . . . So will you marry me?"

Ever since I've known him, Jeff has been noticeably married to a strong-minded lady in Wales. I jumped to conclusions and assured him: "I'm listening. I've been hanging on your every word. Only, Her Majesty has come in—I can see her over your shoulder . . . She's looking this way."

Jeff mumbled something that sounded surprisingly like *Oh shit watch my stand* and evaporated through the gap between his bookshelves and mine, vanishing into a group of our fellow antiquarian book dealers who had congregated momentarily in the next aisle.

I replaced my underpriced volume of H. G. Wells on the shelf. Then I pulled it off again, opened the front cover, changed the first digit of the price from a "1" to a "3," and printed "TRUE FIRST—US EDITION TAKES PRECEDENCE OVER ENGLISH" underneath. The Modern First Editions market is full of these little surprises. At least Jeff had made sure that I'd discovered this one before selling the book, rather than embarrassingly afterward. I owed him.

Though I really ought to have known about it. The thought left me with the gloomy suspicion that my professional knowledge was full of holes, that my whole stock probably consisted of wrong editions, that nobody in her or his right mind would have the slightest interest in buying anything from me, and that in short I had no right pretending to be an antiquarian book dealer. The normal paranoia. It was just one thing in a whole mountain of reasons why I wasn't enjoying my weekend.

The Oxford Autumn Book Fair was in its opening hours. We had set up our stands in rows along the hotel ballroom, and by now two hundred bargaining voices were in full clamor. *Dido Hoare—Antiquarian Books and Prints (London)* was represented, as usual, by six slightly rickety folding shelf-units, heavy with books and balancing nervously in vertical pairs. There was also one chair, for which I had to compete with the neighboring stand, and one proprietor: me—only too aware that my back ached from heaving boxes of old books around, that my new red shoes had rubbed a hole in my right heel, and that a double gin and tonic would probably do even more for my morale than a really good sale. Maybe thirty-three is too old to do book fairs? Or maybe it's just that mothering a small baby is the most tiring activity in the universe.

The only reason I was here at all was that I'd been trying to take myself in hand.

The Oxford fairs are usually profitable ones, and a year or two ago I used to enjoy them. The University provides us with hundreds of customers for academic volumes and mid-range collectibles; also the big book dealers in the city use the fairs to refresh their own stock. So I'd booked my stand, though when the form arrived it had taken me a little while to decide. To get up my courage, that is.

The problem was that the fair is held at the Randolph Hotel, a Victorian Gothic edifice in the city center which holds some nasty memories for me. I hadn't been sure that I ever wanted to see it again, but I'd told myself not to be so childish. And at first I'd been too busy buying and selling to brood. Much.

I pretended to be staring with professional satisfaction at my own shelves while I watched Her Majesty's progress out of the corner of my eye. I'd seen her before at these Oxford fairs. There was something ancient and eccentric about her that suggested she might be, say, the wife of a retired don. The nickname was certainly Jeff's invention, and I knew that it wasn't particularly friendly. I tried to remember something I'd heard that would explain his sudden flight. She was his customer though I thought I could remember selling her something, once . . . My anxiety level rose when I realized I hadn't the faintest idea of her real name. Yet it wasn't as though anybody could possibly forget her—a battleship under sail, a stately juggernaut, a chain-smoking, ash-scattering volcano . . .

I got hold of myself.

She was tall, perhaps five feet ten, and her massive

body strained the seams of a tailored blue suit which had been fashionable in the fifties, though its elegance at this moment was modified not just by time, but by a serious dip in the hemline and the cascade of cigarette ash down the front of the jacket. She was obviously in her late sixties, but her pale, heavy-jawed face was topped by a confection of bright red hair which was beginning to escape from pins and spray. The orange lipstick was too bright for her skin, and eye shadow only heightened the lines around her watery blue eyes. Her unhurried course brought her directly to me.

"Miss . . ." she angled a glance at the sign above my shelves, making it obvious that she didn't remember me. I relaxed. ". . . Miss Hoare?" She hesitated and frowned as though something puzzled her. "I was hoping for a word with your neighbor. Is Mr. Dylan about?" The accent was educated, the tones as musical (and carrying) as any opera singer's.

I lied, "I think that he had to go out on business for a moment. I'm minding his stand—can I show you something?"

She frowned down at me from her six-inch height advantage.

I started to babble: "I know Jeff's stock pretty well. What kind of book are you looking for?"

I was being examined from top to toe. Sized up. "Actually . . ." Her voice lowered to a confidential boom. *"Actually, I was hoping to show Mr. Dylan something."*

Her handbag, though small, might just have held a pamphlet or a miniature book. I decided to go along with it, though Jeff's vanishing act probably meant he'd found the lady's previous offerings more trouble than they were worth. "If you want to show me," I said to the looming figure, "I'll make a note of the title and your phone number and get him to ring you when he comes back."

She was still hesitating. Even at the time, I felt that hesitation was a stranger to her.

"It isn't one book," she said at last. "More a library. My late father's collection. I don't want to sell *everything*, but a friend has persuaded me that I really must begin to think about slimming things down, clearing out . . . well, we don't get any younger."

She ground to a halt, leaving me to reconsider. It's quite normal for people to wander into book fairs looking for a dealer to clear out a houseful of books, their own or a relative's. Half the time, you find a pile of dusty paperbacks only good for pulping or passing on to a charity shop; but the other half is more or less worth the trouble. Occasionally you strike a treasure. An old private library in a university city is always worth looking at. Feeling noble, I set about making sure that Jeff wouldn't lose out by his cowardly flight—though a tiny internal voice kept asking just why he had vanished so abruptly.

To drown it out I said loudly, "He'll be disappointed that he missed you. Does he have your phone number? If not, perhaps I'd better take it and he'll ring you later to arrange a time to visit. Do you live in the city?"

The watery eyes fixed on my face: I was being inspected again—was my ability to pass on a telephone number in question? A pin gave way abruptly, and a coil of red hair hovered on the point of utter collapse. Her expression hardened. She snapped open her bag and hooked out a little leather case holding visiting cards. "Mr. Dylan has been to the house before. Please tell him that I now wish to show him some other things." She blinked. "I've seen you here before, haven't I? If for some reason he isn't buying at the moment, perhaps you'd be interested? I shall be at home at tea time. He could ring then."

Feeling strangely as though I'd been run over by a train, I watched her stately departure. She made her way without hesitation down the main aisle, scattering the crowds as she went and pausing only once, under a No Smoking sign, to light a cigarette. I watched fascinated as she looked hard at a nearby stall holder who visibly decided not to protest, and continued without haste through the doorway of the big room, turning toward the lobby.

The engraved card in my hand said that her name was Clare Templeton Forbes. But the really odd thing was I knew the address on her card. I could feel my stomach knot up.

"What did she want?"

I looked up at Jeff slightly breathlessly. "To sell you some books." I held out the card. "She says to phone her at tea time."

Jeff's hand remained firmly by his side. "What else did she say?"

"They're her father's books. She says 'some other things.' You've been to her house before?"

"Um."

I sighed theatrically. "What's wrong?"

"Haven't I told you the story? Old Oxford family? Pre-historic family house? She came around last year . . . Ah—you weren't here that time, were you? She had some books that she wanted to sell, and I went to have a look."

"Rubbish?"

"No. Well, some. Some really good stuff, too. I bought a couple of things."

"But?"

"Well, didn't you see? She's a bloody monster! Everybody in Oxford knows her—all the local dealers. Her father left her his collection of oriental art and travel, and it's all sitting in this ruin where the family lives. She knows all the recent auction prices, and some of it isn't in very good condition. I mean, you have to count the plates: I suspect that she rips out the occasional nice print to sell to a dealer when she has to pay the milk bill. She's twice as tough as old boots, and she's a tease, too. She'll let you get half a look at some lovely stuff, and then she says it isn't for sale."

"I said you'd phone."

Jeff hesitated visibly and muttered about not having much money to spend this month.

I thought again about my fear that the stock on my shelves was boringly familiar to everybody in the trade, especially me. "She invited me to come around if you couldn't." This was a delicate matter. You don't steal your friends' customers—and this wasn't just a customer, this was a private library.

Jeff looked gloomy and remained silent.

I said, "Why don't you just phone her and find out?"

He pulled a face. "Honest, I can't take the hassle. You go and have a look if you like, but don't say I didn't warn you. And hang on to your check book. If you do get something, good luck. I'll eat my words, and you can buy me a drink to wash them down . . . You aren't going, are you?"

I told him that I thought I probably would, though I'd be careful. It's not that I thought he was lying, but I wondered whether Jeff might be a little overwhelmed by Her Majesty. In a business sense, of course. I thought it might be harder for her to bully another woman. Besides, the card said that she lived on Campion Road. I grew up on

Campion Road, though I hadn't been back there since I'd flown home from New York for my mother's funeral. I thought I'd just have a look, for old times. It didn't even occur to me to remember that curiosity killed the cat.

2

Home

By ten past six I was sitting at the wheel of the Citroën, waiting in the queue that was trying to exit from a bleak car park near the bus station and enter Oxford's vehicle-choked one-way system. I'd hit some kind of early Saturday-evening traffic jam, and so it took me nearly ten minutes to get as far as St. Giles.

It had been a cloudy, windy, damp day. Something between rain and a heavy mist had left the pavements slippery, and the air raw. Typical Thames-Valley-October weather. The walls of Balliol College and St. John's and the elegant pale stone of the old houses glimmered in the darkness beyond the street lamps and big trees shedding their last leaves. I joined a stream of cars and double-decker buses inching northwards and concentrated on bullying my way into the right-hand lane for the lights at the top of the road. It took another five minutes to escape into the wide streets north of the University Parks.

Campion is a typical North Oxford street, lined with

sprawling mid-Victorian brick houses in overgrown gardens. The University had built them originally to house respectable married academics while they raised half a dozen children with the assistance of a dedicated wife, a maiden aunt, and three or four domestic servants. It struck me that the original leases had all fallen in years ago. If Clare was still living in a family house, it must be the last in the road. The ones I could see had obviously been converted into student hostels, flats, or overflow accommodation for University departments. The area had changed almost out of recognition, even in the time since my sister Pat and I had grown up here in our shabby home with neighbors we knew on either side and the spare bedrooms rented out to my father's research students.

There was space at the curb outside number 6, so I pulled in, lowered my window and leaned out.

Our house had been refurbished, and the heavy old front door now wore what looked like dark red paint instead of chipped black, with a brass plate that I couldn't decipher in the gloom. There was a light in the second-floor window that had been my bedroom. I almost got out of the car, climbed the steps and rang the bell; but they say you can't go home again. The clock on the dashboard told me I was already ten minutes late. I'd left the engine running. I headed on up the road.

Modernization had passed by number 42. A semi-detached pile, four tall stories high counting the dark semi-basement, it gave the impression of clinging for support to its refurbished twin. Except for the faint light seeping around the drawn curtains in the ground-floor bay, the place looked abandoned: flaking paint, dirty windowpanes and crumbling stonework were half hidden by the faint light from the nearest street lamp. I'd put my money on a

leaking roof and extensive wood-rot both dry and wet.
Whoopee: just the place to find dust-stained, useless trash.

*Dido, you were warned about this. Now look what
you've got yourself into.*

I could just go straight home.

Oh?

All right, I'll have a look. Two minutes.

I dragged myself away from thoughts of my own flat
and its waiting occupants, gritted my teeth, and solved the
problem of parking in the car-lined street by rolling the
Citroën straight into the driveway, over the weeds that were
growing through the gravel, to a spot beside an abandoned-
looking Ford. The stone steps to the front door were crumbling at the edges. I stabbed at the bell without any audible
result and thumped the knocker until the door squeaked
open and my hostess loomed out of the shadows.

"You're just in time for coffee," Clare trilled. "Shut the
door behind you!"

I stepped into an unlit entrance hall with its clutter of
old coats, stacked boxes, and a stepladder leaning against
one wall; the black-and-white Victorian floor tiles clattered loosely under my feet, like shingle on a beach. I had
a panicky feeling that I'd lose Her Majesty in the darkness
unless I stayed close, but once we reached the inner hallway, there was just enough light from a fixture on the wall
by the wide wooden staircase for me to get a quick impression of loosening wallpaper and stair carpet worn
through on the edges of the treads.

A dark-haired man stood on the stairs just above the
half-landing. He was turning away when I looked up, but I
saw him hesitate, glancing over his shoulder, and our
looks crossed before he stepped into the shadows of the
upper floor. Clare was already vanishing into the room

across the passage. I dashed after her before the weighted door had a chance to swing shut in my face.

She had led me into the dining room. At least—it had been a dining room. The central space was still filled by an oak refectory table, its top scarred by heat marks and circular damp stains (as far as anything was visible between the sliding piles of women's magazines, assorted newspapers, two reading lamps, a telephone, an antique portable typewriter, what looked like a year's supply of old letters and bills in ragged piles, and three overflowing glass ashtrays). A smeared plate revealed that baked beans had figured on a recent menu. My stomach rumbled.

"Coffee!" she said again. "The kettle's just boiling."

A battered electric kettle was squealing in the hearth, in front of a prewar gas fire with ceramic elements half lit against the dankness of the big room. Two cups, a very large jar of instant coffee, a packet of white sugar and a battered milk carton occupied a tin tray. Being close enough to read the expiry date on the carton, I said that I took mine black, thanks, with a bit of sugar.

Clare sat herself ponderously in the carver, so close to the gas fire that I could smell her woollen skirt singeing; I slid onto a straight-backed dining chair with a slippery hide seat, which had been squeezed in at a corner of the table with just enough clear space in front of it to let her set down my cup. It was hard to see how anybody could find the space to join my client at her meals.

Perhaps Her Majesty dined in regal solitude. Perhaps the man I'd seen had been a plumber, or she wasn't speaking to her family. She certainly wasn't chatty.

The kettle kept failing to boil.

Right. Well. I reminded myself that I was only here because I hadn't taken what was starting to look like sensible advice from Jeff. I leaned patiently against the unforgiving chair back and used the time to try to identify the books I was here to inspect.

The room, even in the window bay, was crammed with heavy oak furniture: cupboards with carved doors, a rolltop desk so stuffed with papers that it obviously hadn't closed for decades, a sideboard or two, and even an old wardrobe with a coat dangling in one gaping door and what looked like a blanket trailing from the bottom. Clare must be more or less living in this room. A very small television set which balanced on a little carved octagonal table near the window, its wire trailing perilously across the faded oriental carpet, was the only thing in the room that looked less than fifty years old. The yellowing wallpaper was punctuated by framed Victorian steel engravings of mythical scenes. They'd probably hung there since the house was built. I modified that while Clare was scrabbling in the bottom of the coffee jar with a battered silver spoon: the picture over the fireplace was different from the others.

I was looking at an enlarged black-and-white photograph, the only modern picture in the room. Its frame was surrounded by a rim of pale wallpaper, as though it had recently replaced one of the old engravings. It showed a scene in a cafe or bistro. In the foreground, half a dozen figures at a table were caught in the midst of an intense conversation. Two women and four men, dressed in the fashions of forty years ago, were visible in a haze of cigarette smoke. I modified that: the smoke was there, but whoever had copied and enlarged the old photograph had partly masked and faded the edges of the image, so that the nearest figure seemed sharper and clearer than the others. Perhaps that was why I didn't recognize the picture at once.

The foreground figure was a man with a thin face, a small beard, and dark eyes. He leaned gracefully against the back of his chair, legs stretched forward and crossed. His left arm rested on the table; the other lay carelessly along his thigh, but his fist was clenched. He had placed his hat on the table, beside his empty glass, and seemed to be half listening to a conversation as he stared intently at something beyond the frame.

There was something familiar about it.

"A family friend," Clare said. The sense of familiarity faded. "Sugar?" She dumped a hearty spoonful of white grains into my coffee and gave it a stir.

If only I'd gone straight home. I said, "Perhaps I should have a look at those books? I'm not staying in Oxford."

She stared at me over the second cigarette she had lit since my arrival. "You're driving to London tonight?"

I smiled cautiously and confessed, "I have a baby son. I'd like to get back before he goes to sleep."

Clare smiled faintly under her drooping red locks and clattered her cup into the saucer. "Well, then, if you're really . . . they're in the next room."

She pushed against the arms of her chair with both hands to lever herself up, her cigarette stuck precariously to her lower lip. I scrambled out of her way. Outside the door, a dim electric light seemed to switch itself on, and a woman waited for us: a kind of pale copy of Clare, thinner and younger, with dark hair instead of the unlikely red locks. I wondered how long she had been standing just within earshot and whether my hostess had known she was there.

She said, "Mrs. Georgina Laszlo. My daughter."

The dark-haired woman muttered unintelligibly at me

and turned to her mother. "You're going to show her the books?"

"Just a few of your grandpa's, that's all."

I was watching Georgina and saw a shadow cross her face. Someone didn't approve of selling the family heirlooms. But we were already passing through an adjacent doorway into another of the big, dim rooms.

It bore the same relationship to a living room that the other one did to a dining room. True, a rickety standard lamp and two stuffed chairs, with loose covers so faded that it was hard to see any pattern in the chintz, huddled at the far end in front of yet another vast fireplace blocked by an antiquated gas fire. A matching sofa had been shoved into the corner. The rest of the space was lined with bookshelves. A few old brass and carved wood figures of Hindu gods and rearing cobras punctuated the rows, but essentially I stood among old books: thousands of them. Book cases crowded around a big desk and clustered behind a couple of faded tapestry screens. The overwhelming impression was of dust.

There were thousands of them: not paperbacks, not old magazines, not Reader's Digest anthologies or book club editions—books. My heart thumped. Real books with faded spines. Enough to stock a moderately ambitious antiquarian book shop: mine, for instance. How the floor held under their weight I couldn't imagine. I swallowed an exclamation, decided rapidly that I'd better arrange a bank loan on Monday morning, assumed my poker face, and said mildly, "It's going to take me a little while to look at all this." A day, I thought: or better still two.

"Of course you're very welcome to look around," Clare said musically, "but we weren't thinking . . . not all of it . . . I've put a few things on that table under the window . . ."

My bubble of excitement burst. I located the pile she was indicating and picked my way among obscure objects littering the carpet, managing not to collide with anything more delicate than an elephant-foot wastepaper basket.

"Grandpa lived in India for a long time," Georgina remarked unnecessarily behind my back.

The volumes laid out there were mostly mid-nineteenth to turn-of-the-century quartos with engravings or photographs of palaces, Mogul miniatures and ivories. There was one absolutely smashing volume with bright chromolithos of Asiatic birds: a little foxed and dusty, but I reckoned it was all cleanable, and I just happened to remember the price on that item in Wiener's last catalogue. Underneath it were a couple of volumes of Victorian travels and one very familiar natural history title . . .

Mentally I crossed my fingers. For the second time in five minutes, I stopped to take a couple of deep breaths before I said the wrong thing. Then I looked, counted, calculated, stretched and looked around me again. Aside from one small case which appeared to hold mid-twentieth-century hardbacks, some in faded dust jackets, the whole room was full of this old stuff. Oriental art. Travel. Natural history . . .

Oh yes, I wanted it. I even knew just which specialist dealers would take all or part of it off my hands if I wanted a quick profit instead of drawing up eight or ten good catalogues.

The two women settled in the chairs by the fireplace and twisted around, watching every move I made. Suspicious people. I thought hard and made a calculation based on my assessment of the Forbes family and their crumbling house: enough to be a little generous and encourage future dealings, but not to arouse unrealistic expectations. Then I remembered what Jeff had said and stopped to check the bird plates against the index. All present. I named a tactful price and waited for Clare to start the haggling—say by demanding twice the amount.

"Really?" she trilled from the depths of her armchair. "That's splendid! Thank you very much indeed! Would you like a cardboard box for them?"

I was so taken aback that I almost asked whether she was sure it was enough, but I stopped myself in time.

3

Housing Problems

"Forbes?" Barnabas repeated. "*Forbes?* No such people."

"They're at the northern end of the street," I told him reasonably. "Why would you remember them?"

I edged around the playpen that occupied the middle of my sitting room, trying not to spill coffee from the mugs I was carrying. At this point in the morning, the playpen's owner was falling asleep in his cot in the bedroom. I'd made a pot of coffee preparatory to switching on the baby alarm and going downstairs, but at this point on the Monday morning, after a two-day book fair more than fifty miles away with all the driving, packing, lifting and shifting that implies, I was in no hurry to do more of it. It was my first chance to sit down and tell Barnabas about the odd inhabitants of Campion Road.

"Still," my father said firmly, watching me sidle through the narrow passage between the desk and the armchair. Barnabas at seventy-four has no trouble with his memory. He recalls with deadly accuracy all the details of a lifetime in Oxford. "Did you happen to pass the house?"

I knew that he wasn't talking about Clare's anymore. "I stopped outside for a second. It's been redecorated. It looks nice. I think they're using it as a hostel." It was time to change the subject. "Don't you want to see what I got from her? There's a good two-volume *Malay Archipelago*, and a very pretty bird book with lots of plates. Perhaps if you have time you could look that one up for me in last year's *ABPC* or Junk's recent catalogues?"

My father conceded that possibly he could manage that among his other duties, and stared hard at the surface of his coffee, like a man who had something to say.

To be honest, I knew that he was feeling tempted to complain about a number of things other than my frivolous invention of some nonexistent neighbors: the state of this room, for instance. The state of my life.

I live, as I have for the past six years, over my antiquarian book shop, which is tucked around a corner or two off Upper Street. Islington is an up-and-coming—or nowadays you'd definitely have to say an up-and-come—area of North London. My two-story Georgian-style terraced house had been converted, long before I bought the lease, into a ground-floor shop with a flat above it. My living quarters consist of a long room across the front, furnished, during my short and unsatisfactory marriage, with good Victorian pieces from the local secondhand shops; and a similar space at the back divided between a cramped bathroom, a kitchen I can only eat in because I'm small, and a bedroom just large enough for two people in an intimate relationship. A baby in a drop-side cot had not been in the original plans. Although it went without saying that sooner or later I would be going to have to move, Barnabas had recently taken to saying so repeatedly.

Property values in Islington have shot up during the past five years, and most of my capital is sunk in the business, or in a trust fund that Barnabas insisted on my setting up on the grounds that without it I would probably starve in old age. On the other hand, Ben was now ten months old and the owner of enough toys, furniture and clothing to equip a small-sized kindergarten. My daily life had become a struggle to circulate through narrow pathways between toy baskets and settee, clothes airer and playpen.

Which was roughly what had been preoccupying my father ever since he had inserted himself into the tangle. I wasn't sure whether he'd noticed the sleeping bag that I'd bundled out of sight under the writing bureau when he arrived. The simple fact was that my nightly entry into the bedroom had begun to wake Ben up. All right, I was going to work something out, but for the time being I was sleeping on the settee. It wasn't something that I needed to discuss, so I'd tried the subject of Clare Forbes as a distraction.

"Of course, they might have moved in since our time," Barnabas conceded eventually.

Of course they hadn't. Number 42 had obviously been moldering for decades, and I said so. My father sighed and attempted to slide his mug onto the lamp table between unread sections of the Sunday newspaper and a small wooden elephant. I sulked. His own little flat on Crouch Hill, a mile or two north of where we sat, was no tidier. The only difference was that it was his working library of scholarly texts that occupied every flat surface and always threatened to rush like a tidal wave across the sitting room floor, whereas here . . .

I wrenched my eyes away from the mound of laundry waiting on the sideboard for a miracle. "It's a family house. I told you, the books belonged to her father, and she . . ."

"Templeton!" Barnabas snapped. "I don't know where you got the 'Forbes' thing. It was Templeton, of course. I did know them. I knew Fred. Brother. About my age. Clare was his younger sister. Big girl."

I finally remembered the middle name on the visiting card and said, "She married, of course."

"To the contrary," Barnabas said. He cleared his throat. "There was a mysterious infant, but no sign of a husband. Your mother always thought it was rather brave of her: middle-class single mothers were less common in the fifties than nowadays, and there was a kind of unlikely story that she had married some foreigner she met on the Continent, though we never saw him. Clare Templeton . . ."

"Did you know her well?" I had to ask.

Barnabas shrugged.

"And they all lived at number forty-two?" I asked, still angling for information. "I don't remember any of this."

"Fred married during the late fifties and moved out to South Oxford or perhaps Abingdon to run a small haulage company. The girl—Clare, I mean (how could I have forgotten?)—remained at home. The parents died at some point. I can't recall just when. The baby grew up. As they do. It was a girl, I remember that. Rather older than you and Pat, of course. No reason for you to have known her." He hesitated. "I remember . . . it was the most extraordinary thing: the daughter left home when she was about twenty, I suppose, and turned up again with a baby two or three years before we left Campion Road. Called herself Mrs. . . . Mrs. . . ."

"Laszlo."

". . . Laszlo, indeed. She was supposed to have met and married a mysterious Mr Laszlo in France, but there was never any sign of the man, and it seemed to your mother a curious coincidence that her life should have so mirrored Clare's. In fact, your mother once said to me that she was trying to outdo Clare in . . . in 'the exotic life,' I think your mother said. As though it was a competition. However, that is beside the point. Clare and I continued to nod to one another in the street."

I said, "Well, if I can persuade her to show me some more of those books, I'll remember you to her."

"Indeed," said my father. He sounded vague. I waited and watched him: the tall, thin, old man, upright on my sofa, gray eyes inward-looking and preoccupied under a thick shock of white hair. "You say that she still has all those books there?"

"And bits of Indian art. I didn't really have a chance to look, but if I could get the lot, it would be a real treasure." I tried to push down the uneasy memory of Jeff's warning by promising myself that I'd phone him as soon as I had the chance. And the privacy. Maybe there were some more questions I should ask.

Since my father's recovery from his heart attack, we'd become working partners in the antiquarian book business. It had happened almost accidentally. Barnabas had researched and taught English literature at Oxford University until his reluctant retirement, and he knew more about early books than most professional dealers. My own area

is the nineteenth and twentieth centuries, so we comple-
ment each other. Barnabas had fallen into the habit of
turning up to lecture my customers on bibliographical
matters while I was pregnant with Ben. He had taken to
writing entries for my postal catalogues even earlier—and
a single working mother with a small baby needs all the
help she can get. That doesn't mean I always feel happy
about it. I like to run my own life. It's just that doing so
fills thirty to forty hours of every day.

"Let me see what you came up with, then," Barnabas
said suddenly, and we made our way to the front door and
down the stairs.

On Mondays, I never open the shop. That gives me a
chance to catch up with chores. Today I needed to unpack
the books I'd brought back from Oxford and re-shelve
them, checking my weekend's purchases as I went, and
deal with the last few days' mail which had been collect-
ing on my desk.

First things first. I settled at the desk with four catalogues, skimming them hopefully (as you always do) for
an unrecognized treasure. Barnabas was mumbling to
himself as he examined my Oxford purchases at the packing table and made notes. I listened to him with one ear,
and to the baby alarm with the other: and had got to
"Pound" in the catalogue, where I stopped to contemplate
with admiration the price of £750 that David Andrews
was asking for the May 1918 issue of *The Little Review*
("spine chipped, paper tanned") when my father's
"Ahha!" coincided with a noise like a steam whistle from
the speaker of the baby-alarm.

I jumped and dropped a pencil. "What's wrong?"

"Ah-ha, nothing's wrong," Barnabas assured me.
"Rather, ah-ha, these are nice. I can't see any major fault,

and I've just added up this lot to about eight thousand pounds' worth. In short, ah-ha!"

"Ah-ha," I agreed, weak with relief and realizing that I'd been expecting the worst ever since I'd handed over my check.

"That baby," Barnabas added: "do you think he's all right?"

Knowing that he was, I said I'd make sure.

Half an hour later, I hung up the phone and joined Ben on the sitting room floor.

"Do?" he inquired, switching attention from his attack on the playpen's bars with a plastic hammer.

"I guess it's all right," I said. "That was Jeff. I told him about Her Majesty. I think he was pissed that everything was OK after all, but he was all right about it." Being a gentleman, he'd even tried to camouflage his annoyance at hearing what he'd turned down. I'd listened to his recital of his own dealings with HM, but it didn't tell me anything that I hadn't already guessed. The thing is: if you buy a book from another bookseller and discover it's faulty, you expect to be able to return it. If you get it from a member of the public, you're stuck. You're the professional: you're supposed to know about these things.

Ben handed me the hammer with an imperious gesture, and I obliged him by doing a little half-hearted banging while I considered. I trusted Barnabas' sharp eye, and if he said that my purchases were all right, then they were.

In which case, (1) I'd made a really good deal, and (2) there was a still better possible deal—the kind of huge, satisfying, once-in-a-decade deal that we all dream of, the one to establish *Dido Hoare—Antiquarian Books and Prints* as a real player in the London trade.

"I need to talk to the bank," I explained. "I'd better get

them to increase my overdraft facility for a while. And I have to get back to Oxford to have a proper look at the rest of those books and persuade Clare to sell them. She needs the money. If it goes well, I'll be able to buy you a pony and send you to university next year."

"DO!" Ben shouted.

I said, "All right, then. But Jeff still doesn't trust her, he says she's crooked and malicious, and Jeff's pretty sharp."

"Shup!" Ben agreed.

"I'll phone her," I said. "Just to let her know I'm interested. Not today: too eager. Tomorrow."

But later that afternoon, when I left Ben and Barnabas resting and descended alone to the shop because I couldn't put off reshelving the books from the Oxford fair, the light on the answering machine was flashing, and there was no mistaking those ringing tones.

"Miss Hoare? Clare Forbes here. Something has come up. Please ring as soon as possible." There was a long pause. When her voice came again, it had modulated to a vibrating stage whisper. *"I wonder, though: could I ask you to keep this confidential? I'll explain when I see you."*

She made it sound like a delicious secret; and whatever treat had "come up," she was intending to share it with me. Confidentially.

I reached for the phone.

4

Confidentially

Daylight in Campion Road revealed all the dilapidation that a damp Saturday evening had only hinted at, right down to the tufts of weed dying in the gutters under the slipping roof slates, and a little pile of stone fragments that had fallen from one of the window sills into the long grass at the side of the bay. I slid the Citroën up behind the resident car and cut my engine.

As he tends to, Barnabas tugged fiercely at his door handle before I had a chance to kill the central locking. I was watching him unfold his lanky body from the passenger seat, staring at the face of the old house. He looked impressed. After a moment he admitted, "You will not often see this kind of thing nowadays—not with North Oxford property prices as they are. Of course, just after the war . . ."

His speech on the theme of Oxford As It Used to Be was abruptly halted by the opening of the door. Clare loomed inside.

I had the chance to watch her for a long moment, because it was Barnabas who held her attention. She had expected me to arrive alone, and at first it seemed that a
second person baffled her. I waited to see doubt, then pleasure at recognizing an old friend . . . Instead, I could have
sworn there was something else: annoyance? alarm? A
moment later, and her expression had smoothed itself into
polite curiosity.

"My father," I said quickly, "and business partner.
Barnabas." It seemed that she still didn't remember him. I
opened my mouth, but Barnabas was clearing his throat,
striding up the flight of broken steps, and taking her hand.
He half turned and threw a glance in my direction, and
then he was nodding, shaking her hand, beaming, and taking charge.

"Mrs. Forbes? Clare? I know that you aren't expecting
me, but I was interested in the books you sold Dido, and at
the last minute I decided I'd take the chance to see the rest,
if you don't mind. And you too, of course, after so long."

She looked at him sharply then, her eyes narrowed, and
suddenly she was holding both his hands in what looked
almost like a feverish grip. "It's Barnabas Hoare! Good
Lord . . . I should say Professor Hoare." She leaned forward heavily, and Barnabas received a warm kiss which
visibly discomposed him, followed by a close look which
I could only describe as flirtatious.

It isn't often that my father is silenced.

We edged our way through the encumbrances of the
entrance hall and into the room with the books.

"Sit!" Clare commanded us both. I suppressed the impulse to bark. "I could make some coffee if . . ."

"We had some just before we set out," I said quickly,
the memory of her coffee-making still very clear.

"You'll stay to eat. No, of course you will. There will be quite enough for six, and I shan't take No for an answer."

Barnabas muttered while I speculated: three of us, and presumably Georgina, left two unknowns. I had the sinking feeling that we were about to be faced by two local book dealers, that Clare had set up a little informal auction. That would fit what Jeff had said. I made up my mind that if this happened I'd walk out. Which would leave my competitors to gather the treasure. Damn!

I heard Clare say, "I beg your pardon?"

I fixed a polite smile on my face and pretended not to understand. Then I noticed Barnabas watching me. I ignored him and got to my feet. While I was trying to decide my moves, I'd better take a closer look at the objects of her scheming. I drifted toward the nearest rank of shelves, digging into my shoulder bag for a pen and notebook.

In daylight, the room looked even more ruinous. The books that covered the walls, on the other hand, were just as tempting as before. Three tall bookcases alternated with the two big windows overlooking the garden jungle. Someone had lined the wall opposite the fireplace with dark wooden shelving from floor to ceiling, and an assortment of smaller bookcases were ranged against the remaining long wall and beside the old-fashioned mahogany desk. One of them was a four-sided rotating library bookcase, an antique of some value in its own right. There were old-fashioned built-in cupboards on either side of the fireplace, and one gaping door hinted at further books stacked inside along with a pile of old magazines. To put it crudely, I had at least five hundred shelf-feet of books to look at, which meant perhaps two days' work if I really had to check the condition of all the important items before I made my offer.

I threw a furtive glance at the others. They ignored me, involved in their dialogue: Do you remember? I was sorry to hear about . . . Before long they were deep in reminiscence, Clare leaning toward my father, engaging in a running description of her brother's funeral. Barnabas appeared deeply absorbed. His presence was going to be much more useful than I'd realized when he had announced, two hours ago, that he was coming with me. I'd thought at the time that he was intending to lunch at the Randolph. I'd doubted whether renewing an old acquaintance would make baked beans an acceptable substitute.

I tried to look attentive to the conversation while I drifted toward the bookcases on the window wall. I needn't have bothered. Clare stopped herself in mid-flow. "But I need to talk to you," she said, as though that was not what she was already doing.

I indicated that she had my utter attention. "You said on the phone that something has happened?"

"Yes." She sighed. "Good news . . . Though I haven't made up my mind yet, not finally, no . . . And so I must insist again: what I tell you is confidential. Perhaps we should talk now, before the others get back. We are alone in the house for the moment."

I went back to my chair, murmuring something about respecting her wishes, and hoping she was going to come to the point.

"I have been offered . . ." she hesitated momentarily and whispered, ". . . a flat." Barnabas looked blank; so did I, probably. "Of course, the lease on this house expired many years ago, but there is a protected tenancy, so the college which owns the freehold is unable to turn me out. And if they attempted to I should certainly go to the newspapers: College Expels Aged Tenant from Family Home,

Old Gentlewoman Turned Onto the Streets . . . Imagine!"
There was more than a hint of relish in her voice.

"But they want the house?" Barnabas prompted her.

Clare giggled. "They've been wanting the house ever
since Father died. Of course I've never paid any attention.
The family solicitors are a *very good* firm."

"And now?" Barnabas prompted her. He leaned forward, looking so sympathetic that I felt an odd pang of
anxiety: just how well *had* Barnabas known Clare in the
old days?

She looked from him to me and back again. "I have to
accept that I am not getting any younger. No, no, though it
is kind of you to say so . . . Nor is the house." She stubbed
out a cigarette in the overflowing glass ashtray at her
elbow. "We have one of those repairing leases, but obviously I couldn't afford renovations on the required scale.
You could say that, in a sense, I am *trapped* here. But you
see, they have made an offer."

"One that you can't refuse," Barnabas mumbled.

She looked at him sharply, hesitated, and reached for
her cigarettes. "The nub of it is that they have offered me
a modern flat, not very far away, at an affordable rental.
They will waive the repairs clause—of course I insisted.
My solicitor advises that I have no option but to accept,
that my life would be a great deal easier . . . It is
small . . ."

"Easy to run?" I said, copying Barnabas' attitude of attentive sympathy.

"Important in later years," Barnabas offered.

Clare stared at him.

"You will need to get rid of a good many things."

Judging by the size of the house and the furniture

crammed into the two rooms I'd seen, that was an under-statement. Though most of it looked as though it would be no loss if she just walked out. As for the books . . .

I assumed a poker face; it struck me that I was going to owe Jeff more than just a drink when I got around to telling him about this business. If it worked out. I crossed my fingers furtively. Of course it would be totally irra-tional for him to resent the deal that he'd insisted on send-ing my way: but only human.

"I shall need a good deal of money to equip the other place and give me the income to cover the rent," Clare agreed cheerfully. "That is, if I go at all, because I've not entirely decided what to do."

I pulled myself together. "I'll be happy to make an offer for the books. I'm sure I can handle the whole collection."

I couldn't keep my eyes from traveling around the dusty corners of the room. In the daylight you could see the damp stains on the wallpaper. And the tattered spider webs blowing in the drafts.

A thump shook the house as the heavy front door was slammed. I could hear voices. Clare was whispering, "They're back. Please: not a word . . ." and as the sitting room door opened she added in her normal tones, "And now we can eat."

Georgina stood in the doorway holding a supermarket shopping bag, and I guessed at a last-minute errand. After a moment's thought she decided to smile at us, but her eyes swiveled to Barnabas. Behind her stood the man from Saturday evening, the man who had been on the stairs—the husband, perhaps? Or a boyfriend?

Clare was purring, "Miss Hoare and her father have both come, you see, and it turns out that Barnabas is a very old friend. Barnabas, do you remember Georgina? Dido, my dear, of course I shall call you Dido because we are old neighbors, Dido, this is Professor Jay Roslin. Professor Roslin is an American. He is staying here for a few months to do his research."

Roslin crossed the carpet. He was a tall man, almost as tall as Barnabas, with longish, dark hair. His hand was tanned and square, and the fingers almost of a length, and his palm felt so warm that for a moment I thought he was running a fever; it made me look at him more closely, and I realized what had seemed strange about his appearance when I had glimpsed him the other night: he was dark except for his eyes, and those were an extraordinarily yellow-green color. It was a moment before he released my hand.

Georgina was saying, "Perhaps we should eat before this ice cream melts?" There was an edge to her voice that made you wonder.

5

Sacrificial Lamb

Somebody—presumably Georgina—had made the dining
table usable. Piles of newspapers still filled the window
end, but the reading lamps, the ancient typewriter, and the
overflowing ashtrays had been banished, and the telephone had joined the electric kettle in the hearth. A
slightly threadbare damask cloth hid the ruined table top.

After all, there were only five of us at the table. Barnabas had been squeezed in between Clare and the stack of
newspapers. She was still monopolizing him, her manner
increasingly flirtatious. Georgina, sitting opposite with an
unexplained empty place setting to her left, appeared to be
paying little attention as she hacked slices of meat and fat
from a thoroughly roasted shoulder of lamb. It took me a
while to see that her eyes kept sliding back to my father's
face. I was reminded of an anxious mother, furtively in-
specting her teenager's new boyfriend. I began to wish
that somebody had offered a drink.

Jay had inserted himself between Clare and me. When

I threw a glance in his direction, I found him looking back. A little feeling I'd almost forgotten, like a tickle, located itself in my rib cage.

I'd sworn off men recently, having finally admitted to myself that I'd packed two fairly destructive mistakes into my recent sex life. Anyway, sensible celibacy is the obvious lifestyle choice for the mother of a small child, as I keep telling myself. I threw him another glance and found him grinning at me. Not a mind-reader?

"Can I pour you some water?"

I cleared my throat, nodded and found myself watching his hands again as he tipped water into my glass, and searched frantically for some polite conversation. The best I could manage was, "Have you been over here for long?"

He looked at me. "I'm on sabbatical. I'll probably stay in Oxford until Christmas. There's enough primary material here to keep me happy for a few months." He glanced deliberately from Clare to Georgina. "I guess you can imagine how I feel about meeting these ladies . . . actually getting to know them in person."

I must have missed something.

Clare noticed. "The professor is writing a critical biography of Georgina's father." Her eyelashes fluttered. "You know—Orrin Forbes, the American poet?"

She gestured vaguely, but I had already turned to the framed enlargement above the fireplace. I'd nearly recognized it on my last visit: Forbes, the young American follower of Eliot and Pound, known as "the last of the Modernists," who had tragically drowned in Italy in the sixties? And of course the picture was a worked-up copy of the well-known Avedon photograph, taken at a cafe in Paris immediately after the war, with Cocteau, Sartre and de Beauvoir. I recognized the faces now. No wonder the thing had seemed familiar! Forbes . . . Georgina's father? I managed to keep myself from staring at her by looking quickly at Barnabas instead. My father was examining the food on his plate as though trying to work out when it had arrived. I followed his example, making quick connections. Those unexplained, modern-looking books in the small bookcase in the other room: not Forbes first editions? I was finding it hard to breathe. I knew that the earliest Forbeses were rare: *very* rare, very much sought after by American collectors. Even examples in only reasonably good condition had been making huge auction prices, and I had the impression that these copies might be almost unopened. And manuscripts? I thought quickly: there had to be manuscript material, nothing else could explain a long stay by an American researcher.

I'd eaten every mouthful of my fatty roast without even noticing. Conversation had picked up, but nobody was mentioning Forbes. Dessert was home-baked apple crumble with vanilla ice cream: pretty good.

We were facing up to Clare's instant coffee when the front door once again emitted its characteristic thud. I watched Georgina and Clare exchange meaningful looks. Georgina stood up stiffly, threw down her napkin, and marched out, banging the dining room door behind her. It was a heavy door, but not solid enough to blot out the sound of voices, one rising in anger and the other mumbling.

Clare looked at the ceiling and said, "It's a difficult age."

Jay laughed and explained, "That's Gina. She's quite a girl."

"My granddaughter," Clare offered dryly. "She specializes in missing school, and meals, I'm afraid."

"She's a clever girl," Jay was grinning, "and pretty. I guess she'll turn out all right."

I turned out of Campion Road intending to head north toward the Marston bypass. It would be busy, now the afternoon traffic was starting to build, but faster that way than driving through the center of Oxford.

"Stop!"

I stood on the brakes and caused a cyclist to swerve around the car, ringing his bell and scowling.

"What's wrong?" I scrutinized the face beside me, and felt a twinge of worry. Barnabas looked pale. My anxiety about his health, about his heart problems, is never very far away. "Do you feel all right?"

"Turn off your engine. I want to say something."

Barnabas had never before revealed an inability to speak over a running engine, but I did as I was told.

"What? Are you all right?"

Barnabas muttered unintelligibly.

"WHAT?"

"I said, I wonder whether that girl was always so crazy?"

"Clare?"

"And the house. The Gothic monstrosity? Those women . . . What was it all about?"

"What?"

Barnabas blew a sigh and said, "Don't pretend you're stupid: what the devil were we doing there? I have rarely spent a more frustrating day."

I bit off the suggestion that if he had been bored it was his own fault for inviting himself along. Because I knew what he meant.

For something like an hour after lunch, we had sat

within yards of what was supposed to be a collection of books that I was supposed to be valuing. They had all sat there, even the tardy and sulking Gina. She had followed us in from the dining room, after refusing to eat anything except a large plate of ice cream, and curled up at one end of the settee, all long hair, heavy boots, and silence.

I'd made two visits to the leaking toilet facilities opposite the front door simply in order to give myself a chance to walk slowly past the little bookcase with the modern books and run my eyes furtively over the top shelves. Now that I'd identified the collection, I could see that it probably included all the early small-press publications. I thought I'd glimpsed the incredibly rare pamphlet publication of Forbes' experimental verse drama, *Black Rimini*. If I wasn't sure, it was because no dealer had seen a copy of that book for about twenty years. I would have killed to pick it up, but I couldn't because Clare made no move to get rid of the others. Impressions are no grounds for planning to buy expensive books. Not in the real world.

Gina had spent the time glowering at all of us, especially her mother; Georgina had reacted by making occasional remarks about the rain driving against the windows to anybody who would respond, mostly Jay Roslin. Clare had reminisced relentlessly, and Roslin gave the impression of making mental records of every anecdote, everything even remotely related to his research. From time to time I had the weird feeling that all three women were watching him.

It was Barnabas who had decided when to give up. Clare, escorting us to the front door, had whispered loudly, "Thank you so much for coming. I will be in touch," and shut us out.

I suggested tentatively, "It was unlucky that . . ."

"Luck," Barnabas remarked heavily, "had nothing to do with our experience. It was planned: all of it. My unexpected presence just gave her an extra excuse. She knew they would all be there—even the bad-tempered grandchild was expected. You were being manipulated."

Jeff's hints and warnings had never been very far from my mind, but I pretended to disagree. "Why would she do that?"

Barnabas shook his head. "Possibly because, as I now recall, she was always a . . ." he glanced at me and censored the description ". . . a tease. Obviously, she is dangling bait to make you eager to close a deal. There is something you are not supposed to notice. When she calls you back you are supposed to be anxious, eager, and uncritical."

I said, after thinking about it, "I am anxious, eager, and pissed off."

Barnabas snorted. "I'd seriously advise you not to go *near* Clare again. Certainly not unless I am with you."

I could feel myself glaring. Silence would be best, at least for a while. I had my own thoughts and impressions to sort out before I started an argument.

"There is one thing," my father said abruptly: "the business about not saying anything to the others . . ."

"Part of her scheme?"

"Not entirely." Barnabas pursed his lips. "Have you considered: if she really does sell up and move herself into some little retirement flat somewhere, where do you suppose the others will go—Georgina and that remarkably unpleasant granddaughter?"

That silenced me for a moment. ". . . Surely she wouldn't."

"Wouldn't she?" Barnabas asked.

We considered the question silently. There is no way to judge the secret motives of a comparative stranger, but her hints, her whispers, certainly might suggest that she was intending to take the money and run, leaving the others to whistle . . . I shook myself out of that speculation and started the engine.

"Where are you going?"

"Home?"

Barnabas consulted his wristwatch. "It isn't four o'clock yet. Phyllis won't be expecting you until six or six-thirty."

Phyllis is my long-suffering sitter. Although she has been working for me for less than ten months, she has discovered that my life is full of accident and seems perfectly able to deal with anything that fate or I hand out.

"We are going to the Randolph for tea. I was able to eat very little of that meal and feel that I need to recover my strength before we face the motorway again."

It was tempting. Perhaps it would be best not to set out on a fifty-mile drive until I had stopped worrying about those three weird women and a pair of green eyes . . .

I gulped and tried to pull myself together, but the little tingle in the rib cage had come back. I dug for the mobile phone in my shoulder bag and said, "Yes, sir" so meekly that I caught my father watching me with raised eyebrows; so I added, "I'll just give Phyllis a ring and make sure it's all right. And you're paying."

6

Bedroom Eyes

An amused voice above my head said, "So I guess you can't come out and have lunch with me?"

I remained squatting inelegantly in front of the Illustrated Books section, where I'd just managed to squeeze two newly purchased volumes of Doré engravings onto the folio shelf. Took a breath. Allowed my eyes to drift upward over a pair of boat shoes, jeans-clad legs, a briefcase, and one of those fluffy zip jackets which are more protection against American frosts than English rain, until I encountered Jay Roslin's eyes.

Can't have lunch? To the contrary, I thought. "To the contrary," I said. He grinned.

I surveyed the five or six customers distributed around the shop. It was nearly noon on the Saturday following the Oxford stand-off, and there was nothing happening here that Barnabas couldn't manage single-handed. The throngs would arrive from about two o'clock onward. Hopefully. It had been raining too hard all morning for me to be sure of any decent trade, though Saturdays are normally the busiest days of our week.

I explained about Barnabas as I was scrambling to my feet. "I'll warn him—he's in the back room, working on the new catalogue. I can take an hour, no problem." I added cautiously, "It's nice of you to drop in. I didn't realize that you knew the address."

He looked at me. "I've been wanting to meet with you. There are things we have to talk about."

I found myself staring at his serious face, and my curiosity moved into overdrive. I said, "Ten seconds," and went to get my raincoat.

Barnabas was at the desk, surrounded by piles of books, making industrious, semi-legible notes on a stack of cards. He didn't look up. "Emissary from Clare?"

"I'm not sure."

He said, "Well, go on, but stay awake."

"Will you be . . . ?"

He snorted.

I found Roslin outside, in the street. He seemed to be examining my window display of nineteenth-century natural history books. For a moment I thought he was staring at the copy of the Indian birds that I'd bought from Clare and propped open in the center of the display. On second glance I wondered.

I stood at his shoulder and waited until his eyes focused on me before I asked, "Something wrong?"

"Wrong? No . . . I just came up to London to look at some manuscripts in the British Library, and I thought I'd better drop in. You don't mind?"

I assured him that I didn't.

"Good. Because there is something I'd like to clear up, if possible. Look: have you bought the Forbes stuff?"

I hesitated, wondering. "No." Or maybe it wasn't that simple. "But I'm certainly interested in it." I chose the words carefully: "She obviously needs the money."

Suddenly he seemed to notice that it was raining. He hunched his shoulders. "Can we go somewhere? I don't know this area. Is there a pub or something?"

"Around the corner in the main road. But it gets a bit noisy on Saturdays, if you want to talk. We could walk over the other way and try there."

He nodded abruptly, and we set off eastward, past the row of little shops and along the Georgian terraces that led to the less trendy reaches of the Essex Road. It was a year or more since I'd gone into the Red Lion, and I was pleased to find it still unaffected by the gentrification of Upper Street, though capable of providing good sandwiches and an acceptable choice of drinks. We settled at a table in the inner recesses.

"This is OK," he said. He looked at me. "I like traditional pubs."

I looked back at him. "Where are you from? We didn't have much chance to talk the other day."

He hesitated. "Colorado originally. Right now, I'm teaching at a little private college in Ohio. I don't suppose you've ever heard of it—Macklin?"

I agreed that I hadn't. "Though I did live in New York for a couple of years. Liberal arts college?"

He nodded. "It's a nice place. Small town, pretty campus, no drugs worth mentioning . . . Safe."

I wondered at his description. "Do you like being there?"

He shrugged. "It's quiet. A good place to live—you know: active church life, good sports facilities with a fair basketball team, close faculty, pretty good library."

"It sounds old-fashioned," I said aloud, and for the first time he laughed.

"It's not Chicago."

I thought it sounded comfortable, as though you could raise a family there, and asked him whether he was married.

He laughed again, and this time I was sure that I caught an echo of bitterness. "Was. Not at the moment. You?"

"Was," I said. "Any children?"

"One boy. You?"

"Me too."

We talked that way through chicken salad sandwiches and a couple of drinks, exchanging the kind of background information that you need to start to know one another. The pub was untraditional enough to provide filter coffee, and it was at that stage that I asked him why he had wanted to know about Clare's books.

When he hesitated, I said carefully, "Judging by the state of the house, she needs to sell them." I'd been enjoying our talk, but she had asked me not to say anything about her plans. Though if Barnabas was right (and he usually was), the embargo probably applied to her own family rather than her lodger.

"That house," he said, cutting to the obvious point. "I keep expecting it to fall on my head. It's a shame, but there you go."

I asked what I'd been wondering: "Where did she meet him? Was Forbes studying at Oxford?"

He shook his head. "I don't know how much you know about Orrin Forbes. He was in the U.S. Army, and he stayed on in Paris at the end of the war. Of course it wasn't the way it had been in the thirties, but he got to know the natives, took some philosophy courses at the Sorbonne—

that sort of thing. He was beginning to publish in the little avant-garde literary magazines that started up again after the war, and in the *Cahiers*. His French was good, and he sort of settled in. He married a minor French film actress, Simone Black. That had finished by the mid-fifties, when he met Clare through the British Council there, where she was working."

"And they married?"

He shrugged. "No, and I don't think Forbes was divorced from Black. Anyhow, she moved herself, Georgina and all the stuff in their apartment back home in nineteen fifty-nine, after he went off to Italy with another lady he'd got involved with."

"So that's where the books come in."

He looked at his coffee cup. "That's where the books come in. All Orrin Forbes' author's copies, presentation copies of work by his literary friends—everything. She wouldn't give him a scrap, said that he'd given them to her. I'd guess that she thought he owed her. I found a letter he wrote to her three years later, pretty heated. I've found a lot of stuff from him in Campion Road, letters that have never been published. Clare says they were reconciled before he died."

"When was that?"

"Sixty-four. He drowned himself. Soutter's biography hints at it, but I know from the letters I've been reading. Nothing to do with Clare: he was a manic depressive, that's obvious. Your traditional mad poet." He ground to a halt, which was just as well because I'd stopped listening.

I was trying to think how to react. Every word Roslin had said only deepened my problem.

Orrin Forbes was a second-rank poet, but he's a collected author nowadays. After the usual decade or so of neglect following his death, he was rediscovered, especially by American university departments and collectors of modern first editions, and his prices have been solid and climbing for the past fifteen years. With manuscript materials of the kind Roslin was hinting at, every research library in the States would be interested in Clare's collection.

But who actually owned it? If Jay's story was accurate, it wasn't at all clear that it was Clare's to sell.

My problem was only complicated by the family books. If she wanted to sell me those, and they were like the ones I'd already bought, I'd be crazy to let them go. I'd have to float a temporary bank loan, but it was all within the bounds of normal business—solid, money-making business I wouldn't abandon without a fight.

That meant handling Her Majesty with kid gloves.

On the other hand, it was starting to look as though that weird lunch in Campion Road was part of some scheme to entice me into paying good money for a mouth-watering stolen collection. Jeff had warned me pretty convincingly that Clare was a con-artist, and an antiquarian book dealer with a reputation for buying stolen property is in ten different kinds of trouble. The more I thought about it, the more I knew I ought to walk away. Or find out the truth.

I watched Roslin fiddle with the handle of his coffee cup, apparently thinking his own thoughts, and asked how long he had been working on Forbes.

"Too long. I did my Ph.D. thesis on *Remember Me*. That's his long autobiographical poem about the aftermath of the war, the one he was writing just before he went to Italy." Roslin shrugged. "Afterward, I edited the *Selected Letters*. That came out six years ago. I was working on a biography, but when Soutter's was announced they canceled my contract. Soutter's book is full of holes, but he mentioned a daughter born in Paris, and I connected that with a couple of references in letters I'd seen at Yale. I guess Soutter had read them too. They gave me the name Clare Templeton, and Oxford, and I decided that I'd try to write the whole story about Forbes, all the things that Soutter had missed including, hopefully, the real background of *Remember Me*. You could have knocked me over with a feather when I turned up to do some detective work and found Orrin's Clare still there after all these years."

"Incredible luck," I agreed absently. And that wasn't the end of the luck. I asked carefully, "Does she have a lot of manuscript material?"

"I've seen quite a bit and there could be more. Some manuscript poems, but mostly letters from Forbes to her, and to Forbes from a lot of people, especially literary and motion picture figures in the States and Europe. You know he got into the movie scene in Paris after he met Cocteau? He hoarded everything."

"And you're writing a new critical biography." I made the final connection: "That is, if you have enough time with the manuscripts."

"I want to make you a proposition." He was speaking quickly and seriously now. "I think she's got some idea in her head—I don't know what her rush is, but there's something going on and Georgina won't tell me about it. I think Clare means to sell the collection even though she promised me . . . The thing is, if you get it, will you give me a month? I'd just want you to let me see everything and photocopy some material for publication. Then I'll take a general description of the collection to the MLA in December. You won't know, but that's a big annual jamboree back home for staff and students in university language departments. So I can guarantee you enough publicity that fifty college libraries will be banging on your door to buy it. I'll work on it here in London, or wherever you say. And I'll do you a short catalog so you know exactly what you've got. What do you think?"

I pretended to be considering the question, because I really wanted to agree. But of course what he didn't realize was that both academic libraries and collectors usually prefer their manuscript purchases to be unpublished. It seemed Jay Roslin was going to lose all his work for a second time, and I've met enough university people through the trade, not to mention my father, to understand what a blow that can be to an academic career. It wasn't fair, of course.

I said evasively, "That's interesting. But . . . well, I'm not as sure as you seem to be that she's going to sell. We haven't even talked about it. She's probably going to ask me to offer for the rest, I hope—the family books. Don't you think she might be intending to keep Forbes' things? They must mean a lot to her."

He leaned back in his chair and looked at me through the cigarette smoke that was drifting across from the next table. After a moment he smiled slightly. "Maybe, but I wouldn't bet on it. I sure hope so."

I said sadly that I hoped so too, and then we were getting to our feet. It was just after one, and the place was beginning to fill up, so I had to strain a little to hear him saying, "Anyway, I'll be in touch." But I wasn't prepared for him to lift my hand suddenly and plant a kiss on my knuckles before we parted. Oh.

7

Books

The clouds sat low over Oxford and drizzled stubbornly. I stood at Clare Forbes' front door with my hand on the knocker, and the image of a yo-yo popped disconcertingly into my head: The idea of Clare jerking my string and sending me bobbing up and down the motorway between London and Oxford. It's a pleasant drive through the Chilterns even in the wet late autumn. It was just that I suddenly felt that no good could possibly come of this.

But a bit of profit had already come, and I have a living to earn.

There had been another message on my answering machine, coincidentally when I returned from having delivered the Indian bird book personally to a specialist bookseller in Bloomsbury. He had just given me two thousand pounds for the volume; and he'd handed over his check so cheerfully that I suspected I could have got three or four hundred more. So when I'd heard Clare's musical tones suggesting that I should pay her an urgent visit, sheer relief ensured that I'd be there. After break-fast, I'd left Ben in the competent hands of Phyllis Digby, and Barnabas in deep consultation with Ernie Weekes and my computer about the design of my autumn catalogue, and driven up the motorway and into what was beginning to feel like my personal parking slot in Clare Forbes' driveway.

I shook myself mentally and reached toward the knocker again. It receded. Clare was already opening the door; she must have been watching for me from the dining room window.

The first thing I saw was that the fluttery, indecisive woman of my last visit had vanished. She wore the blue suit, with her red hair under rigid restraint and her ges-tures brisk. Even before she reached out a hand and al-most pulled me into the house, I knew that something had happened.

"You're early. Good! We need to talk. Will you make an offer for my books?"

I took a deep breath. "I'll need to look at them thor-oughly if I'm going to make you a fair offer, I may not even finish the work today. You are going ahead, then?" She looked at me a little blankly. "Moving, I mean."

She winked. "I've decided. I could be in the flat by the New Year. I expect you'd like to make a start?"

No little chats? No offers of instant coffee? I said, "Yes, I would."

"Take as long as you need to," Clare urged hospitably, leaving me alone in the cluttered sitting room and vanish-ing into the depths of the house.

I said faintly, "I will," but the door had already swung shut behind her. "Just as soon as I can take my jacket off . . ."

Left to myself, I went straight to the small case with Orrin Forbes' books. There were no manuscripts here, they would be stored in some cupboard. I concentrated on what I had.

The oldest items were thin booklets printed on hand-made paper and bound in marbled covers with flaking edges: *The Rock, After the Fire, Fatherland*, published in editions of a hundred or two by small French art presses after the war. So rare I couldn't remember ever having handled a copy in the six or seven years I've been in the business. A copy of the famous, elusive *Black Rimini* of 1949 leaned casually among the rest. Afterward the fading dust jackets of *Songs of a Dead Man*, and *Remember Me*, the Faber *Poems*, and the American collections. They were shelved in order of publication, and appeared untouched. Author's free copies, obviously. Which supported Jay's story that Clare had fled with her lover's books.

I extracted a copy of Forbes' major work, the unfinished poem, *Remember Me*, and opened it curiously. There was no inscription, but I read the dedication: *To C my demon angel* . . . I knew there had been some speculation about the identity of "C"; presumably Roslin was about to reveal the truth to the world, or at least to anybody who still thought that it mattered. I tried, and failed, to picture Her Majesty as the "demon angel" to that young poet in the photograph.

The lowest shelf of the little bookcase held books by other authors, Forbes' friends. Some of them were written by French cinema people whose names were obscure, but I caught the names of Camus and Beauvoir, Cocteau, also Eliot, cummings, Pound, Williams . . . I extracted a copy of *L'Etre et le néant* bound in dark red leather, and gingerly opened its cover. Fading handwriting inscribed the copy to *"notre cher American."* It had been signed by both Sartre and the book's dedicatee, "Castor": Simone de Beauvoir. I exhaled quietly and whispered, *"Bullseye . . ."*

Then I sat on Clare's threadbare oriental rug trying to work out what to do.

I ought to be over the moon.

I *was* over the moon; yes, I was.

Except for the voice in my ear which insisted on pointing out that there was something I still didn't understand about the situation. They were not the kind of books you normally find ignored on somebody's shelf. They were the stuff of auction houses, rich collectors, locked display cabinets in libraries. I edged the Sartre carefully back into place and repressed the impulse to dig out my mobile phone and ask Barnabas for advice.

The one thing I had to believe was that Clare knew what she had. Jeff had described her as someone who understood prices. I leaned back, propped on my hands, and focused on the problem instead of the books: time to see the wood instead of the trees.

Orrin Forbes' collection.

Consider his own books: the posthumous American editions weren't worth more than a few tens of pounds (more likely dollars) each. Add something for provenance, of course. The slim early volumes were another matter, and the presentation copy of Sartre's great work . . . My eyes scurried along the bottom shelves: there were also a Beckett (my heart jumped) . . . a Camus . . . I didn't bother to examine them, not yet.

Clare *knew*. I'd better give her credit for understanding that the best thing she could do was to call in one of the major auction houses. They would have senior staff from Books and Manuscripts knocking at her door within twenty-four hours. *And assuming Clare knew this, why had she sent for me?*

I wanted to talk to Jay Roslin again. She might have said something to him, and he was more likely to tell me the truth. The only sounds were the rain on the window panes and the distant traffic hum from the Banbury Road. I could have been alone in the house. But with just a little luck my American professor would be returning soon from whatever library he was working in, and if I could catch him alone . . .

My familiar internal critic muttered, *Don't touch these. The others are all right, so for goodness' sake make sure you get them! Forget these.*

Oh, good advice. And yet . . . and yet . . .

Clare hadn't actually *told* me that Forbes' books were to be included in the sale.

But she hasn't said that they aren't.

I compromised by scrawling a list of the titles into the back of my notebook. I didn't even touch the books again; I just wanted a record of what was there. The examination could happen tomorrow, after I'd looked up *ABPC* and made a few phone calls to people in the trade. Instinct wouldn't be a safe guide here. The job took me five minutes. Then I turned my back and moved to the far end of the room with my notebook. I wrote a heading, WALL SHELVES OPP. FPLACE, dragged a wooden chair over to the left-hand corner, and climbed up to where I could reach the top shelf.

The first book that I touched dumped a small spider into my hair, along with a teacupful of dust so ancient that it had coagulated.

I climbed down and went over to the door. Out in the street a bunch of people were walking past the house, laughing. For some reason, I felt like calling for help. I remembered that there was a fraying pink hand towel on the rail above the little basin in the lavatory. Armed with that, I returned to my perch and began the process of finding out just what Clare's father had collected during his Indian residence.

When I heard the clock over the fireplace announce five-thirty with an unbeautiful ding, I knew I'd had enough. My thighs ached from climbing on and off the chair; my head and my notebook were stuffed with detail.

Outside the grimy windows darkness had fallen, and it seemed to be raining harder than before. I'd been working for over six hours, barring a twenty-minute break for a cheese sandwich, half a cup of Clare's coffee, and a one-sided discussion of what one might need to buy in order to organize oneself for a new life in a small retirement flat. None of the other residents had appeared. My casual questions elicited the information that Clare's American lodger was "at the library," and presumably it was a school day for the troublesome Gina. Where Georgina was lurking wasn't clear. It occurred to me that she must have a job, since I couldn't imagine even this ramshackle household running on Clare's old age pension.

I wasn't really prepared to talk about Orrin Forbes.

Clare had displayed the unexpected tact to leave me alone to work all afternoon, though I'd been aware for the past three hours that she was ensconced in the dining room; she had propped its door open slightly, and when I emerged in the early afternoon for a visit to the lavatory, I'd caught a glimpse of her sitting at the table in a cloud of cigarette smoke, writing in a pad of blue notepaper. She must have been catching up with years of correspondence, because she was in exactly the same position two hours later.

I yawned until my jaw cracked, decided I'd done more than enough, and stretched my back and shoulders while I tried to assess the situation. I'd circled the whole room, surveying the shelves and examining all the books that looked interesting. I'd been a lot more thorough than usual: at a book fair, I'd rush around this much shelving in half an hour, but at a book fair I wouldn't be buying the whole lot from a dodgy owner. I remembered Jeff's warnings after discovering that a seventeenth-century edition of Peeters' *Views* was missing three plates. After that, I collated every volume that I thought was worth real money. Then I counted the rest and valued them at one nominal pound each. That way, I couldn't lose much if they all turned out to be discards, and I could hope that all my surprises would be pleasant ones.

I'd been working on that system ever since the cheese sandwich.

When I put my head around her door, Clare looked up, finished licking an envelope, then was ready to say, "If you wish, we'd be very happy to have you stay to eat."

I expressed proper gratitude, but reminded her of Ben.

"And how have you got on?"

The time had come. "Are you wanting to sell everything? All the books, pamphlets . . . ?" She raised a quizzical eyebrow, and I said quickly, "I wasn't sure whether the Orrin Forbes should be included . . . the books . . . and of course any related papers or manuscripts, if you have them." Time to be economical with the truth. "I've concentrated on the older books today."

"You're being very thorough," Clare said flatly. She hesitated, and then obviously decided to give me a pale smile. "Orrin's books . . . Well, I . . . yes, I suppose so. They're worth quite a lot, I believe. Professor Roslin says many libraries would like to buy them."

So I'd been right. And there was something in her voice that made me wonder whether this was some kind of test. I thought quickly. I also thought about her claim to ownership. When I was ready for a gamble, I said, "Perhaps you'd like to auction them all in New York? I think that might be best. I can help you to arrange it: Sotheby's or Christie's would do it."

I watched her hesitate.

"Wouldn't it take some time?"

"But," I explained, "you'd probably get more than I could offer." Much more, in fact; though I didn't feel that I needed to be quite that honest.

Clare lit a cigarette from the remains of a previous one and frowned at the little pile of stamped envelopes which was her own day's work. She took a minute before she asked, without looking at me, "What do you think they're worth?"

I told her, perfectly honestly, that I couldn't be sure until I'd examined them, and watched her narrow her eyes behind the fug of tobacco smoke.

"I would be interested in having your estimate. Then I can decide, can't I? Will you be able to do that quickly? I'll need to know soon, time is short."

Even at that instant I had enough sense to hesitate: but one way or the other I was going to do it. Tomorrow? I told her that I couldn't get back to Oxford until the afternoon.

The thud of the front door shook the house like a distant bomb. Clare began the process of heaving herself to her feet. "We'll speak tomorrow, then. Dido, I should tell you that I've already signed documents. A lease." She looked at me with what seemed almost an appeal. "You see . . . you must see that my situation here is impossible. And frankly, I owe a bit of money to various people, including Professor Roslin, so . . ."

She was interrupted by a knock. She mouthed, "That will be him," and called, "Come in!"

I found myself watching the door open with mixed feelings. It's not every man who has the foresight to kiss my hand. I needed to talk to him again, but not here or now. And there were things to work out beforehand.

8

Rain

It might have been bad luck.

Georgina herself had met me at the front door with the news that Clare was in bed with a headache. Then she slipped away, leaving me to amuse myself and worry about the two envelopes I was carrying. One contained what I thought was a fair offer for the Templeton books. The other held a written offer for the Forbes collection with the sum left blank. I still hadn't decided what I was going to do. I wanted to corner Clare in a long, frank conversation. Depending on what I learned or guessed, I'd either finish pricing those particular books or tell her to call in somebody else.

I'd spent the morning squaring my bank manager and getting my new overdraft limit in place.

There was no sign of Her Majesty. At random I picked a book off one of the shelves (a nineteenth-century treatise on temples in Ceylon) and carried it over to the settee to count the plates while I listened to the rain falling softly. It had been a dry, hot summer, and we certainly needed the rain.

Gradually I became aware of two people talking in the hallway. The tone was unmistakable: they were having a blazing row. I identified Georgina's voice, urgent and demanding, and her daughter's sullen, monosyllabic responses.

The Victorians knew how to build houses—none of those paper thin walls and cardboard doors that let you hear every word and snuffle. But whatever was happening by the front door was growing louder. The first words I could actually identify were a kind of hoarse shout from Georgina: "I WON'T HAVE IT! You are barely eighteen, and while you're living under this roof . . ."

The grand parental cliché. I tried to switch off and lose myself in the pictures of the Temple of the Tooth, but the voices, though quieter again, were intrusive. I heard Gina being sulky and stubborn, Georgina's voice turning from angry to placatory.

They had obviously forgotten about me. Had Georgina ever actually *told* Clare I'd arrived? Was I going to spend the rest of my life sitting in this dank room listening to the squeal of the gas fire and waiting for somebody to appear? If the argument hadn't been raging on a spot between me and the car I'd have been tempted to escape, except that of course I wouldn't, not after I'd spent so many hours on this business. I was embarrassingly trapped.

The voices shifted back into top volume.

"You will KEEP AWAY from him! What do you think it has to do with you? He's . . ." Georgina's voice sank into a mumble, and I heard Gina say "No, I won't," very distinctly.

More mumbles. I yawned.

Georgina: "You . . ." Mumble.

Gina, shouting, "I will, then!"

There was a stir as somebody (two bodies?) clattered off upstairs. Silence. I leaned back against a lumpy cushion and tried to focus.

One thing was clear: Clare *had* to sell the books. She needed the money. I was musing about the decaying house when the first drops of water fell: suddenly my forehead was damp, and then rain was falling, a shower that turned into a downpour, filling the air with water, blotting out my view of the shelves and books and pictures, soaking my hair and my clothing. I shivered . . .

"Miss Hoare?" Something brown loomed over me. Georgina, peering down with her colorless eyebrows arched.

Gasping, I scrambled to my feet. "I'm sorry—I fell asleep." I slid a glance at the noisy mantel clock, realized that I'd only been out of it for about ten minutes, and promised myself I'd get home to bed on time for once.

Georgina had cooled down to what I was starting to think of as her normal bland manner. "Mother says would you come upstairs? She's having one of her migraines, but she would like to see you. I hope you don't mind."

In these circumstances minding seemed unreasonable. I followed Georgina out of the room, across the corridor, and up the dusty staircase.

On the half-landing, she pointed into the shadows overhead. "It's the first door on your left. The room right above the dining room. She's waiting for you."

I nodded and edged past, successfully avoided a worn hole in the stair carpet which threatened to catch my toe and catapult me back down, and found myself listening at another heavy oak door. Silence. I glanced back, but

Georgina was already retreating. My mother used to have migraines when I was little, so I tapped gently; on this occasion I must have been too quiet because the silence behind the door was unbroken. Instead, another door banged and there were footsteps downstairs and what sounded like an exclamation.

"Georgina? Listen . . ." It was Jay Roslin's voice, and it had an urgency that made me freeze.

The response was a mutter: "What's wrong?"

"Is she here? Has she seen Clare yet?"

A mumble.

Any inhibitions I might have felt vanished. I froze and listened to the exchange downstairs growing louder as the speakers assumed they were alone.

"Listen, I want to talk to Clare about the archive. I really need to speak to her today."

Mumble.

"But why not?"

"She still isn't feeling well. She might see you this evening if she's feeling better. I'm sorry, I can't . . ."

"But she *has* to!"

Georgina sounded impatient: "She's ill, she doesn't want to see anybody."

"Except Dido Hoare?"

Silence. When I strained my ears I thought I heard movement, but it was perhaps half a minute before Roslin spoke again.

"I'm sorry, I'm just worried. Orrin Forbes' books mean a lot to me. And the manuscripts . . . I just want to get your mother to at least let me photograph those before they go, that's all. Let me talk to her. She won't mind."

There was another silence, then: "I'll ask her. As soon as Miss Hoare leaves her. I promise, I'll try."

"Good girl. Look, when Miss Hoare comes out, can't I go upstairs and just find out how your mother's feeling? Ask if she wants a cup of tea? Maybe I can find out what she's decided to do."

I heard a sound like a pretense at a laugh. "All right, why don't you try? She'll probably tell *you* about it."

Whisper. Silence. After a moment I heard a door close somewhere and the sound of a footstep on the bottom step. I tapped quickly on Clare's door and was opening it and slipping inside while she was still saying, "Is that Dido? Come in, be careful, it's dark . . ."

The master bedroom was dim rather than dark, with thick velour curtains pulled across the windows. There was a strong smell of musk and lavender. I made out the usual clutter of old oak furniture and scattered clothing, and found myself thinking that if anything could reform my own housekeeping it might be Clare's example. She was a mound on top of the double bed, reclining in a pink chenille bath robe with her eyes closed.

A hand fluttered. "So sorry . . . Do . . . sit . . ." She belched.

I found the bedside chair and lowered myself cautiously. "I'm sorry you're ill."

Her voice grew stronger: "Not too bad this time. I shall be all right by the morning. Don't concern yourself, I've been having these for years. The doctor says I drink too much coffee."

I mentioned my mother's migraines, and waited while she stirred. She cleared her throat. "I hope you have good news for me?"

I dug into my handbag, made sure that I had the right envelope, and pushed it into her hand. "I thought you'd want this in writing. It's my offer for all your father's books." I hesitated, but what the hell. "There are five thousand, nine hundred and seventeen on the shelves downstairs. I don't know whether you knew that." My unspoken text was supposed to be that, even if she didn't, I'd counted them carefully. People who sell private libraries often make the assumption that the dealer who is buying won't mind if they extract a few books after getting their check. In this belief, they are wrong.

Clare's eyelids fluttered. "I don't think I can read anything just at the moment. How much . . . ?"

I told her: thirty-eight thousand pounds. Her eyelids fluttered again. We were silent. Eventually I said, "Of course you don't need to make up your mind yet. If you want to have somebody else look at them . . ."

"No, no." Her voice was definitely stronger. "I will accept."

I knew instantly that she'd already had at least one of the Oxford dealers in, whose offer I had just generously surpassed.

Tough.

I took a deep breath and said, "Then there are the Orrin Forbes books." When she didn't respond, I added, "I've been thinking about those quite carefully." Still no answer, but I'd worked out my approach and went on, "According to Professor Roslin, there are manuscripts too, but I haven't seen them. Presumably you're going to keep those?"

I held my breath and waited through another of those long, invalidish silences.

Suddenly there was a glint from under her eyelashes. "I don't think you should assume that."

"Then I'll need to look at them."

"Obviously. I keep the papers locked in the cupboard

beside the fireplace in the dining room. Will you ask Georgina to come up? I shall get her to unlock it for you. Will that be all right?"

Apparently she had said something to Georgina after all. The news was a relief. There was nothing that I could do but agree, though as I let myself out of the darkened room and onto the landing I found myself hoping I was doing the right thing.

What's wrong with me?

Nothing was wrong with me. Though I felt that I didn't want to bump into Jay Roslin just at the moment. But it certainly wasn't *my* fault that Clare was selling up. Whatever I decided wouldn't make any difference to his problem.

I heard my voice say, "Oh, shit," took myself in hand, turned to go downstairs, and ran into a body, all elbows and scratchy bits: Gina. We let out simultaneous gasps, and I was saying, "Sorry! Are you all right?" a fraction of a second before I wondered whether she'd been listening at the door.

She mumbled and turned.

"Wait a minute."

She froze. I stared at her for a minute, but the light on the landing was too dim for me to be able to see her expression. I thought, *Damn the house, why isn't there ever enough light anywhere?* saw the switch on the wall and pressed it: a forty-watt lamp flickered over our head. It was just enough to let me see that she was in a black temper. Apart from that, she was wearing jeans, a heavy anorak and boots, and her hair, since I'd last seen her, had acquired dreadlocks and beads. She still managed to use it to hide most of her face. It was about time for her to be going back to school for the afternoon, but there was something about her expression which made that destination seem unlikely.

Time to mind my own business. "Do you know where your mother is? Her Majes—Clare would like a word with her."

Gina said, "Downstairs," pointed briefly and dashed ahead of me, looking like a stork in flight. I heard her shout, "I'm off" in a voice that was probably audible halfway down Campion Road, and the heavy front door slammed dangerously, leaving me wondering why the house was still standing and whether that had been a normal disagreement for this family. Not that this looked like a very normal family, whatever that is.

There was a window on the landing. I slipped down to it, craned my neck, and located Gina. She was wheeling a bicycle into the road. I watched her stiff back as she set off northward, pedaling furiously. It was still raining. Feeling slightly middle-aged, I distracted myself by descending in search of her mother.

9

A Life

The door that Georgina finally opened, after several sticky attempts, revealed the tidiest space I'd yet seen in this house. I nearly commented, before I remembered that an emotionally battered mother could probably do without my adolescent jokes.

The cupboard had a single shelf. The space beneath it held three old cardboard boxes of various sizes which seemed to be filled with newspaper-wrapped bundles. Curious, I reached in and unwrapped a round shape which emerged as a soup bowl decorated with blue lilies. I looked around me and shuddered. The room was full of cupboards and drawers, and beyond it there was obviously a house full of drawers and cupboards. It would be miraculous if Clare ever got herself moved out of here. The whole place reminded me depressingly of my own flat. Multiplied.

The shelf held not the untidy bundles of papers I had been expecting, but a row of gray box-files labeled in black ink. The first, "1946," was succeeded by single boxes for every year until 1959, the year when Forbes had left Paris. The last box was marked: "1960–1963." It took me only a second to realize that I was looking at Jay Roslin's handiwork. My heart sank.

I leaned hard against the dining table to shift it back a couple of inches and pulled two of the chairs over into a space by the window. That gave me a square of carpet where I could sit crosslegged and pile the boxes around me.

At first I assumed I'd found a huge store of documents, but the 1946 box contained only three items, each enclosed in a clear plastic envelope: two single-sheet letters handwritten on lined paper, and a manuscript of eight handwritten stanzas, thick pen-nib in pale ink on lined paper. The title was "Ballad":

> *Alpha, I am*
> *the worm in the heart of fire*
> *in the sharpness of ice*
> *the melting, moveless earth-center . . .*

I scanned it rapidly, deciphered a couple of handwritten corrections, and concluded that although this juvenilia might interest a scholar, it wasn't going to advance Forbes' reputation much.

The letters both began "Dear Orrie" and were signed "Love, Mom."

I listed the items in my notebook, shut the box, and returned it to the shelf. Then I pulled down "1947."

It wasn't until 1951 that I struck pay dirt. By the spring of that year, Forbes had published *The Rock,* and the correspondence with other writers had started: Jay Roslin's plastic sleeves held a dozen letters from Zukofsky and MacLeish. Through the next few boxes, I followed lines of correspondence with various other American poets, including Ezra Pound writing disjointedly from the mental hospital in Washington, and with the editors at Faber. By now, the letters were about authors and poetry, including his own fifties publications. I could understand why a scholar would be fascinated, and it was all beautifully marketable.

By 1955 or 1956 I was out of my depth. I'd found the typescript of *After the Fire*: a thin bundle of the kind of cheap pulp that newspapers were printed on in those days, with the familiar lines of uneven typing from the machine with the bluish ribbon that Forbes had acquired in the summer of 1950 and used until the end of his life. The handwritten alterations, made with a thick-nibbed fountain pen, in handwriting that was also familiar by now, consisted merely of typographical corrections. This looked suspiciously like Forbes' fair copy prepared for a printer. Still, I knew several American collectors who would be happy enough to buy it. I'd also found a series of short letters from T. S. Eliot, mostly on business matters, and some notes from Wallace Stevens. I'd even found a single undated sheet from Samuel Beckett which merely contained a date, the word "Merci" and his signature, and would probably sell for more than almost anything else in the boxes.

In a funny way, it was disappointing. I'd hoped for manuscripts, preferably unpublished poetry. What I'd found, neatly preserved and labeled, were letters written to him by friends and literary acquaintances, both famous and not-so, and a few scraps of verse all typed on that old machine with the bluish ribbon. They had been identified by labels stuck to the plastic sleeves. Several were labeled things like "early version of 'Cenotaph,' " or "first version of final two stanzas 'Walking in the Auvergne,' " and I tipped my mental hat to Jay Roslin for saving me time and trouble while at the same time feeling unhappy.

The only letters actually written by Forbes were dated after the break-up and addressed to Clare, and as Jay Roslin had already suggested they weren't particularly friendly. The poet hadn't kept copies of his own letters. However, he had corresponded with dozens of important Anglo-American literary figures, and their replies would be just as valuable as anything of his.

Too valuable, of course. I'm not a manuscript specialist, but I could see that Clare would be expecting a sum for the archive that was beyond my limits, despite the cooperative bank manager. I thought of Jeff, but he had made it clear that he wanted nothing to do with any scheme involving Clare Forbes, ever. We were old friends, and I wouldn't pressure him to change his mind.

I drummed my fingers on an empty plastic sleeve lurking at the bottom of the 1959 box until a name popped into my head: Howie Masters. A big, rich, honest bookseller in California whom I've known for a couple of years, and a modern-firsts specialist. I could ask him for advice about Jay Roslin's request to be allowed to photograph the papers. He might even have ideas about the ownership question, and if he liked the look of things I knew he'd offer financial backing. I was already reaching for my mobile phone when it struck me that it was about two a.m. in San Francisco. I had time to find out more before I spoke to him.

I dialed the shop instead. After the phone had rung long

enough for me to start worrying it was answered by my nineteen-year-old part-time computer guru, Ernie Weekes. I reflected that Ernie's telephone manner could do with some polish as he cleared his throat loudly, but he announced "Dido Hoare, Books and Prints" formally enough.

"Ernie, are you getting a cold?"

He obliged me by sneezing into the mouthpiece. I groaned: I could do without being short-staffed just now. We established that, fueled by frequent doses of a lemony cold remedy, he had nearly finished my Christmas catalogue.

"But you got some prices to check," he croaked.

"If I do that tonight," I suggested—who needs sleep?—"can you get it printed out tomorrow?"

Ernie thought that this would happen unless his mother made him stay in bed; Ernie lives with his mother and two younger brothers while he is finishing college, and Mrs. Weekes keeps her sons on a pretty tight rein.

I asked for my father. Ernie was still explaining that he was dealing with a customer when Barnabas arrived and took over.

"Trouble?"

"How did you know?"

"Experience," Barnabas said grimly. "I remember Clare."

"Actually, Clare has a migraine and is being pretty cooperative, though other people have made it a lively day." Not to be described over the phone, though. "Tell you later. She's accepted the offer for her father's books."

Barnabas said, "And?"

"And I'm going to arrange for somebody I know here in Oxford to help me pack, and drive most of it down for me."

"What about . . . ?"

"And I'm still working on the Forbes stuff." I lowered my voice. "There are papers. The ones Professor Roslin is working on."

"What?"

I repeated myself in a slightly louder whisper. "I can't talk now, somebody may come in. But I've had a look through them, and they're pretty good."

"How good?" Barnabas demanded, reasonably.

I hesitated. "Almost certainly six figures. We'll need to take somebody into the deal if we go ahead. The trouble is I'm still not sure. I still think they might not be hers to sell."

There was a silence, broken only by the usual mobile phone noises.

"Have you thought," Barnabas suggested eventually, "that Forbes might have given her the things at some point? He may have decided it wasn't worth the struggle."

"I'll have to ask her. I'll suggest that she tell me exactly how she got the stuff, and see what she says. I may get a feeling for it. Whether she's telling the truth."

"Ideally, you want to find a letter from Orrin Forbes saying, Fine, they're yours, go away." He sounded abstracted. "I wonder whether he made a will? If he died intestate, either Italian or American law might dictate that they belong to this French lady you said he was married to. What happened to her?"

"I'll try to find out. I was thinking that they might belong to Georgina, if she was his only child," I said glumly. I wasn't going to enjoy asking about that.

I told Barnabas I'd see him later and switched him off in the middle of his farewells, because I realized suddenly who might be able to help, and he keeps office hours.

Leonard Stockton is a scary, respectable solicitor with offices about half a mile from my shop, over on Essex Road. A couple of months earlier, when I was in a patch of trouble, he'd put up with my questionable behavior and had even aided and abetted me in some tough negotiations. As a result of which I'd decided that I should have him for my regular solicitor and programmed his telephone number into my mobile. I punched buttons, got his secretary, and persuaded her to put me through. We hadn't been in touch since we'd attended a funeral together, but he sounded glad to hear from me.

I said, "I can't talk easily, I don't want to be overheard."

"How nice of you to phone me, in that case," he replied. I caught a chuckle.

"This is . . . a ranging shot," I laughed. "I have a problem, part legal, part people, if you know what I mean. It's really terribly important for me to talk to you about it. I don't suppose that if I dropped everything and drove from Oxford as fast as possible you'd still be in the office?"

"Sorry, but I have theater tickets." My heart sank. "However, my first appointment in the morning isn't until eight-thirty, so if you'd like to come in for coffee . . . ?"

It was a measure of my desperation that I promised I'd arrive at a quarter to eight. "I may have Ben with me, though," I said doubtfully. In fact, that seemed a certainty. And said goodbye.

There was nothing else for me here, and suddenly I just wanted to get home. I shoved the last three box files back and surveyed the tidy row without much real pleasure. I'd better decide what kind of message to send upstairs. I scowled at the dusty carpet which had rubbed patches of dirt into my pale gray trousers. At the gas fire which was burning my right cheek. At the old dishes stored in the box in the bottom of the cupboard . . . it struck me that they looked like a rather fine china, and I reached in gingerly and pulled the little bowl out again, turned it over, and rubbed some of the grime away. The maker's marks said that it was porcelain from a French factory I'd never heard of. Part of Clare's Paris loot? There were two more boxes crammed into the cupboard, and I wondered suddenly what else they held.

A floorboard creaked, and I shoved the bowl away and pushed the door shut. I was expecting Georgina; but when I scrambled out from below the tabletop, it was Jay Roslin who stood on the other side. He examined my face and grinned. "Your forehead's black. And your nose."

I rubbed my hands on my trousers without thought, and completed their destruction. "I'd better go. I think I need a bath."

He edged around the table and threw a look at the cupboard door. "What do you think of it?"

I hedged. "There are some nice things."

"So she is selling up? Damn it!"

"I think so. I've bought the rest of it—her father's books."

"Well, I'm glad it's you. Good luck with them." The eyes gave absolutely nothing away, and I wasn't prepared for him to lean down and kiss me lightly. "They couldn't go to a nicer lady." He looked at me thoughtfully. "You aren't just going to bundle it all up and vanish from my life, are you?"

I managed to admit that I saw no reason to do that.

"Well." He rubbed a finger down the bridge of my nose, held it up to display the black mark, and smiled.

"Anyway," I said, keeping my voice level, "I'm still

looking at the manuscripts. I wondered if we could talk about those?"

"The archive? Have you bought that too?"

"Not yet." I thought quickly and said, truthfully, "I haven't made up my mind whether I want to handle it."

"Will you be here again?"

"Tomorrow. I'll probably take a car-load of the books back to London, and I'll make arrangements for somebody with a van to do the rest."

"Can you take time off to have lunch with me? There's a great little restaurant up the Banbury Road where I eat sometimes, when I feel like celebrating."

I looked into his eyes and asked casually, "What are you celebrating?"

He looked back and told me, "Perhaps we can talk about it tomorrow."

10

Breathless

When I got to the offices of Wisby Finch, it was just after eight. The parking restrictions wouldn't start for half an hour: I left the Citroën at the curb and staggered across the pavement, carrying Ben with a red wooden dog on wheels. Either he or his toys were getting heavier or I needed a good night's sleep: probably all three. I rang the bell and was buzzed in by the secretary, who knew me by sight and waved me past her door and down the long passageway toward Leonard Stockton's office.

The room was an oasis of peace, elegance, and the smell of newly brewed coffee. I stopped in the doorway and said, "Yes, please."

Stockton looked at me, laughed, and crossed to the electric coffee maker on the walnut side table by the window. "Black?"

I told him, "Milk, no sugar." Ben informed me that he would explore, so I sat him in the middle of the Chinese silk carpet, fell into the visitor's chair, received my cup, and said, "I've got a problem that I don't even begin to know how to deal with. It's probably all lies and international law, and it goes back thirty-five years."

Stockton settled lightly into his desk chair, gave his coffee two precise stirs, and looked at me. He is a little blond man, not much taller than me, with a pale face and gray, intelligent eyes. His dark suit, a solicitor's working uniform, was freshly pressed. If I hadn't discovered, months ago, that he possessed a wicked sense of humor as well as the willingness to stretch a legal point in the cause of fair play, I would probably have felt intimidated. I told him the story and watched him lean against the high back of his chair with his eyes closed, as though he was listening to an inner voice. In about thirty seconds, the voice came up trumps.

"An American citizen, but resident in Italy?"

I assured him that was the case.

"And with a wife who might still be alive, an illegitimate daughter and a possible will."

I sighed.

Stockton laughed. "And you want to settle the legal ownership of this more-or-less pilfered property, presumably without spending a fortune?"

I agreed.

"Right. I'll make a few phone calls this morning. The Italian embassy should have somebody who can give general guidance, and I'll see if I can get anything useful from the Americans in Rome. We do have a contact in a law firm there who could fax us a copy of the will if such a thing was filed in Italy."

"And if it wasn't?"

"If it wasn't, then it's problematic. I'll have to determine whose laws of intestacy apply. Don't worry, I know somebody who will be able to give me an answer. The American professor must know whether the wife is still alive? Did you say there's a recent biography? You might find something in that, if you can locate a copy."

Soutter—that was the name. Library work for Barnabas if he was willing, and I had the feeling he would probably agree. Not to say insist.

"Frankly," he added, "I doubt you should touch this archive, but that's just my suspicious mind. Maybe it's . . ."

There was a jangling crash. Ben, wrapped in the telephone lead, sped off on hands and knees across the expensive carpet pursued by Stockton's telephone, his desk diary, and the contents of a pen holder. Stockton's secretary arrived at the door to find the three of us crawling on the carpet trying to retrieve the pieces. To her credit, she merely announced, "Mr. Thomas is here, and your extension seems to be disconnected."

Back at the flat, I deposited Ben and the wooden dog in the playpen together and leaned back on the settee while I tried to plot my next move, if not my plan for the day. Mr. Spock stalked into the room, paused, sniffed delicately, and landed unhurriedly on my chest, where he stood eyeball to eyeball.

"I forgot to feed you," I agreed. "But you're getting fat, hanging around the house all day just because it's raining."

Spock opened his mouth in a soundless protest, and I tipped him onto the floor and went to open a tin. From the kitchen I could hear Ben experimenting with the noise made by rubbing a wooden toy against something hard. He just failed to drown out the ringing of the telephone. I slung some lumps of meat into Spock's dish and sprinted back to answer Barnabas' morning call.

"You sound breathless," he greeted me.

"I am breathless." Despite the fact that I already knew it was one of those days when everything goes wrong, I assured him that I was under control, or would be when Phyllis Digby arrived to take charge of my son.

"Oh, lord," Barnabas muttered.

I took a deep breath. "What?"

"I can't think how I forgot. Perhaps age is at last rotting my brain? She rang last night, just before you got back. Her husband is coming down with flu, and she wanted you to know that she'd be a little late today. She said an hour or two—she's taking him to the doctor."

Phyllis Digby's husband, whom I'd never met, was a semi-invalid with (I guessed because Phyllis was vague) lung problems, and occasionally this meant she needed to make last-minute changes to her schedule. Normally I could cope with any problem: other days, not today.

"I'm supposed to be going back to Oxford."

"Do you ever feel," Barnabas asked distantly, "as though you might be neglecting the shop?"

I gritted my teeth and reminded him that this was going to be my final visit, unless I could bring myself to ignore Leonard Stockton's doubts, to say nothing of my own, and return for the archive. I didn't mention that I wanted him to go to the British Library that morning to look for the Soutter biography and find out what he could about the end of Forbes' life. Never mind: if he had to cover for me, the library could wait.

"I take it we aren't going to the party?" Barnabas interrupted.

"Party?" I thought frantically and fruitlessly.

"Your nephews' Halloween party? Fireworks, apple-bobbing, childish mayhem? Pat phoned yesterday to remind us."

I held the receiver away from my mouth and did a little quiet cursing: of course I'd forgotten. I noticed Ben watching me with interest and wondered whether I was going to have to change my vocabulary before he started talking. "Barnabas, I forgot."

"Really?"

"Don't be like that. You didn't want to go anyway."

"I know."

"I'll phone Pat," I said grimly.

"You don't have to. I told her yesterday that we were up to your ears in a huge deal that would either make our fortunes forever or tip us into bankruptcy. She wished you luck and remarked that perhaps Ben is a little young for Halloween anyway. It may even have been a relief, as she appears to have invited half a junior school. And by the way, I'll be with you in half an hour."

I said, "Oh. Good." And hung up.

Ben had curled up on the floor of the pen with his dog. For a while I watched his eyes trying not to close; then I switched on the baby alarm and tiptoed down to the shop.

The next hour was full of activity. There was nothing to help me solve my real problem, so I read two booksellers' catalogues, ordered three books by telephone, and finally supplied some missing prices for our own pre-Christmas catalogue. I'd been too tired the night before, and a phone call from Mrs. Weekes had assured me that Ernie was in bed and keeping warm for a day or two, so that I was still ahead of the game. In a flurry of industry I wrote out a couple of checks, stuffed them into envelopes, and paused to wonder why I never had any stamps.

It was just after ten when the rattle of the door reminded me that I'd locked it behind me. I listened at the baby alarm, heard noises which suggested a wakeful but not unhappy son, and decided that I was ready for business. Ready and eager, in fact, with a thirty-eight-thousand-pound check already—I was very certain of this—sliding through bank clearing toward my account.

By ten-thirty I'd slung a heap of empty boxes into the back of the car, left the shop in Barnabas' protection and Ben with the apologetic Phyllis, and was making what speed I could in the outside lane of the Marylebone Road. My mobile rang as I was creeping across the lights at Baker Street.

"Dido?" It was Jay Roslin's voice. "Professor Hoare gave me this number. He says you're on your way."

Already anxious, I said, "I'll be there in about an hour, unless the motorway is jammed up."

"The thing is . . ." the voice was lost for a moment as the car passed some electronic interference ". . . warn you that something's happened."

I forced myself to speak calmly. "What's wrong?"

"It's Gina: she's run away. Or Georgina chucked her out. Or both."

I said stupidly, "Run away?"

"There's been some boy around all fall—long hair and a guitar, and Georgina doesn't like him. She and Gina have been fighting. Anyhow, when she didn't come downstairs for school this morning, Georgina went up and found a note."

"Perhaps I shouldn't come today?" I said doubtfully.

"No, no, Clare says come on anyway, she's anxious to see you. Anyhow, you're coming for your books, aren't you? It's just that things are pretty upset here, and Georgina's in a real state. I guess I've got to hang around, and that means postponing lunch. I'm really sorry about it."

I said I understood.

"So come on, but be ready for tears, OK? Of course the kid's all right. She might even be back by the time you get here."

That seemed a little optimistic: Gina wasn't a little girl, and she must have run away *to* somewhere, presumably to the boy with the guitar. But that wasn't my business. Without commenting, I said, "I'll be there as soon as I can. Tell Clare that of course if I can do anything . . ."

"Sure." His voice broke off for a moment, but then he said again, "Sure. And look, in case I can do anything to help you, I've taken the day off."

I said, "Wear some old clothes, then," and switched off, feeling confused.

I pulled over before Magdalen Bridge to make my own phone call to the man I know who works in one of the smaller Oxford book shops. It was his early closing day, and we'd arranged for him to turn up at Campion Road with a van and his partner, and take my purchases up to London. Considering that everything else I'd organized for the day had somehow gone wrong, I wanted to make sure that this arrangement was still on.

Having done that, I remembered something else. "Richard, there's one thing: weren't you people advertising for a Warren Hastings *Memoirs*, first authorized? If you still need it, there's one in this library I've bought. I'll take seventy-five."

The price was more than fair, but I listened to silence until I began to wonder whether I'd made a mistake.

"I thought I recognized the address. You got the Templeton books?"

"You knew about them?"

"We made an offer about a month ago, but I heard that Blackwells outbid us. Somebody said they offered her forty thousand."

"Somebody was trying it on," I suggested in a voice that sounded almost natural. "Maybe you were supposed to raise your offer?"

"Maybe." The voice was doubtful. "But I'll take the book, anyhow, thanks. See you about two-thirty?"

I was late, but I stayed there for another minute. It seemed all too likely that Clare had tried to manipulate two of the local dealers into an informal auction by telling each of them that the other was offering more. The attempt had failed either because she'd been too greedy, or they had decided not to play. It was, let's face it, improbable that I would out-bid a firm like Blackwells if they were really interested.

Well, perhaps I'd given her a few hundred more than the others had actually offered, but I wouldn't believe forty thousand. Would I?

Shying away from the thought that I'd made a horrible mistake which would somehow end in ruin, I shifted into gear and drove on toward Campion Road.

11

Halloween

I listened with my eyes shut to sounds outside the sitting room: someone asking a question, somebody else replying. Then the front door banged and the engine of the overloaded van coughed into life in the driveway.

We'd had four hours' hard labor, packing and carrying boxes outside. Enough. The big van now leaving for London was crammed from floor to roof, and the back of my Citroën was similarly stuffed with the cardboard boxes I'd set aside, the ones holding what I'd thought were the most valuable items, which I didn't feel like letting out of my sight. The muscles in my shoulders and thighs had turned to water. I couldn't bear to think about the unpacking.

We'd stripped the sitting room. The shelves had become skeletal frames for dust and the little bunch of Indian figures which I'd huddled into a corner out of the way. Even the cupboard by the fireplace where ancient magazines had been stacked was empty, its door swinging. My own inclination had been to leave them, but

Richard had assured me that ancient copies of *Country Life* do sell. Nostalgia.

The Forbes collection were the only books left, apart from a copy of an Edgar Wallace thriller, due back at the public library last July, which I'd dumped onto one of the armchairs in the heat of the fray.

The door squeaked and Jay was back. He'd worked beside me for most of the afternoon, except for vanishing occasionally to check on the residents. Although Georgina and Clare had together opened the front door when I arrived, Clare had seemed unnaturally subdued and Georgina, tearful. It was hard to understand the emotions. Gina had seemed to me a tough and devious young woman who was perfectly able to look after herself while she gave her family a hard time. I tried to imagine Ben, six feet tall with long hair and a rucksack, stomping down the stairs and out of the flat in a tantrum. And failed absolutely. There are a lot of interesting things I still have to experience. The women had simply left us to get on with the packing; they had obviously spent the day quarreling somewhere upstairs.

"Listen, do you really make your living like this?"

"Constantly," I said to Jay. "Weight-lifting and step-climbing are what keep me fit."

Jay joined me on the sofa and draped his left arm ambiguously over my shoulders and the back cushions. "I didn't realize that book selling was such hard work. Listen, would you like a cup of tea? I guess the ladies could use one, too."

"I'm parched," I admitted. "Are they all right?"

"Clare's napping. She says she has another migraine coming on. Georgina's crying in her bedroom."

"I'd better just go home," I decided.

The arm across my shoulders grew heavier. "I have a good idea. You can't go now, not till you've got your breath back. Stay and eat. You don't have to be there while those guys unload, do you?"

I twisted around and looked at him in astonishment. The green eyes were watching me intently. Talk about bedroom eyes . . . I gulped, "They won't want an outsider around this evening."

"What about me, then? Anyhow, it isn't doing them any good, stewing upstairs and blaming each other. Maybe it's better to have somebody here for an hour or two who'll make conversation."

"Have they contacted the police?"

"Clare phoned them an hour ago. They say if Gina's still missing in a couple of days, they'll send somebody around. They're not too interested, I guess they think she's an adult. Clare tried to put her foot down, but it didn't work, and she got mad."

I almost laughed. Clare would certainly have tried to put her foot down.

"Look, I'll phone out for a takeaway, if you like. Please stay? I owe you a meal. It isn't what I planned, but if you'll take a rain check for lunch, it would cheer them up to have you stay for a while. Me too; cheer up. Look, what about the tea? Or do you want something stronger?"

I said honestly, "I think I want both."

"I've got some bourbon, if you drink the stuff."

I managed to avoid suggesting that just at the moment I would be happy to drink anything. When I opened my mouth to say something more civilized than that, I was drowned out by a series of explosions.

"Hey! It's just fireworks," Jay laughed. "It's Halloween, remember? The kids around here do fireworks on

Halloween. Clare says it's an awful American custom that got mixed up with Guy Fawkes Night, and nothing's the way it used to be when she was a kid. Listen, you're all tense. You sure can't drive while you're in this state."

It was just an excuse, but I knew suddenly that I'd like to spend more time with Jay Roslin. Especially exploring the problem of Orrin Forbes' books, I reminded myself virtuously.

Obviously a mind-reader, he extended his hand and pulled me to my feet. "Come into the dining room and help me stare at the kettle. I'll get the bottle, and we can have a drink while we're waiting for it to boil. I think I'll buy them a new electric kettle as a leaving present."

"You're going away?"

We were standing just at the door, and he hesitated with his hand on the knob. "Well, sooner or later, maybe sooner. I know Clare has some scheme in mind—hasn't she? I've been talking to Georgina, and she swears she doesn't know anything about it, but it's obvious Clare has some plan for selling up and moving. I don't think this is news to you. I'm not pushing you about the Forbes stuff if you don't want to say anything." He shrugged.

So did I. "It's not that I don't want to."

He leaned against the closed door and looked at me. "She's asked you not to talk about it."

There was nothing that I could say.

"Got you, haven't I!" He grinned slowly. "OK. So, what happens to the Forbes?"

"I'd like to ask you about that," I said, "privately."

He looked at me and frowned. "Now? Look, you go into the dining room, and I'll go get the bourbon, and check for signs of life. We'll probably get half an hour before one of them shows up."

His plan, like everything else that day, went wrong immediately. Stepping into the hallway, we were assailed by a draft. The inner door was propped open, and cold air was whistling through the cracks around the front door. What was propping the inner door was a box of books. We looked at one another in disbelief.

"They forgot it. Give me your car keys," Jay said. "I'll take it out."

"Leave it," I groaned. "Dump them. I don't want any more books. The car's full."

He threw back his head and laughed. "Come on."

"Honestly," I said, and flicked back a flap. The first thing I saw was an eighteenth-century plate book in a calf binding, worth two hundred pounds if it was worth a penny. I sighed and dug into the pocket of my jeans for the car keys.

Desperate shoving eventually allowed Jay to wedge the final box through the side door of the Citroën, into a space just behind the passenger seat which I could have sworn didn't exist. He started to fumble with the lock. "Central locking," I said wearily, and limped around to the driver's door to engage it. "I'll kill Richard. How could he?"

Jay laughed, and after a moment he followed me around the car and gave me a light kiss which started to turn into something else. The wind blew a shower of water out of the branches overhead. I gasped and looked up, which was why I noticed a movement of the curtains at Clare's bedroom window. We were being watched. Jay laughed again, and we stumbled up the broken steps and slammed the door behind us.

Afterward, huddling at the dining table in the mean circle of warmth, we faced one another more soberly. He had found a tray of ice cubes in Clare's little fridge, then vanished for a few minutes and returned with his bottle of Jack Daniel's and a couple of thick tumblers.

"What's worrying you about the Forbes?" He glanced at the cupboard just at our elbows. "You know, I thought you'd be more excited."

"Oh, it's fine," I assured him. "Lots of good things. I'm sure you know that."

"Hasn't she accepted your offer?" He saw me hesitate. "Don't tell me if you're not supposed to."

"It isn't that," I said quickly. And told him what my problem was.

As I talked, he lowered his head and stared at the glass in his hands. "So you're asking me whether they're hers to sell?"

I hesitated, but he wasn't a fool.

"I guess you are. You wouldn't handle anything that was stolen."

No, I wouldn't. And it wasn't just Jeff's warning that made me hesitate now that I knew Clare a little. There are some people who drop you in it every time.

"Have you read the letters from Forbes? The ones in the last file?"

"I looked at them."

"Well, all I can say is that they're sort of . . . more friendly. According to her, the two of them were always in love really, and Orrin came to see that when his new lady dumped him. There was Georgina, too. Clare says they were getting back together. Who knows? Look, what do you really want to hear?"

"I want to know who else might own those books and manuscripts, if Clare doesn't."

"I can't say. I know Forbes' parents were both dead, and he was an only child. He had no money. The embassy arranged his burial in Rome."

"What about his wife—Simone somebody?"

"She died in nineteen sixty."

"He didn't sell all his manuscripts to some American library, or anything like that?"

"I'd know if he had. There's no big Forbes collection anywhere in the States, just scattered bits and pieces."

My glass had emptied itself. He dug out the rest of the ice and poured seconds.

"So there's nobody with a legal claim? But what about Georgina?"

He looked at me, frowning. "You think that Mrs. Forbes is cheating her own daughter? Well, she's always talked as though the collection belongs to her. I guess . . . I mean, Georgina is illegitimate."

That didn't mean she had no claim in law. It was the kind of thing that Leonard Stockton would check, though, so I could let it go. Was it beginning to sound all right? Or did I think so because I really wanted the collection?

We both heard the noise on the stairs, and a moment afterward the door creaked open for Clare, her hair immaculately pinned and a look of determination on her face. We must have looked like conspirators, huddling there with our drinks.

She stared at me solemnly. "My dear Dido, you must think we are making a terrible fuss about that naughty girl. I'm afraid we've forgotten our manners. I hope that Professor Roslin has made up for it a little."

I told her demurely that Professor Roslin had been a tower of strength, and caught a twitch of his mouth.

"I'm glad. Now, it is time to eat, and you will stay and have something with us."

It was more a royal command than an invitation, and I might have refused on principle if Roslin hadn't winked. I said weakly that I would have to check on Ben, and Clare dragged her telephone out from the pile of rubbish on the far side of the dining table, pushed it at me, and stood over me while I dialed.

Barnabas answered at the first ring.

"It's me," I said. "Is everything all right? I'm just checking."

"Everything is normal, if not all right." The voice in my ear was exasperated. "Young Ernie is still missing, presumed flat on his back in bed, and Phyllis has just left. Where are you?"

"I'm still here at Campion Road. Two men and a van are on their way with a million books. Give them another hour to arrive. Let Richard and Adam unload, don't you dare try to help. Just unlock the shop and leave them at it, please. And, Barnabas . . . could you put Ben to bed?"

There was a brief silence, then. "Do I deduce from this that you are plunging into the night life of Oxford?"

I said carefully, "I'm staying for a while to talk to Mrs. Forbes and Professor Roslin. We're going to have a bite to eat before I start back."

The voice grew sharper. "The Forbes books . . . ?"

"Yes," I burbled, "she's right here with me now, I'll give her your regards."

Barnabas said, "I see. Don't wake me up if you get back in the middle of the night; you'll have to sleep on the couch. As usual, I believe?"

"I won't be that late," I said weakly and hung up.

But it was nearly two hours before I managed to disentangle myself. We'd avoided the topic of Gina, though her bereft mother's silence dampened the conversation. I noticed that both Georgina and Clare ate heartily, but it was an awkward meal, full of long pauses. When I mentioned the Forbes collection in passing, Clare glared at me.

One thing became clear: this wasn't going to be my last visit. Jay and I would look at the manuscripts together as soon as Phyllis and Barnabas were prepared to live through yet another of my day-long absences. Not to mention Ben. As the front door closed behind me and I stood alone on the damp steps, I felt a sudden pang: I missed my son.

The wind had veered to the east, bringing a hint of winter, and the sky above the trees had cleared. Even in the glow of the street lamp beyond the hedge I could see a few bright stars. At least I wouldn't have the unpleasantness of a rainy drive home. And by now, I encouraged myself, both the motorway and the Marylebone Road would be free of traffic and I'd get home in fifty minutes if I pushed it, and maybe Ben would wake up. With a sudden cheerfulness I descended to the car, unlocked it, let myself in, turned the key in the ignition, and listened to the sound of something trying to happen. Stupidly I tried again, but it was perfectly clear that the car wasn't going to start.

I pulled the collar of my jacket around my neck, closed my eyes, and tried to remember the number of my emergency service. People were approaching in the street. I was distracted by a cheerful babble of voices and a sudden shriek of "Trick or treat!" from just beyond the hedge, laughter, and the slam of a door. Then I noticed the music. The neighbors were having a party.

Something brushed against the car. I opened my eyes. Jay was standing against my door, watching my face. "What's wrong?"

Resigned, I opened it and fell out. "It won't start."

"Do you want me to have a look? I don't know this make, but it might be something obvious. Pop the hood for me, and try the ignition when I say. And stay inside—this wind's freezing."

I shivered, crawled back, and released the catch. He lifted the bonnet and vanished behind it. After a moment, he called, "Try it!"

I turned the key with the same result as before.

"OK! Stop! Stop!"

After a pause, the bonnet snapped down and Jay shrugged at me through the windscreen. "I'm sorry, I'm not great with cars." He came around and reached for my hand. "Come on. We'll get out of the wind and call around, see if there's a garage still open that will send somebody out."

I explained about the Automobile Association, remembered their emergency number before I'd stopped speaking, and used my mobile before I relocked the car and faced the fact that I would be spending more time in Clare's depressing house.

The women had vanished again. We sat in the hissing warmth of the sitting room fire, and after a while the conversation faltered and Jay lifted my chin and kissed me in an enquiring sort of way. I let him understand, appropriately, that this was fine with me, and the time passed pleasantly after all until a clatter in the hallway roused us both. I cast a quick glance at the mantel clock and was shocked that ten o'clock had passed unnoticed by either of us.

"They said 'about an hour.' I'd better ring and find out what's wrong."

Jay had followed the direction of my look, then checked his watch. "I don't much want you to go."

"I know. Under other circumstances I wouldn't want to either, but I'm getting a little crazy about being here. And there are people waiting for me."

He laughed. "All right, don't get crazy. You phone them, and I'll see if I can find some more coffee."

I stretched, watching him go, then retrieved my mobile and found myself complaining to a dispatcher that I was still waiting for my rescue.

The voice became harassed. "I see that you cancelled your previous call-out. Is it the same problem as before?"

I blinked. "I phoned you at about eight-thirty because I couldn't get the car to start. I'm still waiting . . . I'm still at the same place—this is Dido H-o-a-r-e . . ."

"According to the computer," the voice interrupted, "you phoned again at eight-fifty-two to say that the problem had cleared and you no longer needed a mechanic."

"But I *didn't*!" I wailed.

The voice became apologetic. "We'll be with you as quickly as possible, but there's been an incident near Woodstock, and it will take at least an hour, I'm afraid. You said you aren't alone?"

I knew that for a quick response I should explain that I really was entirely isolated in the wild reaches of North Oxford with packs of tigers, bears and rapists circling, but it had been a long day and I wasn't thinking clearly. My watch said that it was nearly ten-twenty. I decided not to phone Barnabas. If he got worried, he would ring my mobile. Maybe I'd get home before he realized I'd been delayed again. In only about a hundred minutes it would be another day, and maybe my luck would change.

It was Clare who reappeared first, sweeping into the room enveloped in her pink bathrobe. "Professor Roslin says that your car has broken down and you're waiting for help? I'm so sorry, I should have come down."

I forced myself to sit up. "Yes—sorry. There was some kind of mix-up, and they'd canceled my call, but they say they'll get here in an hour or so." I glanced furtively at the clock, but it hadn't got any earlier. I stumbled into another apology, but she shook her head vigorously and looked oddly coy.

"Not at all, not at all! In fact, it's a blessing you're still here, because I've remembered something." She had been holding a large brown envelope behind her back, and now she thrust it at me. "I'd like you to look at this. As you are interested in buying Orrin's things. You haven't seen this yet."

I said, "Professor Roslin will be back in a minute . . ."

She nodded insistently. "Look."

The flap of the envelope was tucked in rather than sealed. I dug in and carefully slid out some typed sheets. The paper was rough to the touch and slightly fragile, and I knew even before I saw it that this was more of Orrin Forbes' coarse, yellowy-gray typing paper.

I was expecting more letters to Clare from her lover. What slid into sight was a poem: the irregular, free-form verse of his mature work. The typing had faded in the intervening decades, and I had to hold the pages directly under the standard lamp to get enough light to read them. The top sheet was headed: "Canto 8—for C," underlined in thick blue ink. The first line began characteristically in mid-breath:

sitting on the steps above the river
> *Remember me*
> *remember   me*
the bateaux mouches stammering above the Seine
> *stuttering Remember . . .*
That was in '54
> *looking across to Notre Dame*
the seagulls dipping over the water
> *crying   crying   remember*
palm against palm
we whispered, sang, we weeping sang

Something moved overhead, explosively. Jay was back, leaning over, his eyes fixed on the page. He gripped my wrist hard and I couldn't be sure whether what I saw in his face was anger or just excitement. I let the papers fall into the hand he reached out, and he straightened and faced Clare, holding them.

"What's this?"

She smiled girlishly. "Just another poem. I came across it among some things in my bedroom, and I thought that Dido would like to see it."

"You know . . . You *knew* that this is the lost Canto, Canto Eight of *Remember Me?*"

"I suppose it is." Clare sounded unsurprised. "He sent it to me, you see. It was never published because it's a personal communication."

Roslin pulled himself together with a visible struggle and laid the typescript quietly on my lap. "I'd like to read it when you've finished looking at it. Canto Eight, like Mrs. Forbes says, was never published. Everybody thought he burned it when he left Paris."

I was doing my own remembering. I had actually heard

of the famous "Missing Canto," though I couldn't say that I'd have thought of it in other circumstances. In the early editions of *Remember Me,* the publishers had even left a single blank leaf to mark the missing section. Once, a few years ago, somebody had returned a copy to an auction house on the grounds that it was faulty, and I'd seen a condescending paragraph in one of the booksellers' newsletters under a heading "Whatever Next?", or something like that.

I needed to talk to Barnabas.

I shuffled the sheets of the poem gingerly. Apparently the typescript had not always been kept in its envelope, because the typing grew darker on the second and third sheets of the poem, as though that first page had faded in sunlight. Not that it mattered: it was all legible, the missing canto could be published now, the scholars could have their field day. I could picture the excitement in universities and literary reviews all over the United States. Which reminded me, naturally, of Jay.

I checked that the work was complete: eight and a half pages, numbered, all present. Why wasn't I more excited? If my hair wasn't curling in bibliographical ecstasy, I must be dangerously exhausted. I heard my voice say flatly, "What do you want to do with this? Obviously, it's very exciting."

"It must be valuable," Clare said then in a tone of mild encouragement, and I looked up to see her and Jay glance at each other. They were both wearing poker faces.

I said, "Oh, yes, quite valuable."

She turned her attention to me and cleared her throat. "Then perhaps I ought to sell it, along with the rest."

"It would certainly increase the price of the collection as a whole," I agreed, keeping my voice neutral. Now that

I was quite sure the archive was too rich for my pocket, it didn't seem to matter. I did a little deep breathing. It had no effect. Of course the archive would go to auction, and I wouldn't even bother to bid for it. I slid the sheets carefully back into their envelope, and handed them back. The mantel clock chimed the three-quarters, and I needed to go home.

"Are you all right?" Jay asked hesitantly. "You don't look too hot."

"Just tired."

"Stay the night," Clare said suddenly. "I feel I can trust you, Dido, and I certainly trust your father, since we've been friends for years. I need to think. By morning I shall decide what I'm going to do about this. The guest room is empty, and as it happens the sheets are clean today. You can sleep there."

It felt like a good idea, if only because I was too tired by now to drive safely. Today had gone on forever. With my present luck, I would probably finish it in a ditch. I realized I was staring at Clare blankly.

"We shall have a nice cup of hot chocolate now," Clare announced gently, "and you'll get a good night's rest and leave at first light. Doesn't that make sense?"

I phoned the rescue service for the last time and told the dispatcher to postpone my rescue for a few hours more. Then I retreated to the guest lavatory by the front door and examined my face in the little mirror over the basin. The glass had been installed high on the wall for a tall family. I looked coldly at my image: what looked back bore an unflattering resemblance to a severed head: brown eyes, slightly bloodshot, staring at me out of a face that was washed out under the harsh overhead light, curly dark hair sticking up here and there and needing brushing, and a dust smudge on my forehead that I must have overlooked.

The memory of Jay Roslin's eyes swam uneasily into my mind. I wasn't looking quite as sexy as I would have liked: he was obviously attracted, but at the moment I couldn't understand why. I dabbed at the dirt with the damp edge of the hand towel, thought about it, washed my face with cold water, and tried running my fingers through the wilder portions of my hair. The result wasn't flattering. What I needed was two baths, a long sleep, and a visit to a beauty salon. Since I wasn't likely to get any of these on the spot, I gave up.

Out in the hallway, I nearly ran into Georgina, arriving from the basement kitchen with a tray that held four mugs. I caught the flash of her eyes as I held the sitting room door for her. The look said that I was rubbish, and I decided on the spot that she guessed more about my business there than Clare realized. Georgina didn't like me. Not at all.

She dumped the tray silently on a little table beside Clare's chair. The smell of chocolate suddenly scented the stuffy air in the room.

"Thanks," Jay said hoarsely. I thought he looked absorbed. Not surprising . . . "Not for me. Thanks."

Georgina shrugged and distributed three mugs. The chocolate was dark, strong and comforting. A bit too sweet. I thanked her, as she retired to the far end of the settee, but she gave no sign of hearing me. She was holding her own mug in her lap, as though she had forgotten what it was for.

Clare watched her, frowning. "You'd better get off to bed," she said suddenly. "Try not to worry, it will be all right." It was the first time I'd heard her say anything sympathetic to her daughter: whatever had been exercising them all day had apparently been resolved. Georgina nodded, replaced her untouched chocolate on the tray, and stood up. We all watched her go.

"She will be all right," Clare said to nobody in particular. She put her mug down empty and picked up the envelope holding her poem. "If you're ready, Dido, I'll take you upstairs."

I stood up and pulled myself together. There was no sign of Georgina on the stairs, and it was left to Jay to turn out the lights behind us.

At the landing, Clare paused and gestured. "The bathroom is there, and your room is to the right, the door opposite mine in fact. But will you come with me for a moment to say good night?"

I looked at her blearily, and she held up the envelope in a way that seemed meaningful. Dreamily I followed her into her bedroom. The only light came from a small lamp on the bedside table, and I tripped on the edge of the rug. Clare lowered herself ponderously onto the bed. She positioned the envelope on the table, under the lamp, and stared at it for a moment. I watched her fumble another cigarette out of the packet that was lying beside it. She lit it with a disposable lighter, and a wreath of white smoke curled into the lamp's rays. Everything was in slow motion. Her face was in shadow, except when she drew on the cigarette and the tip glowed briefly.

"It must seem to you that I'm being impossibly slow about all this." I felt my mouth smiling stupidly. "The simple truth is that I know I must sell Orrin's things, yet I want to keep them. They represent . . . the very best time of my life. But yes, I do *know* that they must go. Be patient with an old woman. I thought I should just tell you not to worry, I'm sure that you're the person to look after it all for me. And Barnabas." She hesitated, and a shadow crossed her face. "Such memories . . . Good night, my dear: we will talk in the morning."

I said good night and turned to leave, but an exclamation stopped me. She was struggling to get to her feet. She wheezed, "My pills! I nearly forgot. I don't sleep a wink without my pills. Could you . . . ?" She pointed.

There was a bottle of prescription tablets on the chest of drawers beside the door, and a glass of water. I turned and carried them to her. She shook some pills into her hand and swallowed. Then she sighed, smiled faintly, and placed the tumbler beside the ashtray. "I'll say good night. You'll find your way across the hall all right? Sleep well."

I said good night again and closed her door behind me. The only light in the passage was what shone in through the landing window. I stood for a minute, waiting for my eyes to adjust, and heard a key turn behind me: Clare locking herself into her room with her memories.

A dark figure loomed between me and the stairs, and I heard Jay Roslin's laugh. "Dido?" I started to giggle: everything seemed unreal. "I'll show you the room. Come on."

He took my hand, and led the way around the stair well toward the dark rectangle on the opposite wall. I could feel his hand shaking, or perhaps it was mine. The door was slightly ajar, and a faint light shone inside. Somebody had left the gas fire on, and the room was hot. It was a tiny room holding a single wardrobe, a chair and a bed opposite the window. The sheets were turned down over a thick, old-fashioned quilt. My attention was not on the room.

Jay said, "I could stay . . ." as I'd known he was going to, and put his warm hand on the nape of my neck and pulled me down onto the narrow bed.

12

Smoke

I drifted into the sitting room. The brightness lit every corner with cruel clarity. The shelves were full of books once more, but these were tattered and damp-stained paperbacks. Clare stood at the fireplace. She was pulling Orrin Forbes' books from the revolving case and flinging them into the fire. The pages fluttered and blazed up, but the chimney must have been blocked, because black smoke gusted back into the room. I coughed and watched her scooping the papers from the filing boxes, scattering them into the flames, where they flared and became flakes of drifting ash. When she saw me, she cried, "Dido, I've made up my mind! Everything has to burn, Dido!"

I choked, and the voice went on saying, "Dido!" I opened my eyes on darkness. I was being shaken.

"Dido! God, will you wake up?"

I blinked and croaked, "I'm awake."

A light came on suddenly, not the blinding lights of my nightmare but the bedside lamp. For seconds I had no idea where I was; but Jay was standing at the side of the bed. He had dragged me into a sitting position and was holding my shoulders, shaking me so hard that my head snapped back and forth, shouting. I put up a hand to catch his arm, and he let go.

"Get up! Put some clothes on, there's a fire somewhere. We've got to go downstairs and—we may have to get out!"

I shook myself, took a deep breath, and found that it was real smoke. He had got his clothes on. I stared and tried to understand what was happening. My head wouldn't work, but instinct or adrenalin kicked in then and I fell out of the bed and looked dizzily for my clothes.

Jay flung my jeans at me. "Put on your outer things and your shoes, never mind the rest. We'd better make sure the others are awake. Come on, don't hang around!"

I said, "I'm not," but I was fumbling with the button on my jeans. I pushed my bare feet into my shoes, and then Jay was opening the door and switching on another of those dim lights. The stairs were full of smoke.

"Wait a minute." He thrust something at me—a bunched towel. "Breathe through this. Keep low." Then we held hands and pushed out into the reek and he was banging at the door across the passage. Silence. I watched him twist the knob and push fruitlessly against the solid oak. "Mrs. Forbes? Clare! Fire! You have to get out of there!"

There was a noise behind us: Georgina, half falling down the other stairs, huddling a coat over her nightdress. She said something I didn't hear and pushed past us, and Jay was twisting the handle of Clare's door again, banging and shouting.

He turned back. "It's locked. The fire's inside. You go down. Call the fire department. Go!"

Georgina had run ahead down the staircase, and I started to follow her but stopped on the landing, thinking confusedly, *She needs air, we need to breathe* . . . The window was stuck. There was a stand on the half-landing holding a heavy brass pot. I used the pot to smash at the windowpane. It cracked on the second attempt, and I pushed the shards outward. At the same time there was a bang above me and I realized that Jay was kicking at the door. I struggled back.

He kicked again. "It's no good, it's too solid." I joined him and banged with him at the solid oak, thinking maybe we could still wake her and she would open the door, and we could pull her out. I could smell the sickening reek of feathers, hair . . . We stopped.

"We'd better get out," Jay rasped and burst into a paroxysm of coughing. I pulled him down to the landing, and we leaned our faces to the broken window.

"We can't just leave her there," I said. I could only manage a whisper.

He put his arm around my shoulders and held me. "There's nothing I can do. That door's solid, I can't shift it. The fire department will have to smash it open." He hesitated and said again, "There's nothing you can do. Listen!"

More air.

Georgina was staggering up toward us. "They're coming. I've left the front door open."

Jay said, "Don't go up."

Georgina's face was set. She said, "She's dead," as though she could see what was in the room, and already there were sirens at the bottom of the road and blue lights flashing against the tree outside the window, and before any more time seemed to have passed there were people pouring up the stairs toward us. The three of us flattened ourselves against the banisters as they pushed past. The first of them turned his head and yelled, "Get out!"

Jay was stepping forward. "The door's locked," he croaked. "She's in there."

Somebody called, "Bring an axe! Get a ladder up to the window. I want . . ." and then Jay was dragging Georgina and me away down out of the front door, and we stood in the cold, clean air to watch a ladder being twisted and raised to Clare's window before we were pushed away from the house.

Dawn brought a cold day with clear skies. The students in the adjoining house had taken us in. I was sitting numbly in an armchair, among the remains of their Halloween party, wrapped like a refugee in somebody's duvet. Jay and Georgina sat a little apart on the couch opposite, not looking at one another. The girls had made us tea, strong and sweet, and two of them had stayed with us, silent and embarrassed. I had been hearing, without wanting to, the cars and fire engines arriving and departing at the front of the house, and an ambulance wailing. At some point a police officer had come into the room and spoken quietly to Georgina. He had asked if her mother had been in the habit of smoking in bed. Georgina had stared at him speechlessly. It was Jay who had said yes. Yes, Clare had been in the habit of smoking everywhere. I closed my eyes. When somebody stood over me and shook my shoulder gently I opened them again.

Jay said, "The man's come about your car. Have you got the keys?"

For a moment I thought that I'd left them in the house, and then I felt them in the pocket of my jeans and handed them over wordlessly. Time passed, and someone in a brown jacket came, sayi.... Vould you mind signing this?"

I reached dreamily for the paper he held toward me. "Is my car fixed?"

"It's all right. I've taken it around the block. I left it out in the road."

I said, because I thought I ought to know, "What was wrong?"

"Nothing. It started up as soon as I tried it. An air lock in the fuel line, something like that."

"But," I said, but it didn't matter. I signed in the space he showed me and received my keys and stood up. I said, "I'm going home."

Jay looked at me from a distance. "Will you be all right?"

I said, "Of course." I looked at Georgina, who did not look up. "I'm sorry," I said clearly, "I'm very sorry. Will you let me know about the funeral?" She remained silent.

Jay said, "Think you should stay for a while?"

I wanted to laugh at him. I said, "No."

The Citroën was at the curb on the other side of the street. Like everything else, it looked sharp but unreal in the cold light. I got into it without looking back, feeling the rawness of my throat, and thinking that I should drive carefully but that the traffic was still light and I would be all right if I was careful. As I was fastening my seat belt, I remembered that my shoulder bag was still in the Templetons' sitting room. There was nothing in it that I wasn't prepared to do without, not even the mobile phone. Jay could send it, or bring it to London.

The car started as soon as I turned the key in the ignition, and I drove away in a dream without looking back.

13

Remember Me

The bedroom was bright with sunshine when I woke up the first time. A motorbike passed in the street. I listened to it and let myself drift away with the sound.

Later, I could hear voices. At least three people were talking in the front room. One of them was Barnabas. I couldn't make out any words, but the sound was peaceful. I yawned and coughed painfully and remembered.

I'd got myself home. I could remember dragging upstairs, and the feeling of relief when I found Barnabas and Ben having breakfast together. I could just about remember holding Ben and telling Barnabas that there had been a fire and I wasn't hurt, but sleepy, so sleepy . . . I remembered questions, but couldn't remember answering. My brain still felt like turkey stuffing.

I crawled out from under the duvet and stood up experimentally. That was all right, so I tottered over to the wardrobe and dug out my terry robe, because a hot bath seemed essential; and I was almost decent when the unlatched bedroom door burst open and Ben arrived at high speed on hands and knees, expressing delight, pursued by Phyllis Digby.

"Sorry, Dido. Are you up? He can't understand why you've been in bed all day, and he's got impatient. Dido, are you . . . ?"

I told her I was fine. It was very nearly true. I retrieved Ben as he started to scramble up me like a climber on a cliff face. Then Barnabas arrived, preceded by Mr. Spock at a gallop. One of them had no hesitation in pushing past Phyllis and yelling at me. Phyllis scooped up my squalling cat, said briefly, "I'll feed him," and made way for my father. I sat down on the edge of the bed and gave Ben a cuddle.

"What happened to you? What the devil did you mean by driving home in that state?"

I decided to ignore the last question, because what it implied was probably correct. "Didn't I say? There was a fire. Clare was . . . she's dead."

Barnabas frowned. "Yes, you said that much. You didn't explain what you were doing there, why you weren't on your way back here. We went to bed. When you hadn't arrived by the time Ben woke up, we both assumed that you had done something very, very silly. I tried your mobile: there was no answer."

"I had to leave it in the house when we got out. The car broke down," I said. "I couldn't get it started, and there was some kind of mix-up about the emergency service, and then Clare and Georgina had been in a state all day because of Gina running away, so I thought I might as well stay for a while and be supportive; anyway it was awfully late . . ."

"This is not," Barnabas commented, "the clearest of accounts."

I remembered something else, and interrupted in my turn. "Did the books get here all right? Did Richard manage to get everything into the packing room? Why isn't the shop open? Is Ernie there?"

Barnabas clutched his brow dramatically. Phyllis reappeared at the door with a mug of tea and said, "You drink this, Dido. I'm sorry, but I have to go. I'll be here tomorrow at nine."

I said, "We'll be fine. I'm all right now. Or I will be when I've had a bath and washed the smoke out of my hair." Then the four of us interrupted each other for a couple of minutes more before Phyllis finally clattered downstairs toward the front door. As it slammed behind her, I remembered something else and screeched, "Where's the car? I can't remember where I left the car!"

Barnabas removed Ben from my arms and said loudly, "Bring your tea out to the other room and you can see. And for goodness sake, explain what happened, in order, without squealing!"

I followed him edgily. Barnabas waved an invitation for me to look out of the window, and I was relieved to see the Citroën parked on the yellow line outside the shop at a sharp angle to the curb. It looked a little as though it had been abandoned by a drunken driver.

"What's that on the windscreen?"

"I put a notice there when I saw it. I considered that you might be alarmed if it were towed away. It says 'Broken axle, gone for help.' I thought that was quite credible, considering the load you're carrying, and would prevent any effort to tow it away."

"Not bad," I said weakly. "I'd better get it into a residents' bay, though. Perhaps Ernie would help me unload."

Barnabas hesitated. "Ernie wasn't here today. Mrs.

Weekes has agreed he will be well enough to come in the morning to help. She'll wake him up herself before she leaves for work. I've promised you'll pay for a taxi. If he walks here in his usual eccentric fashion, it could take half the day."

"Who's minding the shop?"

"The shop didn't open today."

I stared at him. "Barnabas, Fridays are . . ."

My father raised a hand commandingly. "Dido, your friends from Oxford unloaded the Templeton library yesterday evening, remember? The office is full of boxes. Although it is just possible still to get to the desk. The right-hand aisle is blocked. The left-hand aisle is passable, no more."

I mirrored his raised hand. "Sorry. Sorry."

"And the car will be all right where it is for another night, especially as you can see it from here. I presume you have set the alarm?"

I said I thought I must have but ought to go down and check. Not that I was expecting thieves to target a car full of old books, but you can never be sure.

"And now," my father commanded, "put that child down, drink your tea, and tell me, clearly and logically, precisely what happened."

It took a long time, with interruptions. At the end of it I wanted a bath and to stop thinking about last night.

Barnabas noticed. "Go on," he sighed. "We'll talk about it later. While we eat. If you have anything here that's fit to eat."

"We won't," I said just as firmly, though I didn't believe it.

But when I was lying back in the hot water with my eyes closed, the shadows and the smell were still with me.

It would take a while to start forgetting about what had happened.

Cigarette packages carry government health warnings: *Smoking Kills*. Not that any smoker takes that personally. I sank under the surface of the water, came up with my eyes shut, and felt for the shampoo. Something lingered like the stink of smoke in my hair and clothes. I couldn't think what it was, and yet by the time I'd finished soaping and scrubbing and soaking, I hadn't got rid of the feeling. *Remember me . . .*

14

Book Jam

"Wossup?" Ernie demanded protectively, and I turned and watched him lift a book-filled carton that must have weighed sixty or seventy pounds and deposit it lightly on top of a stack of the same that already reached head height. At nineteen, he is even shorter than I am and about five times broader, a powerhouse of bone and muscle and therefore a perfect assistant for any book dealer.

Ernie is black and dresses like a streetwise school kid with touches of gangster. He is working his way through a business course at college; we were introduced by one of my oldest friends who is a lecturer there and who reckoned that I was in particular need of Ernie's skills, because Ernie is a computer genius and I am a computer idiot. During the past few months, Ernie had not only saved me from probable back strain—and worse, on at least one occasion—but computerized my business. He was beginning to threaten to put us on-line so that we could sell books on the Internet. On days like this one, I feel tempted. Sometimes real books seem more than I can cope with.

I sighed, "How much more?"

Ernie had arrived uncharacteristically on the dot of eight and was unloading my car while I supervised with assistance from Ben because Phyllis wasn't due until nine. So far, Ernie had labored for fifteen minutes without stopping: I couldn't think how I'd originally got all this into the car, even with Jay Roslin's help.

"One, just," Ernie reassured me. "Big one." He looked about and added enthusiastically, "Gotta lotta new books here."

I clutched Ben, who was investigating the inside of my left ear, and couldn't answer. I've noticed before that books in boxes take up a lot more space than the same ones on shelves. Why this should be is beyond me; but what had seemed in Campion Road like a good big collection of interesting books had become, by their arrival in my shop, a terrifying mountain. Never one to fear stating the obvious, I said, "I've got more books here than possible. What am I going to do?"

Ernie cast a calculating glance around the shop. "Trouble is," he mused, "you got so much you can't move it around."

He had put his finger on the problem, of course. There wasn't enough space for me to unpack boxes and find out what they held, much less cope with the occasional customer. If only I'd sorted as I packed, I could have sold whole boxes of the ordinary books to a certain second-hand shop on Charing Cross Road. But that wasn't an option; in this book jam I had no idea where anything was. I had to work out how to start. And quickly. It was Saturday, my busiest trading day of the week, and I was deep in debt and effectively out of business.

Ernie went for the final carton. Ben and I looked at each other thoughtfully. I said, "I'm going to stick a notice on the door. I'm going to say that I'll be closed until next Thursday and then I'll reopen with a hugely expanded and wonderful new stock. What do you think? Then we'll go and move the car before the traffic wardens turn up. Want to come with me, or stay here with Ernie?"

The man himself was back, edging the last box onto the pile. There was something sitting on top of it. "Found that onna floor jus' behind the passenger seat. Musta fallen outa some box."

He pushed the big brown envelope into my hand. I forgot to breathe. I dumped Ben on the floor between my feet, fumbled clumsily and frantically at the flap, and pulled out the top sheet with its faded lines of typing, the steps above the river, and bateaux mouches and the seagulls . . . *Remember me* . . .

Somewhere beyond the roaring that filled my ears Ernie was saying, "Dido? You OK?"

15

Arrivals

Barnabas arrived in a taxi, looking imperturbable.

I'd been watching for him. Ernie and Ben had gone upstairs, though neither of them wanted to miss the fun, and I'd been jittering in the shop for the past twenty minutes. I'd abandoned the manuscript in its envelope on top of the mess on my desk and spent the time sitting out in the shop on a box of books, trying to think what I was going to tell my father. Or, for that matter, Georgina. How to explain an impossibility.

"Ghosts," I said to Barnabas, unlocking the door for him. "Miracles."

Barnabas raised both eyebrows. "Show me."

We picked our way between the stacked boxes, edged into the office, and stopped at the desk. My father looked at the envelope with an expression of distaste. "I don't need to say that I discount both miracles and spiritual intervention. This is it? There's no mistake?"

"Not unless I'm hallucinating. Look for yourself." I watched him retrieve the manila envelope, clear space on the desk to spread out its contents, and settle himself in the chair. There was a box of books on the visitor's chair. I dumped it somewhere and edged myself in to watch Barnabas separate the pages gingerly. Nine limp typewritten sheets, all numbered and all precisely as when I had seen them in Oxford. With the air of a researcher he set about the examination. I could see that he wasn't reading but concentrating on the physical document. He was treating it the way, in his earlier research career, he would have inspected a newly discovered sixteenth-century manuscript exhumed from some dusty drawer in the Bodleian Library. I got the impression that he was finding something deeply interesting about the pages, but I kept my mouth shut and let him get on with it for as long as I could. Eventually I said, "The point is, it's here and that's impossible."

Barnabas hesitated. "The point is not that it's impossible, but that it *mustn't* be here. I'm not sure you've thought of the implications. Apparently you have stolen an extremely valuable manuscript. Or . . . well, perhaps I would prefer to call it a manuscript of commercial interest. Value is in the eye of the beholder."

"I did *not* . . ."

"Don't yell at me. Of course you didn't. I am merely stating the obvious, while in this case the truth appears to be obscure." We looked at each other as I started to picture a whole new disaster area. "I think you had better spend the next ten minutes bringing me up to date."

I spread my hands helplessly. "I've already told you everything."

Barnabas closed his eyes and leaned against the back of

his chair. "On Thursday morning you left here, late as usual, to drive to Oxford. I am rather wishing I had thought to come with you again."

"If we'd had to carry you out of a burning house," I said grumpily, "it would have been much worse."

"Scarcely," Barnabas said in a tone that allowed no contradiction. "You drove to Oxford. Tell me precisely what happened. You were in no condition yesterday to explain yourself. I believe you were in a state of shock. However, now would be the right time. You drove to Oxford . . ."

"Everything kept going wrong. You remember when Jay Roslin phoned and asked you for the number of my mobile? Well, he was phoning to cancel our luncheon date because Gina had gone missing and Clare and her mother were upset, and he thought he should stick around. So I . . ."

"Upset how?" Barnabas inquired. "And why had Gina 'gone missing?' You mean she had run away from home? I remember when you were three you ran away to make camp in the University Parks."

I began stiffly, "I don't think . . ."

But Barnabas was far away. "And when you were thirteen, there were times when your mother was afraid that you were planning to join a circus. Has Gina joined a circus, do you think?"

I stopped to consider. It seemed possible. "There was a lot of moodiness when we were there the other day, but she's really too old to join circuses. I know she's been quarreling with her mother, because I heard them. Jay says it was about a boy."

"So she has eloped?" I looked at Barnabas and caught a flash of amusement.

"Perhaps."

Barnabas pigeonholed the idea. "Go on."

I got as far as the departure of Richard's van with the books before Barnabas interrupted again. He held up his hand and frowned. I waited.

"At that point, there were four of you in the house and the manuscript hadn't yet appeared?"

I nodded.

"What had you said to them about the Forbes material?"

I thought about it. "Nothing. There wasn't a chance. I wanted to talk it over with Jay before I said anything to Clare. I wanted to ask about provenance and whether he knew anything about ownership. I knew that if we bought it, it would cost a great deal. I wanted to be sure about it."

Barnabas stared at me sharply. "You didn't believe Clare had the right to sell it."

I shook my head. "It felt odd."

"So you were in the house with the two older Templeton women . . ."

"I actually hadn't seen much of them at that point. They were upstairs all day phoning the police, arguing about what had happened . . . I don't think they were paying any attention."

Barnabas frowned. "And then?"

"Clare came down, looking fairly calm, and suggested I should stay and eat with them. That was when I rang you. They phoned for some Chinese takeaway and the four of us talked."

"About . . . ?"

I found I couldn't remember.

"So you . . . ?"

"So when the meal was finished I said goodbye and went out and found that the car was dead."

"Dead? What was wrong with it? You haven't had any trouble with it before?"

"You know I haven't—it's nearly new. It just wouldn't start. The battery was all right, but the engine didn't catch. I phoned the AA . . ."

"Time?"

"About eight-thirty, more or less."

"And waited in the house?"

"Yes. With Jay. The others had gone upstairs again."

"And the two of you talked about . . . ?"

I said, "Barnabas, mind your own business."

"Ah. So you talked until . . . ?"

"After ten. The AA hadn't come, so I phoned again. There'd been some kind of confusion. They said they'd get to me as soon as possible."

Barnabas nodded encouragingly.

"Then Clare came downstairs again and she had . . ." I nodded toward the papers in front of Barnabas.

"What did she say about it?"

"She said something like 'I happen to have found these upstairs . . . ' "

Barnabas snorted. "Just something she'd forgotten?"

I heard myself giggle nervously. "Something like that."

"And Professor Roslin said . . . ?"

I thought back. "He came back into the room and saw the manuscript. He was . . . I think he was furious."

"Go on."

I went on, step by step, a little nervously: Barnabas' interruptions didn't help and I wasn't eager to get to the point where I was going to admit that Jay Roslin and I had decided to spend the night together. On the one hand, I am unpleasantly close to my thirty-fourth birthday, which is certainly the age of discretion if not decrepitude; but on the other hand your father is always your father. The moment came and passed unremarked, though I wasn't sure it would stay that way. Barnabas heard me through my waking up, the smoke, the attempt to break into Clare's bedroom, the arrival of the firemen . . .

He held up an index finger. "Stop. You said she put this envelope down on her bedside table before you left her. Did you see it again?"

"Of course not! She'd locked her door. Later, we found we couldn't get in."

Barnabas scowled. "I suppose that's so. Pity."

I said, "Where would it have gone?"

"Into your car," he said acidly.

"But my car was locked all this time. All night. I had the keys. Obviously I thought about that, and I can remember locking it before I went back into the house."

"Did you set the alarm?"

I tried unsuccessfully to remember. "I probably didn't bother. I mean, who was going to come into the driveway and steal my car?" Barnabas glowered. I added defensively, "I don't remember, I may not have. Why would I?"

"Why would you?" Barnabas echoed in a growl. He was upset. "Unluckily, somebody put something valuable into your car rather than taking it out."

I said, "I had the keys with me all the time until I gave them to the mechanic in the morning. He was the only one who could have got in, and I doubt that he crept upstairs past the firemen and the police to take . . ."

Barnabas snapped, "Don't be frivolous! Are you pretending you don't understand how much trouble you're in?"

Probably. It's become second nature to try to shield Barnabas from my personal problems. We were in the second year since the heart attack that had almost killed him, and he had seemed very well for months now, with his low-fat diet and half an aspirin daily; but a part of me can never forget the evening in my flat when . . . I shied away from that memory for the thousandth time.

Barnabas had fixed the typescript with an icy stare. If it had been human, it would certainly have broken down and confessed everything. "There were four people in the house, assuming that the child wasn't hiding in the attic in which case there were five: but let's assume Clare, Georgina, Roslin, and you. Let us assume that Gina really was away, and that *you* didn't take the envelope."

I muttered, "Thanks."

"So we must consider motives. The professor?"

I thought about it. It was impossible for him to have hidden the thing in my car, but if we were thinking of motives in the abstract . . . "He would have loved to get the poem away from Clare long enough to copy it, I suppose. He was very angry that she hadn't shown it to him."

"Perhaps we should find out a little more about his reputation at his university?"

"But Barnabas, he had no chance to do it!"

"As nobody else did either, that's irrelevant."

I sighed and abandoned the point for the moment. Back to motives: "Georgina? She had nothing to gain."

"Have you considered that she hated her mother?"

I opened my mouth, closed it, and thought about that. There had been something very odd about their relationship, and if Georgina did believe, as I'd started to, that Clare intended to cheat her out of both a home and an inheritance, then she could have decided to remove the best thing from the collection. But why would she put it into

my car, even if she could? It made no sense, and I told
Barnabas so.

"It doesn't at the moment, but I'd say it's worth remembering," Barnabas said brightly. "Now, and more interesting, Clare? We must consider that she is the one who
actually had the envelope in her possession."

"That has been bothering me. If she'd had a key to my
car of course she could easily have gone down and put the
envelope in it, though I can't imagine why she'd want to.
But the car *was* locked. I don't suppose she knew how to
pick the locks without doing any damage, do you?"

"No, she doesn't strike one as a professional car thief.
And yet she has been behaving strangely from the start: all
this secrecy, the calling you to Oxford and sending you
away, her making it almost impossible to buy her father's
books although she obviously needed to sell them . . . Well,
she was a tease. Always. I speak from experience. She
clearly had her own scenario, though I have no idea what it
might have been. And she *did* have the blasted typescript.
Do we know that she didn't break into the car? Have you
looked for damage? You should." He changed direction
suddenly. "Alibis? Gina appears to have a rock-solid one,
though somebody should certainly find the blessed girl."

"So have Jay Roslin and I," I said. "We alibi one another that night."

Barnabas smiled sourly. "Which leaves Georgina
friendless."

"But locked out of her mother's room."

"Nonsense!" Barnabas said sharply. "The more I think
about it, the more possibilities I can see here."

I said desperately, "I have to have a coffee. My mind is
like glue. I can't think this out."

Barnabas looked at me closely. "Are you all right? I was worried yesterday. You got yourself home, arrived at the curb with a screech and a thump . . ."

"I did *not!*"

". . . fell into bed almost without saying a word, and slept for nine solid hours."

"I didn't get much sleep the night before."

"You said that Roslin had to shake you awake. So you obviously had some. And last night?"

"Like a top," I admitted.

Barnabas stared at me through narrowed eyes. I could see him wanting to pursue the matter and deciding not to.

"Then we are down to the final matter."

I said nervously, "Which is what I'm going to do."

"To do?"

"With Canto Eight."

We both looked at the manuscript which should not have been where it was. In either sense of "should."

"I have to take it back."

"Right away. It may well have been missed."

I said rather loudly, "I would love to really burn the thing. I suppose I could post it back to Georgina anonymously."

"Yes?"

"I know. Barnabas, I'm going to go upstairs and change and drink two cups of coffee and eat a piece of toast, and then I'm going to drive back up to Oxford with it. Will you and Phyllis take care of Ben for one more day?"

Barnabas, who happened to be sitting in the strategic position from which a person at the desk can see through the shop, said, "I think you may be too late. I shall answer the door."

I craned forward until I could also see what had caught

his attention. There were two cars stopping just in front of mine, and what looked like a sizeable number of people getting out. Some of them were in police uniform. Some were not.

I croaked, "No, I'd better."

I was unlocking the door just as the first of them arrived at it. The face seemed familiar. I scrabbled through my memory as I opened up and said weakly, "Hello. I met you last year when you were working with DI Grant, didn't I?"

"DS John Baden," the man said. He didn't smile. "Miss Hoare, we have a warrant to search these premises. If we could come in . . . ?"

From behind me, Barnabas was saying, "It won't be necessary. I assume you are looking for this?" He was standing immediately behind me, the envelope in his hand. "It was found in my daughter's car this morning by her assistant. It is a manuscript; I presume this is what you want."

Baden was visibly taken aback. He reached out. "I'll have to look."

"Of course," Barnabas said pleasantly, continuing to block the door. He does this kind of thing with a sort of aristocratic grandeur. "Was there anything else?" He seemed to be expecting Baden, a woman detective who was with him, and the two uniformed constables to retreat. I thought otherwise, and for once I was right. Four emotionless faces considered the two of us.

Baden said, "I think this is what we came for. Miss Hoare, I have to ask you to accompany us to Islington police station. We'll need a statement from you."

I said, "I'll get my coat. It's in the flat. Barnabas . . ."

But when I turned, my father had gone. I could hear him dialing the phone in the office.

The woman detective said, "I'll come up with you."

I kept myself from asking whether she thought I was likely to jump to freedom from an upstairs window, and we climbed the stairs in silence; she positioned herself at the door of the flat and watched me reach into the cupboard.

I caught the movement inside the sitting room and turned to glimpse Ernie's worried face.

"You OK?" he asked hoarsely.

"I'll be out for an hour or so," I said casually. I know how Ernie feels about the police. I caught a look of curiosity on the policewoman's face and said breezily, "The baby sitter." I watched her face freeze. Well, I wouldn't have believed it, either.

Down in the street, I stopped. "I need to move my Citroën. I don't want it towed away."

Baden looked impatient. "We'll see to that. It won't be. Will you get into the back of the car, please?"

I turned to give Barnabas a wave. "Phyllis should get here any moment. Don't worry."

He stood in the doorway of the shop looking more absentminded than alarmed. I had the odd feeling that he was thinking about something else entirely. He pulled himself together and said, "Nor you. I got hold of Leonard Stockton. He will be at the police station almost before you are."

My sudden sense of almost hysterical relief was nobody's business. I turned back to Baden casually. "My solicitor," I said. "Shall we go?"

16

Criminal Cases

"Of course, I don't do criminal cases," Stockton was saying. He turned the wheel and maneuvered his Saab through the entrance to the car park beside the police station. "But your father gave me the impression that if I didn't get myself over here I wouldn't hear the end of it. If they do prosecute, I'll recommend somebody. I wanted to speak to you anyway."

"It was good of you to come," I croaked. Two hours spent trying to explain the impossible in a stuffy interview room had left me childishly grateful for his company. It had all been quite polite, but in the end I could only sign a short statement of the facts as I knew them, and it seemed wildly unsatisfactory even to me. "Are they going to prosecute? I wasn't sure."

"Neither am I."

We made the turn toward Islington Green. I leaned back on leather upholstery and told myself to relax. When

I threw a quick look in the direction of my solicitor, I saw him frowning.

"It's a crazy story. *Did* you take the manuscript, by any chance?" I spluttered, and caught a twitch of his mouth. "I'm just asking. I'm never sure what you'll do next, Miss Hoare."

"I wouldn't do that," I said glumly. "Even if I wanted it, I couldn't possibly sell it without being caught, and I'm not so keen on Orrin Forbes that I want a holy relic. Antiquarian book dealers do have to be careful about this kind of thing."

"That's a point," Stockton agreed slowly. "I hope they'll understand it. To be honest, I think they were startled by the alibi you gave them. The complaint was laid by Mrs. Laszlo, and you certainly did have the material. But if this American backs you up, then they'll have to try to prove that the two of you were acting together. I believe that a successful prosecution would be unlikely. Do you have any idea what actually happened?"

I confessed that I didn't. But that wasn't good enough. There had to be something I hadn't noticed, or something I hadn't remembered, or understood. Yet. All my instincts of self-preservation told me that I'd better dig it out soon.

I changed the subject. "You said you had something to tell me?"

"Yes. I had a phone call last night. It was a good deal simpler than I'd feared. Orrin Forbes left a will."

I sat up, all attention.

"It was proven in Rome, and is valid under both Italian and American law. He left his entire estate to Georgina Forbes, described as his only child."

I turned to him as abruptly as the seat belt allowed. "You mean everything . . . all the books and papers . . .

belonged to Georgina? Not Clare? Do you think she knows?"

"Perhaps you should ask her."

I certainly should. There had been no hint, at Campion Road, that Georgina had any knowledge of our negotiations. She had been very young when her father died, and presumably her mother had acted on her behalf then. Could Clare have prevented her daughter from discovering the truth? She had certainly *behaved* as though the books she was selling were her own. It threw a nasty light on her insistence that I shouldn't tell anyone about the sale.

"Is something wrong?"

"A bad taste," I said. I would have liked to change the subject, but there didn't seem much else to say and when Stockton pulled up behind my Citroën we had been silent for five minutes.

There was a white notice stuck to my windscreen. It said "Police Aware." I said goodbye to my companion, ripped the sticky paper off the glass with a good deal of difficulty, and decided to move the car to a parking bay before anything else happened. I was fumbling for keys in the pocket of my raincoat when Barnabas appeared in the doorway.

"What happened?"

I considered his question. "It was civilized. But they didn't believe me. What have you been doing?"

"Waiting to see whether you needed rescuing. Attempting to bring order out of chaos. Deciding it was impossible."

"You rescued me by getting Leonard Stockton over there," I assured him, "and I don't want you trying to lift those boxes."

Barnabas sighed. "Moving boxes about would merely confuse the issue. However, Ernie and I came up with the solution as soon as Phyllis arrived and gave us a chance to think. She and Ben are still out, by the way."

"The solution?"

"The florist."

"The *what*?"

Barnabas raised his eyes to the clouds. "The flower shop around the corner. You must have noticed that it closed last week? At any rate, Ernie did. I have made arrangements for you to use the place as storage for nearly six weeks. It has cost us a pittance. The agents intend to refurbish it in December before they put the lease on the market. In the meantime, they were more than happy to accept our check for two hundred pounds. The place is yours until December the fifteenth. There is enough floor space, and a counter to spread books out on. Ernie assures me he can get all the boxes around there with the help of the folding trolley, so if you will just get that out before you move the car . . ."

I let out a gasp of relief. "Good for Ernie! You know, I may have to raise his pay."

"Actually," Barnabas said slowly, "I believe that the reward he really wants is for you to let him 'put us On Line' to play computer games of some kind. He claims it is a method of issuing catalogues to American customers. Do you know what he means?"

In my rush of gratitude, I decided on the spot to surrender the point. I told Barnabas so as I was moving around to the driver's door to release the central locking. The folding trolley which I use at book fairs was jammed against the side of the rear compartment. I had trouble disentangling it from a protruding bolt, which was why I failed to notice Barnabas at first. He was moving from one door to another, opening each one in turn and bending down.

"What are you doing?"

"Looking for something. Just a minute."

I waited. He seemed to be examining the frame and the edge of the nearside rear door. "Barnabas?"

His voice was very quiet. "Will you look at this? What do you think it is?"

I went around, crouched down and peered into the hole in the frame where the door latch goes. I could see something small and bluish deep inside, and started to insert a fingernail.

"Leave it!"

"What? Why?"

"It's doing no harm there at the moment, and it might turn out to be a good thing not to leave a fingerprint in there," Barnabas said slowly. "Or disturb anything."

I looked up at him speculatively. He looked back.

"Well, I can see something caught in the works. I don't know what it is. A filler of some kind?"

"At any rate, it doesn't belong there. I am asking myself whether it might be the remains of something that was rammed into the hole and later removed? Perhaps to prevent that latch from sliding in when you locked the car? Or would you have noticed if it didn't?"

I thought. "Probably not, since all the locks work from the key in the driver's door. If that one didn't catch, I would still have heard the sound of the others. I mightn't have noticed anything."

"On the other hand," Barnabas said slowly, "it could be something that has been there since the car was manufactured. It's no proof."

"Proof?" I echoed wildly.

"I don't suppose there's any way of telling," Barnabas said annoyingly. He was talking to himself. "I don't suppose so. Still, we'd better file the fact that your locks may have been tampered with. And don't poke at it! It's doing no harm there now."

I said, "I'm just going to move the car into the residents' bay. Then you can explain."

"Ernie has started moving the books," Barnabas said severely, "though he will get on faster with the trolley. Perhaps we should help?"

I got into the car. It started up, again, at the first attempt.

17

Alarm Call

I heard the bells of St. Mary's clanging beyond the houses across the road, straightened up in the middle of a carpet of books, and surveyed my efforts with pride. Time for lunch.

Ernie had lugged the last of the boxes into my temporary premises yesterday evening by the light of a big torch—electricity to the old flower shop had been cut off when its last tenant left and it didn't seem worth having it reconnected. I'd spent the morning unpacking and sorting, with Ben safely imprisoned in his folding playpen in the midst of it all. I'd ranged the everyday volumes to the east of the playpen, the sound nineteenth-century stock to the west, total rubbish in four black plastic sacks beside the door, and the collectors' items, the heart of my purchase, I'd piled tenderly on top of the old-fashioned wooden counter which the departed florist had left behind. Those piles were pleasingly high. There'd been at least twenty absolute surprises, all good, and now, early Sunday afternoon, I knew that it was going to be all right. In fact, it had been a good purchase. Now I just had to price the parts of the collection I was adding to my stock, and decide what to do with the seven or eight hundred ordinary books that I was never going to be able to find shelf space for.

Inspiration struck suddenly. Jeff's shop in Swansea holds big general stocks, and he rents old stables for storage. I could offer him the books I couldn't use. For free, if he'd come up to London to collect them. Maybe I could persuade my conscience that it was a fair payoff for sending this deal my way, especially considering the side effects. I was reaching for the mobile in my shoulder bag before I remembered that both phone and bag were still sitting (presumably) by the settee in Campion Road.

I'll go out and buy another phone.

Feeling abruptly cross, I shifted Ben into the pushchair and we stomped out, locked up and marched the thirty yards to our own shop with its "Closed" notice on the door. The sign reminded me that I was supposed to be reopening in a couple of days with a new and expanded stock, and still had a lot of work to do carrying a selection back without help from Ernie, who had his classes to attend, and getting them priced. No time to mope.

The cubbyhole at the back of the shop which serves both as office and packing room looked almost normal without the Templeton boxes that had filled it up twenty-four hours ago. I checked Ben, who was sucking a thumb and beginning to look sleepy. He'd be good for a quiet half-hour before he got hungry, so I settled myself at the desk to dial the house in Campion Road and listen to the phone ring for a long time before I gave up.

Well, she wouldn't be staying there now, would she? Presumably some friend had taken pity on her.

The red light on my answering machine was flashing. I put off thinking how I was going to retrieve my missing property while I picked up a series of business messages: half a dozen offers of books I might want to buy, three people wanting to buy books I didn't actually possess. The final one was different.

"Miss Hoare? This is Detective Inspector Dave Ferry, Thames Valley CID. I'm phoning you from Oxford." My stomach turned over. "This is . . . about ten o'clock on Sunday morning. Will you ring me here as soon as possible, please?"

I copied the number onto my pad and sat watching it. I could guess what this was about and wasn't in any hurry to return the call. I needed time to think seriously about the mess I was in. What I was going to do. Because I was in trouble, and at the moment I suspected it could only get worse.

What the hell was I doing worrying about pricing books when I was about to be arrested for theft? For that matter, what was I doing sitting around waiting for it to happen? Maybe Barnabas was right when he said there was something wrong with me. A little icicle slid down my spine. It felt as though I'd been asleep since Thursday night and struggling to wake up. After I'd thought for ten minutes without any particular enlightenment, I gave up and reached for the telephone.

"Miss Hoare? I didn't know whether I'd get you there on a Sunday."

I delayed my answer long enough to wonder about that. Maybe I should ask why he was working on Sunday morning, on a case that couldn't pretend to be urgent. I said, "I'm around. What can I do for you?"

"Islington CID faxed me a copy of your statement yesterday." The voice paused for so long that I thought we'd been cut off and almost re-dialed. Eventually, he added, "I wondered whether we could discuss it. Would you by any chance be coming up to Oxford soon?"

I asked myself what that question meant, exactly, and told him I had no specific plans. Then I had a thought. I said gravely, "I was meaning to come for Mrs. Forbes' funeral, but in the circumstances . . ."

Another pause.

"I—ah—did understand that you were a friend of the Templeton family, as well as a business contact."

"We were neighbors in Campion Road for years. My father knew them well. Perhaps I can just sneak in at the back of the church. I wouldn't want to upset anybody." The idea that I might have a chance of exchanging telephone numbers with Jay Roslin trickled into my mind. I pushed it down firmly. "You wouldn't happen to know where and when it will be, would you?"

This time there was no hesitation. "I don't think they have any plans. The inquest is set for Thursday; the body will probably be released then, so the funeral could be some time the following week. I'd really like to talk to you before that."

I'd forgotten about the inquest, though of course it's necessary to hold one in a case of unexpected death. In the meantime, I had this detective to sort out. I couldn't imagine why he was being so evasive.

I said cautiously, "I might come up. Actually, there's something that you could help me with. When we had to get out of the Templeton house the other night, I left some things behind. I'd like to get them back."

"Things?"

"My handbag. My wallet. My mobile phone. That kind of thing."

"If you'd like to come up, I'll see what I can do."

You scratch my back, I'll scratch yours. But there was something I wanted to clarify. "Should I bring my solicitor?"

The voice became cautious. "Why would you do that?"

"Because," I said, "I'm not quite clear what this is about. Am I going to be charged?"

"No, no," the voice said. The tone grew fatherly; there was a reassuring chuckle. "Not at the moment, anyway. Can I be frank?"

I said he could.

His voice sank a tone or two. "This thing that you're supposed to have stolen: is it really worth what Mrs. Laszlo claims? I hear you're the expert."

I pulled the phone from my ear and stared at it. Was he for real? What kind of question was that? "I really don't know," I said.

He accepted my evasion with a mumble. "Well, anyway, it would be very, very useful if you could fill me in on some points. Call it background information. Frankly, there are things about this situation I don't understand."

Makes two of us.

After I'd let a silence fill out for a while, the voice added, "Between you and me, and don't quote me, you've worried me. You admit you had the poem. You say you don't know how you got it. You aren't a sleepwalker, are you?"

I said, "No."

"Well, but you say your car was locked. And Mr. . . . Professor Roslin says that to his certain knowledge it was impossible for you to get this thing without Mrs. Forbes' knowledge and consent."

I said, "Yes." My alibi was still in place, then.

"But you're saying that you didn't take it at all. You see how I'm puzzled."

"I don't know whether I can help you," I said, having worked out what my line was going to be. It didn't seem the time to mention curious deposits in one of my car door locks. "In an objective way, I'm curious about this too. But you can't expect me to help you prosecute me. Partly because I didn't steal it, and partly because . . . well, obviously. So if you're going to question me, I'll bring my solicitor."

"Miss Hoare, I am not going to *question* you, not the way you mean. I would be grateful if you could explain a few things in the statement we've had from you already. The story you people are giving me—it doesn't make sense."

I threw a face at Ben, who was beginning to ask about his lunch. "Then what exactly is it that you want me to help you out with?"

"We're treating Mrs. Forbes' death as suspicious," said the disembodied voice.

I sat back abruptly. "What do you mean? I thought . . . She must have been smoking in bed. I remember one of the firemen saying so. And I certainly know that the place was full of smoke!"

"It appears that she was, but I'm afraid that doesn't explain everything. Miss Hoare, I have a call coming through on the other line. If you can come here tomorrow, say about twelve-thirty, I'd be grateful. The house is sealed, but I'll try to arrange to get your things by that time. You know where St. Aldate's police station is?"

I did. And I told him before I hung up that I would certainly be there, because I was thinking that he might be able to help me do more than retrieve my telephone.

I said to Ben, "There is something very funny going on, that's for sure. I don't know what, but it involves me: and I don't know why. But I think I'd better make sure that man finds out the truth, don't you? What, if anything, would you say he meant by a 'suspicious' death?"

"Mick!" my son shouted.

It seemed to be as good a suggestion as any. "Mick for you," I agreed, "and a big gin and tonic for me. And don't say anything to Barnabas—not yet."

18

Bad Company

When I asked for DI Ferry, a passing WPC led me up a flight of stairs to an upper floor, and into an open office filled with desks, chairs, telephones, filing drawers, computer terminals, coffee cups, people and papers. She gestured at a desk under the left-hand window, where a big man was struggling with a ballpoint pen and a pile of papers, and gave me a quick glance that looked obscurely meaningful.

I straightened my jacket. I was wearing the charcoal gray Jaeger suit that I'd bought in the spring: clothes to give a police detective the impression of my total respectability. I suppose it's my personal version of Barnabas' grand manner.

Ferry saw me coming. He lumbered to his feet and waited. Upright, he was a formidable figure, a big man of about fifty who looked as though he had played a lot of rugby in his youth but was running these days to a beer belly. His brown hair was smoothed from a side parting across a balding head. I catalogued intent hazel eyes, a wide mouth with dodgy teeth, sloping shoulders and a gray suit which looked lived in. He wore a green shirt and a loosened tie.

"Miss Hoare?" I nodded and watched his eyes do a tour of inspection. He leaned across the desk and offered a hand which clasped mine a little too warmly. Two black marks. "Have a chair."

I took the usual upright office chair intended for discomfort. Ferry returned to his own and leaned across the desk, smiling at me winningly. I remembered the WPC's odd look and decided that I had been given a sisterly warning. I sat straight, remembered not to cross my legs, and looked him in the eye. "You're in charge of the investigation?"

"Immediate charge, yes."

"Good," I said. "You can probably tell me what's happening, then. You say you're treating Clare Forbes' death as suspicious. Why?"

He gave me a meaningless smile and spread his hands. "Any unexplained death is suspicious."

"What's unexplained?" I said. "I was there, remember? There was a fire in her bedroom."

Ferry looked down at the folder in front of him. "Well, we may know more after the inquest. We'd like you to attend that as a witness. I have this for you." He retrieved a sealed envelope from his desk top and handed it to me with the air of somebody conferring a gift. My name and address were typed on the face of it, and I could feel a couple of sheets of paper folded inside. I put it into my handbag. I'd been expecting a summons, and I could read it later.

"What I've come for today is to pick up my belongings.

I need the phone, and it's a nuisance not having my check book or the rest of the things in my bag. I drove past the house in Campion Road on my way here. I see there are seals on the door." He looked at me and nodded. "Frankly, I don't think I know anything about what happened that I haven't already explained in my statement, but if there's anything that I can clarify . . . ?"

"It's clear," he said shortly: "it just doesn't make sense."

"It certainly doesn't," I agreed heartily. "I don't understand it, myself."

"The coroner will be considering it at the inquest."

I said boldly, "I don't see what he has to consider about Clare's death. You're not suggesting that I set fire to the house to cover a theft?" As I was saying it, I realized that was probably just what he was suggesting. The DI wasn't smiling now.

I considered and dismissed it, because the arguments against were the same as those against my having stolen the Forbes in the first place. But also, I reminded myself, exactly the same inconvenient fact applied: I'd had the typescript as well as an apparent motive for trying to prevent Clare from discovering the fact. I could only hope that a forensic expert would be capable of determining the truth about a smoker setting fire to her bedclothes.

Then he did surprise me. "If you're willing, I thought we might go over to the house. We can pick up anything of yours that's still there, and at the same time you can help me."

"How?"

He leaned closer. "Are you willing to take me through events step by step? Show me where everything happened, what you saw? It could help me to get things clear. If you won't be upset going back?"

My impulse was to say that I would be, not from squeamishness but because there seemed something odd about his proposal. It might make sense if he was trying to spook me into revealing holes in my statement. It would make even more sense if he wanted to check it against what Georgina and Jay had told him. I suspected a trap, though I wasn't sure who he wanted to catch. On the other hand, a visit suited my private agenda, about which I had no intention of enlightening Ferry. My memory of the night was still curiously blurred. Maybe I was suffering from the after-effects of shock: but every time I tried to remember things, it was as though a thick woolen curtain was draped over my brain. I wouldn't mind clearing events in my own mind if I was going to give a sworn account at an inquest. I said, "My car is over by the railway station . . ."

He was reaching out an unnecessary hand to help me to my feet. I avoided noticing it. He said, "We'll take a car and driver, it's quicker."

The driver turned out to be the same WPC. Ferry held a door and ushered me into the back seat. By the time he had gone around the car to the other side, I had put my bag down in the middle of the seat. He hesitated and got into the front passenger seat, growling, "Campion Road, then."

I could have sworn I caught a twitch of amusement reflected in the rear-view mirror. I said, "Hello, I'm Dido Hoare."

She didn't turn around. "Hello, Ms. Hoare. WPC Jen Lassalle." She was concentrating on her driving. The DI and I sank into our own thoughts until the car turned left onto Campion Road, avoided a couple of cyclists, and drew up in front of the house.

It was the first time I'd looked at it in daylight since the fire. The air of abandonment was complete. We ducked under the striped tape tied across the driveway and I looked up to the first floor, to Clare's bedroom windows and the landing window I'd smashed, now covered by a sheet of ply which made the face of the house look even more disreputable. There seemed to be fresh damage to the windowsill of Clare's bedroom, and the big nails the workmen had driven in when they covered the broken window on the landing had sent drifts of crumbling brick down onto the steps. A padlock secured the front door, accompanied by a notice which warned that the house had been sealed by the police.

WPC Lassalle said, "I have the key here, sir."

Ferry grunted. She took that as an instruction to unlock the door and stand to one side for Ferry, who in turn stood to one side for me. I caught him searching my face with a quizzical look and reckoned that he was watching for signs of guilt, so I floated past him without letting myself falter.

The entrance hall had been reduced to a kind of junk hole by the comings and goings on the night of the fire, and the stink of burning still hung in the air. I picked my way through it, pushed open the door to the sitting room, and headed directly for the settee. My brown leather shoulder bag was at one end, and I retrieved it gratefully.

"That's yours?" Ferry said. "Will you check the contents? I'd like WPC Lassalle to list them."

I agreed, and found that listing the contents in practice meant Lassalle pulling everything out piece by piece, writing it into her notebook, and piling it to one side. Mobile phone—battery dead, after so long on standby. Wallet, with driving license and credit cards.

"I make it thirty-five pounds and coins," she said, and I told her that seemed right.

The hairbrush was listed, the two pens, check book, my notebook; she ignored a handful of crumpled tissues, credit card slips and a loose mint. The final item was the unsealed envelope. She held it and hesitated.

"What's this?"

"It's an offer for the rest of the books. I hadn't decided what amount to write in, so I never gave it to her." I threw a furtive glance at the book case with the Forbes collection, and found it empty. The overdue Wallace was the only book in the room. I caught my breath.

"What's that?" Ferry asked. "What do you see?"

I explained that it was more what I didn't see. "They were valuable books. Really very valuable—the ones I hadn't bought yet. There were some manuscripts in the dining room which were part of the same collection."

"Would that be . . . ?"

"The document we found in my car was one of them," I said delicately.

Ferry was flipping through a notebook of his own. " 'Forty-nine books and fifteen filing boxes,' " he quoted. " 'Removed and stored at request of householder.' I guess we have them in the warehouse."

I said nastily, "I hope you have them insured, then. If you lose them, she'll probably sue you for a hundred thousand pounds."

The warning caused a flutter. "Really?" WPC Lassalle muttered, and I said yes really.

Ferry laughed. "Who would have thought? A bunch of secondhand books, not even old ones."

I said, "Some of them were new," before I could stop myself.

"Well, thanks for the warning. I'll check it out." His tone said that he couldn't quite believe it.

"That's everything," Lassalle said quietly. "Is it all correct? And would you initial this list?"

I ran my eye down her writing and obliged. Then I shoveled the things back into the bag and crammed my small handbag in on top. I took a deep breath and looked around. It was time for me to be eagerly cooperative. "What do you want me to explain?" I asked the two of them equally.

Ferry threw me a fatherly smile. "It might help if you'd go through what happened on the day in question. Expand your statement. Jen will take notes."

I hid a smile. "What I could do," I said innocently, "is walk you through it. Show you exactly where everything was, what we did and where, all day and especially during the evening. Would that help?"

The DI beamed at me and stepped into my body space. I swiveled on my heel, moved behind the corner of the desk, and said quickly, "When I arrived at about noon, Mrs. Forbes saw me into this room. I'd come to pack and remove books that had belonged to her father. I'd given her a check for them the day before . . ."

I took them through it, step by step. When Ferry began to show signs of impatience with my methodical plod, I explained that I was trying to tell him absolutely everything that had happened, "Because I can't know what you'll find important," I simpered. I caught another of those background glances from Lassalle which said that she suspected me of taking the mickey. She wasn't entirely wrong, but I was doing it for my own benefit. Things had happened on Halloween that I didn't understand. I didn't expect to get another chance as good as this one to go through it.

We worked through the afternoon and the early evening step by step, moving between the sitting room, the dining room, and the front door. The remains of our Chinese meal were on the dining table, the sauces dried and cracking on the plates. I got everything clear in my own mind, even at the cost of ensuring that it was equally clear in theirs. To do him justice, Ferry had the patience to give me his unswerving attention.

We came to the point of my attempt to leave and agreed that it was just before eight-thirty. I told him about the car.

"And what was wrong with it? When did you finally get it started?"

"I had to call the AA. They didn't arrive until the morning, some time after the fire."

He and Lassalle stared at me. "It took them long enough."

I told about the dispatcher's mistake, and the postponement.

Ferry was writing in his own notebook. "There'll be a log," he said. "I'll check it. All right, and what was the problem?"

"By morning," I said, "the trouble had cleared. They said it was probably a blocked fuel line."

Ferry looked at me hard enough to make me uneasy. "There'll be a written report," he said. "He got you to sign something?"

I admitted it.

"Back to the evening," Ferry said. "You were waiting? What happened next?"

"Professor Roslin stayed in here with me, talking. When I'd phoned the AA for the second time, Mrs. Forbes came downstairs. That was when she showed me the manuscript poem. It hadn't been with the other things. We all discussed it for a minute. Then she invited me to stay for the night, and I accepted because I was too tired to drive home. That was when I phoned the AA for the third time and told them to wait until the morning. Then the four of us had some hot chocolate that Mrs. Laszlo made." I looked for the tray, but unlike the remains of our meal, the mugs had been cleared away. "Mrs. Forbes took me upstairs after that."

"Shall we go up?" Ferry suggested. He seemed to catch my hesitation at that point. "We won't go into the bedroom. I just want to get it clear where you were."

He led the way and Lassalle followed us, giving me the uneasy sense of being under police escort. We stopped on the landing. The door to Clare's bedroom was closed. One panel of it had been splintered. I looked away while I gave a summary of our talk.

"And you saw the envelope . . . ?"

"That's in my statement," I reminded him. "She put it down on her bedside table, and that's where it was when I left and she locked the door behind me."

"You say she locked the door," Ferry said slowly. "Are you sure about that? Why did she lock the door? She was at home—it wasn't a hotel."

His question stopped me cold. I couldn't think why it hadn't struck me. It would make sense if she had wanted to make sure I couldn't creep back during the night, but she hadn't given any impression that she suspected me of planning a robbery. I grasped that it looked bad for me, yet it was also the reason why I couldn't have stolen the Canto.

"So you'd agree," Ferry said abruptly, "that any attempt to get into the room would waken her? If the door really was locked, that is."

I decided that it was time to look puzzled, which wasn't hard. "Of course the door was locked," I said innocently. "When the fire started we tried to open it to get her out. Professor Roslin tried; and the firemen had to climb in through the window. I don't understand." My not understanding didn't tempt him to explain.

At Ferry's request, I led them into the little spare room. It had been searched since I'd last been there. Our flight had been too confused for me to remember just how Jay and I had left things, but I was fairly certain that we hadn't folded the quilt, left it hanging over the headboard, and removed the sheets from the bed. I had been hoping to retrieve my abandoned underwear, but there was no sign of it anywhere.

"Please don't touch anything here," Ferry rumbled, and I knew that his forensic people were interested in the room. I was willing to bet that by now there was recorded scientific evidence of my—of our—presence.

"I don't see my things," I remarked innocently.

"We'll return everything when we're finished," Ferry said quickly. I'd been right.

With about a quarter of my brain I listened to his questions and tried to tell him when we had woken and what we had done. I presumed that my story was being checked against Jay's, and explained that I'd been wakened sud-

denly, in thick smoke, and was totally confused. I was trying to avoid traps. I had the feeling that I sounded stupid
but, I hoped, honest.

The remaining three-quarters of my brain was making
a furtive assessment of the room. I would have given my
eye teeth for a chance to go upstairs and have a look in the
bedroom belonging to the missing Gina. If she was still
missing. I broke into a question from Ferry to ask him
whether she had been found.

"Not as far as I know," he said vaguely.

"Are you looking for her?"

"Of course."

"Doesn't she know what's happened to her grandmother?"

"Presumably not. Presumably when she hears, she'll
make contact."

I said, "Georgina must be very worried."

It was Lassalle who said, "She's coping very well."

I looked at her quickly, but she was looking down at
her notebook and I couldn't be sure of her expression. I
would have liked to corner the WPC for a talk.

I said, "If I can make a suggestion, perhaps some of her
friends at school could tell you something. What school
does she go to?"

"Somebody has been there," Ferry said impatiently. "If
we can get back to it . . ."

So we got back to it without my learning the name of
Gina's school. Georgina could tell me, but would she
complain of intimidation if I tried to contact her?

I repeated the story of running down to the window,
breaking the glass, watching Jay Roslin try to open the
door. "You know all this," I said. "It's in my statement.
Then the firemen arrived and sent us out. That's all I saw."

"And you can't remember anything else?"

Not yet . . .

They drove me back to the car park, and Ferry walked me over to the Citroën. He looked impressed. "Nice car," he said. "Isn't it a bit big for a little one like you to drive around?" He smiled and stepped closer. I wondered whether he even realized what he was doing as I opened the driver's door and put it between us.

"It is big," I agreed sweetly. "But then it takes the ton or so of books that I have to load and unload when I carry them to sales, and it's good for carrying the baby's equipment. Baby chairs and pushchairs and nappy bags take up a surprising amount of space."

I gave Lassalle, sitting in the police car a few yards away, a little wave. I gave Ferry a look. "I'll see you at the inquest," I said.

19

Smoke Screen

The small room was over-filled with the coroner's elevated bench, a tiny, empty jury box, the witness box, four rows of tilting chairs, a royal crest, a large wall clock, and sixteen people not counting myself and Barnabas.

The two of us had been sitting there for forty minutes. We'd left George Street early to allow for possible delays and arrived too quickly, which had at least given us a choice of seats. Barnabas had settled us in the last row of chairs. He didn't need to explain that he had chosen these seats in order to be able to watch everybody else.

A gray-haired man, something to do with the court, and three or four uniformed police officers began to wander in and out and pass papers from hand to hand. At a quarter to ten, Ferry and Lassalle arrived. The two of them noticed us and went to sit in the opposite corner, where they sank into mumbled conversation. They surfaced to greet the next two arrivals, a thin dark man with a briefcase and one in the dress uniform of the fire service; the quartet put their heads together and exchanged documents. Two casually dressed young men arrived together and positioned themselves in the chairs along the side wall. Finally, at five minutes to the hour, the door opened for Georgina and Jay. They spotted us simultaneously. Jay flashed what looked like a rueful grin. Georgina hesitated, nodded at a point somewhere between Barnabas and me, and smiled stiffly. They were with a middle-aged man in a charcoal gray suit, who directed the two of them to chairs in the first row and sat immediately in front of them at a desk below the coroner's table. I watched him open his briefcase and extract a handful of papers to spread about.

"Georgina has brought a lawyer," Barnabas observed in a ghost of a voice.

"And some clothes," I said. Barnabas raised his eyebrows. I was starting to explain that the black coat looked new and uncharacteristically expensive when the door at the front of the room opened, and we stood up and sat down for Her Majesty's Coroner, a middle-aged woman with an intelligent face under stiffly permed gray hair, who circled her court room with a sharp and comprehensive glance and got things started briskly.

"I understand it is likely that criminal proceedings may arise in this matter. I will call Mrs. Georgina Laszlo."

Criminal proceedings? I sat back to listen and learn.

The procedure was for the coroner to question the witnesses in detail about statements we had given to the police. Georgina was taken, step by step, through the events on the night of the fire. The coroner wrote her replies down very slowly. I heard nothing I didn't know already, which gave me the chance to notice Dave Ferry throwing significant looks at Jen Lassalle and the uniformed officer sitting with them. It didn't require a genius to see that he thought something was wrong, but I couldn't imagine what it was.

Jay was called. The coroner spent some time picking at his identity and the reasons for his presence in Campion Road. Abandoning that, she took him through the events of the evening, pausing at the assertion that he and I had retired to bed together, and making a long note about the fact. I could hear Barnabas stirring at my side and avoided catching his eye.

"Miss Dido Hoare, please."

Miss Dido Hoare made her way to the witness box between rows of police officers titillated by her sex life, was handed a card to read aloud promising to tell the truth, and faced the coroner. I could swear I caught a look, but when I checked, her face was emotionless.

"Miss Hoare, if I could take you back to the night of October thirty-first . . . Can you tell us why you were at forty-two Campion Road that evening?"

We went through the statement I'd made to the CID in plodding detail but without, as far as I could see, turning up anything new or anything that was even marginally different to what Georgina and Jay had already said. At the point where Clare and I had gone upstairs together, I was on my own. What had happened when the two of us entered Clare's bedroom? What had we talked about? Did anything else happen before I left? I thought myself back into the dark bedroom, saying good night, turning to the door . . .

As an afterthought, said, "I remember that she asked me to hand her some pills, and she took them and said good night again . . ."

Out of the corner of my eye I could see Dave Ferry

doing the significant glances again. The coroner shuffled papers. "Can you tell me what pills those were?"

"Sleeping tablets of some kind; she said that she had to take her pills or she wouldn't sleep."

"Did you notice whether these were prescription pills?"

I called up an image of a brown bottle with a white label and said that they were.

"And can you say how many of them she took?"

I hesitated.

"More than one?"

We danced back and forth for a while and came to the conclusion that it had probably been at least two. I described leaving and, forewarned by my interview with Ferry, described hearing the key turn behind me in the lock.

"You're certain about that?"

I was. I was also certain that Jay Roslin had met me outside the door, and we had been together after that.

"Do you remember what happened next?"

I controlled my inappropriate sense of humor and worked out what she meant.

"Professor Roslin woke me. He was shaking me, and there was smoke . . . he shouted that there was a fire and we had to wake everybody and get out. I don't know what time that was."

The coroner looked at me. "He was shaking you? Are you a very heavy sleeper?"

I looked back. "No, quite a light sleeper usually. I have a baby who sleeps in my bedroom, and I hear every sound he makes."

"But on this occasion you had trouble waking?"

Yes, I had. It was one of the things that had been bothering me on some level. I told her I'd been very tired and explained about the day's work. She nodded and wrote for a long time.

"Then you went with Mr. Roslin and attempted to rouse the deceased?"

"Yes. But the door was locked. The smoke was getting thick. I broke a windowpane . . . We banged and called . . ."

"Don't distress yourself, Miss Hoare; I'm sure that you both did your best. And then?"

"The firemen arrived and sent us out of the house."

She wrote again, and looked up at me. "Miss Hoare, did you take a manuscript or anything else from Mrs. Forbes' room at any time during that night, either with or without her permission?"

I said I hadn't. I'd been expecting this, because Jay had already been asked whether I had been carrying anything when he met me on the landing. Even so, I didn't like the question.

"Is there anything else you'd like to tell us that might help the court?"

But there wasn't, not yet.

"Then we've finished, thank you."

Dismissed, I rejoined Barnabas, who moved slightly for me to pass and whispered, "Now for the interesting part."

One of the uniformed policemen was rising, a constable the coroner described as the "officer on the scene." We got through his description of Clare's bedroom after the fire, supplemented by the evidence of the fireman who had been the first to climb in through the window. Barnabas, at my side, leaned forward. I couldn't see why, yet I knew he was listening with a concentration that rivaled the coroner's.

"I will now read the evidence of my forensic patholo- gist, Doctor James Weir, who is unable to be here today." She took a breath and began. I listened to a description of the body of a "well-nourished woman about seventy years of age" with more detail than I really wanted to hear. Barnabas had extracted a notebook from his pocket and was writing in it. I pulled myself together to listen, and suddenly grasped that Clare had not burned to death. The smoke must have killed her. I hoped that she had been asleep.

The coroner threw a hard look at the court. "At this stage is appended the toxicology report prepared by Dr. S. J. Keates. He reports the presence in Mrs. Forbes' blood and urine . . ." I struggled to keep up with Latin names and quantities in milligram percentages per hundred mils . . .

"Good lord," Barnabas said aloud beside me.

I hissed, "What? What?"

He hissed back, "Listen! Unless I am very much mis- taken . . ."

Somebody said, "Shh!" and my father drew himself up and fell silent again.

". . . and therefore based upon the presence of cyanosis, with the absence of carbon monoxide poisoning or of carbon particulates in the lungs, the consultant pathologist gives as his finding that the immediate cause of death was suffocation. Furthermore he notes that given the blood levels of the barbiturate and flunitrazepam, and the lack of any signs of injury, the deceased was in all probability smothered in her sleep before the fire started."

The report concluded with the last touch: the pathologist reported traces of an accelerant in the carpet near the bed.

The verdict was of course unlawful death. The voice said, "All rise," and we all rose.

I turned to Barnabas and opened my mouth.

"Not here, not now. Those two young men scribbling away over there are obviously reporters."

I threw a look over my shoulder and saw one of the young men looking my way and scrambling to his feet.

"We are," I suggested breathlessly, "leaving as fast as possible. But Barnabas!"

"Lunch," Barnabas said. "At the Randolph. You are as white as a sheet, and it's early enough that we shall certainly get a table without a reservation."

He demonstrated a lively turn of speed, and we had got ourselves out of the building and into a passing taxi before anybody managed to catch up.

"So it *was* murder," Barnabas said. "Well."

"I should have realized. It explains why the police were acting so picky. I couldn't understand why they were so— I don't know—so intense. At least she was asleep when it happened."

Barnabas said, "I wonder whether the Randolph still keeps Irish whiskey in the bar?"

"If not," I said, "I'll buy you a bottle at the nearest off-license." Though when we arrived at the hotel that proved unnecessary after all.

We were sitting at a table in the corner of the dining room with our drinks in front of us and the soup of the day on its way. Barnabas approves of restaurants with real table cloths. He looked comfortable but distant.

"I want you," he said, "to throw your mind back to the night."

"Because . . . ?"

"Because your story strikes me as incomplete in some way. Perhaps we can retrieve the missing pieces."

I looked around. The sound of the traffic beyond the tall windows was hushed by double glazing and the thick curtains, and the carpet muffled the waiters' footsteps. The dining room was almost empty at this hour, and the only customers on our side of the room were a pair of businessmen engaged in what looked like fierce and very low-voiced negotiations.

"All right. Now?" Only half joking, I leaned back in my chair and closed my eyes.

"Think back. You left Clare. You heard the sound of the key turning in the lock. Did you see anybody? Anything strange?"

I was back in the hallway on Campion Road, with its faint musty smell. "The hall light was off, but the street lamp was shining through the landing window. Jay was waiting for me. He said he'd show me to my room. The spare bedroom."

"And then he remarked that he would stay, I presume? What time was this?"

I suggested that I hadn't bothered to look at my watch. When my father persisted, I worked out that it must have been about a quarter to eleven or eleven o'clock.

Barnabas nodded. "What time was it when you fell asleep? I presume you are totally incapable of answering that. Hours later, was it?"

"Hardly. I was so tired I was dizzy. Getting six thousand books into boxes is tough work, even with help."

"Five minutes?" Barnabas asked. His tone was sour.

I opened my eyes and looked at him. "As a matter of fact, more like minutes than hours."

"Despite the circumstances? I find that hard to believe. All right, never mind it for the moment. What's the next thing you remember?"

"I had a dream. Clare was in it and there was a fire. The smoke was in the dream. Then I realized that Jay had pulled me up into a sitting position and was shaking me and shouting and it was real smoke."

We went through the next ten minutes, but no matter how much my father probed or I tried, nothing came to alter what I had told the inquest. The door had been locked—I knew that. I myself had watched Jay try to break it down, had banged fruitlessly.

"But did *you* turn the handle?" Barnabas inquired.

"I don't remember. But the firemen found it locked."

Barnabas frowned and nodded reluctantly. "That's true. For a moment I was playing with the idea that the door hadn't been locked at that stage, but merely . . . But, as you say, the firemen found it locked, and later the police found the key on the inside of the door, which disposes of various other possibilities. We mustn't get side-tracked. The fire engines arrived . . . ?"

". . . Very quickly. And we had to leave."

"You went next door? You waited for several hours? What did you talk about? I presume that both Roslin and Georgina were there?"

"I don't think we talked," I remembered. "It was like being in a nightmare."

"Do you mean," Barnabas persisted, "that despite the excitement, the escape, the tragedy, the adrenalin, it still felt as though you were asleep?"

I shrugged.

"Well, that was perhaps shock. And then you drove home as soon as you could. When you arrived, you gave

Ben a hug, babbled something, and went to bed, where you slept for approximately nine hours. Do you have a comment to make?"

We looked at one another for a long moment. Behind Barnabas' head, I saw the waiter approaching with a tray containing our soups. We waited until they were in front of us and we were alone again.

"That's not like me," I said.

Barnabas said, "There is no point crying over spilt milk, but I wish we'd thought . . . Well, never mind, it's much too late now to get any blood tests done. It is clear in my own mind at least that there was something wrong even after you got home. I would say that you, like Clare, might have revealed high levels of—what was it called?— 'flunitrazepam' in your blood stream." He didn't even stumble over the word, which suggested to me that he had taken some trouble to remember it.

"You're saying somebody drugged me."

"I am saying," Barnabas retorted precisely, "that in all likelihood that was so. Now, how did Clare manage it? That is something to consider. Shall we eat now?"

20

Telephoning

I latched the hook that holds the top of my outdoor bin securely against the front of the shop, propped up the "All in this section £1" sign, and stepped back to look at my handiwork. It had decided not to rain, and I had decided that I would hold a clearance sale. Just on eleven, I was open for business again. I intended to finish the day with a big contribution to the huge sums of interest I was paying every day on my overdraft.

When I looked up the street toward the council flats, I saw Mrs. Acker walking my way with her shopping bag. An old customer. She would be pleased that the bargain bin was out. I reckoned that two or three pounds were probably heading my way right now, and I nipped back indoors partly to give her a free hand and partly because I could hear the phone ringing.

"Hello, Dido."

"Hello, Jay. How are you?"

"I'm not sure." There was a silence, and then a laugh. "It's pretty funny here. How are you?"

I said meaninglessly that I was all right. "Are you staying in Oxford much longer?"

"I guess I'll hang around for a few weeks. I'm not finished here, and I'm not due home for another couple of months anyway."

I could feel my face freeze: this was a weird conversation. Perhaps not surprisingly, considering everything. But there was some information I needed. "Has Gina turned up yet?"

"Not a peep."

I said, "Isn't that odd? What does Georgina say?"

"Not much." I thought I could hear an echo of my own unease. "You wouldn't think a kid could just drop out of sight like that in a country as small as this is, would you? But the family haven't had a word from her. Look, I'm sorry about . . . you know. I should have called you before. Georgina shouldn't have told them you took the poem. It all got out of hand. I told them you definitely didn't, for what that's worth."

I heard myself say coolly, "Oddly enough, that's more than I could say myself. It was in my car. If I didn't take it, who did?"

"When I come to London, could we have that meal together?"

For a minute I wasn't sure. "I'm busy with the Templeton books, but—why not? When were you thinking?"

"Well, next week? Are you coming to the funeral? They released the body, and Georgina's cousin is arranging things. She's staying with them . . . with the family. It's probably going to be Wednesday, but I'll let you know the time and place. Or she will. We could make a date then."

I agreed, and then as I was starting to ask about Gina again, he broke the connection.

"Your face," Barnabas said, "is a study."

I hadn't heard him come into the shop. "That was Jay. He's feeling awkward, and so am I. I'm not sure why he phoned."

Barnabas pursed his lips. "Did he have anything to say about the inquest?"

"No. The funeral is probably going to be on Wednesday, that's all. And there's no word from Gina."

"That is starting to seem peculiar," Barnabas conceded. "I wonder what's wrong?"

"Somebody should find her."

"I suppose that she is all right," Barnabas said thoughtfully. "If I were a policeman I should want to ensure that she is still alive."

I considered the hint and rejected it. "No. She got out before all this started." An idea was starting to surface. "Barnabas, are you here? I want to do a lot of phoning, and I'd better do it upstairs."

"I thought I was here," Barnabas said, "but Dido, you and I have to . . ."

I said I'd be back in fifteen minutes, shot out of the shop, swerved around Mrs. Acker who was delving into the very depths of the bin, and let myself in the door of the flat. Friday is one of Phyllis Digby's regular days, and she and Ben had gone shopping, so I had the place to myself. I stopped long enough to fill a mug from the coffee maker, slid onto the settee in the living room, kicked the toy horse to one side, and located a pad of paper and a pen. There was a light flashing on my answering machine, but I ignored it for the moment and dialed Directory Enquiries.

"Oxford," I said to the operator. "I need the City Council. The Education Department, if it has its own number."

Two minutes later I'd reached my goal and was saying to a man's voice, "I'm moving to Oxford, and I need to find a secondary school for my daughter. I wonder if you could give me a list of the names and phone numbers of all the secondary schools? Both girls' and mixed?"

At the end of two minutes, I had more than a dozen numbers and one empty mug. I took the time to grind coffee beans and put on a fresh pot, and then returned to the phone. I saw no point in trying to guess: I started with the first number I'd been given and dialed the school office.

"This," I lied to the voice that answered, "is . . . Patricia Stephens." My sister could lend me her name for the occasion. "I'm ringing from the public library. We're trying to retrieve some library books which are on loan to a 'Gina Templeton.' Very overdue. But we aren't getting any reply from her home address. I see from her details that she was supposed to be at your school. I wonder whether you could tell me whether she is still on the roll?"

I held on and listened to the coffee maker sputtering the last drops of hot water into the pot before the secretary returned to inform me that no Gina Templeton was registered with them. I agreed with her comment that people nowadays can't be trusted with public property. Then I helped myself to a fresh coffee and dialed the second number.

I located Gina at a big comprehensive on the eastern side of the city. She had been absent for some days, and the school secretary would just ask the Head of Department for the Sixth Form whether she knew anything, if I cared to hold. I held for so long that I began to wonder whether I'd been sussed, but in the end the voice returned to say that "Mrs. Brown says that Gina is away for the time being." I said that no doubt explained her silence in response to our postcards. And hung up very quietly. I could foresee another drive up to Oxford on Monday. What I needed to work out was what I could do once I got there.

I pressed the button on the answering machine and was rewarded by the sound of my sister's voice. She sounded shrill.

"Dido? Are you there? If you are, pick up the phone . . . Dido, it's Pat. Will you ring me at *once* please? I've just had a . . . a *very* odd telephone call from Alice Trent. Do you remember Alice? She was a friend of mine in Oxford. She says . . . Dido, are you in some kind of trouble?"

Ouch. I phoned my sister's number and in my turn got her answering machine. Friday—she was probably at the supermarket. Putting off the inevitable for as long as possible, I tried the second message, heard Jay Roslin's voice, and deleted it.

The phone rang, and my father's voice said, "You might want to know that somebody called James T. Nusser has just arrived."

"The one from Nottingham University?"

"Precisely."

I said, "I do want to know that. Don't let him get away, I have a dozen books he'll want. I'm coming down."

"Just as well . . ."

I hung up, dumped my mug, and skidded out of the door and down the stairs. Oxford would have to wait: I needed to get through Friday first.

Half an hour later I turned to Barnabas and waved a check for sixteen hundred pounds. "We may be able to hold off the bank manager, at this rate."

Barnabas said, "Good. True. Now . . ."

The phone rang. I answered. "Did Hoare . . ."

"Hi! It's Richard."

I grimaced. "Richard, I'm so sorry, I should have rung to say thanks for all you did the other day. I've had too much on my plate. Everything's fine, and I'll send you the Warren Hastings on Monday."

"Thanks . . ." There was a pause. I opened my mouth, but Richard beat me to it. "Dido, I don't suppose you've seen the Oxford papers?"

"What—today's?"

My caller coughed. "Is it true about the Orrin Forbes 'Missing Canto' being in Campion Road?"

I sat down hard. "That's in the papers?"

"That's not the half of it. It says the manuscript went missing on the night of Clare Forbes' death and was discovered in the possession of a London book dealer."

"What?"

"There's a report of the inquest, and it says that 'one of the witnesses at the inquest was Dido Hoare, the owner of an antiquarian book shop in Islington, London . . .' "

I ungritted my teeth long enough to ask, "Does it by any chance say that I shot Clare, burned the house to the ground, and stole every book in it?"

There was an embarrassed titter in my ear.

"Richard, do me a favor: get a copy of the newspaper and post it to me, first class, so I'll get it in the morning."

"I'll send them both," he said, "the daily and the weekly."

I managed to find the words to thank him before I hung

up. It was quite a feat, because what I really wanted to do was scream. It was about as bad as I'd foreseen, and I knew that the London papers would pick up the item by tomorrow.

The phone rang. "Dido Hoare Books."

"Hey, Dido, you got some work for me?"

I must have been silent for a moment, because Ernie's voice said, "Dido?"

I said, "I have. Come. Any time, all the time, today and tomorrow, because it's possible that I won't be able to be in the shop much myself. And Ernie, if you . . ." I caught Barnabas watching me with interest ". . . Ernie, I can use some help on Monday too, if you can possibly find a couple of hours. All right?"

"I got the morning free," Ernie said, "no problem. So, I'll see you later."

I think I whispered, "Good . . ."

"You can hang up now," Barnabas said. "What's up?"

"The business about the poem has got into the Oxford newspapers, and Ernie is going to find Gina for us."

"Ah," said my father.

Mrs. Acker hesitated in the doorway between the shop and the office. She held four hardbacks in her hand.

"You've found something?" I said. "Good. Hope you enjoy them."

Mrs. Acker smiled shyly and handed over four one-pound coins. I put them into the cash box on top of James T. Nusser's check.

21

Chemistry

Gina's school was a sprawl of seventies buildings set among playing fields on the London side of the city. I slid the Citroën into the curb and craned my neck. It was just after nine-thirty, and the place was humming. I'd calculated that it was late enough for classes to have begun, early enough that the staff would still be focused on getting the new week started.

"What now?" Ernie asked in a conspirator's murmur.

"We'll go in together. I'm going to find the sixth-form center—I think there's some kind of separate office—and see if I can talk to somebody called Mrs. Brown. I'd like you to come in with me, but don't do anything conspicuous. It's a big school, and with any luck they'll think you're just one of the pupils; but remember that Mrs. Brown will know all the sixth form by sight, so it's better if she doesn't really notice you. And that probably goes for the other teachers too. Am I making sense?"

Ernie grinned. "I c'n do that. Don't you worry. What d'you really want me to do?"

"What I really want you to do is talk to the kids, because someone may tell you something they wouldn't tell me. Try to find Gina's friends. See if you can get anybody to tell you what's happened to her. She's supposed to have a boyfriend. Is he at the school too? Is he missing? Try to hang around and blend in. Make up a story about how you met Gina at a club or something. The kids will know you're a stranger, but if you can avoid the teachers, you may be able to get somewhere. If you're challenged, tell them that you came with me but lost me when you stopped to look at a . . . a . . ."

"A notice board," Ernie supplied. "There's always plenty'f notice boards. No problem."

I handed him the spare car keys. "Take as much time as you need, and meet me here. If I'm not back, let yourself in and wait. Look—don't get into trouble."

Ernie turned a shining grin in my direction.

By the time I was standing in front of a closed door bearing the nameplate of "Mrs. Caroline S. Brown, Sixth Form," he had disappeared. Silence greeted my knock.

Right.

A row of notice boards holding a formidable collection of lists, notices and small posters decorated the wall opposite. Timetable . . . I explored Monday's and discovered that Mrs. Brown would be teaching until noon in Chemistry Lab I. Not so good. Though on the other hand not fatal, since a lab should be informal enough to allow a short interview, and short-and-slightly-absent-minded suited me down to the ground. I wandered off at random through quiet corridors, looking for either the science labs or a pupil to give directions. I failed on both counts until I had an inspiration and ducked into the toilets, where I caused a stir by interrupting three underaged girls with cigarettes. Their expressions changed from alarm to relief to curiosity as they realized I was a stranger.

I said, "Hi! I need directions. I'm looking for Chemistry Lab I."

"B Block," they chorused.

I indicated ignorance, and they obliged with detailed and only slightly confusing instructions which I followed by walking out of a side door, along a path, through a kind of courtyard, and in at a pair of swing doors at the far side. The sour smell of acid assured me that my navigation had been accurate. A babble of voices led me around a corner to a door marked "I," and I peered through the window above the number plate to find twenty people, in pairs, bending over their projects. The teacher was, to my relief, perched in her lab coat on a tall stool at a side counter with a pile of exercise books, letting them get on with it. As I watched, one of the girls went over to her and spoke. The woman raised her head, answered briefly, and went back to what looked like marking. I took a deep breath and slid into the room, causing a momentary silence.

The woman looked up, her finger marking her place on the page. I smiled and made my way briskly across the room to hover at the end of the bench.

"Mrs. Brown?"

She examined me carefully, and her face said, *Now what?*

"I should apologize for arriving without phoning ahead, but it's urgent. It's about one of your sixth-formers, Gina Laszlo . . ."

Mrs. Brown's expression slid from suspicious to harassed. She was a pale woman, fortyish, with anxiety lines between her eyes. She placed a pencil carefully on the page she had been marking and closed the cover of the book. "I spoke to one of your people last week. I told her exactly when Gina was first recorded absent, and I really don't know anything more."

I took in the phrase "one of your people." My people. *Think, Dido . . .* I made a wild guess and said cautiously, "I believe it was WPC Lassalle who spoke to you?" When she nodded, I had to lean casually on the counter in my relief. I took a deep breath. "You may not be aware that things have moved on. We have a murder investigation on our hands."

I watched Mrs. Brown's expression falter. After a moment, she said, "I saw the newspaper."

"Then you understand why I'm worried about Gina. I've dropped in on the off-chance . . ." That was the point when we both noticed the silence in the room. Nobody was looking directly at us, but we were definitely not alone.

"Please come this way," Mrs. Brown said, and we escaped into the corridor and walked down to the entrance, where she turned. "I'm sorry that I can't help, but I really don't know Gina. She is on the social sciences side, so my relationship with her was purely pastoral, and—well, we never had any particular reason to speak, beyond the occasional review or assessment. I'm sorry."

I said, "Perhaps you could tell me which of her friends was particularly close?"

I caught a fleeting frown. "I did give your policewoman a couple of names. She was supposed to contact the parents and arrange interviews. Hasn't she . . . ?"

I said quickly, "She's doing that. Didn't Jen warn you

I'd be checking that no other names have come to mind since you spoke to her?"

I could see Mrs. Brown start to wonder what was going on, which meant that I wasn't going to get any further; and in fact when she opened her mouth I thought it was time to interrupt, thank her for her continuing help, say that she must get in touch with "us" if she remembered anything more, and promise that I would get back to her if something else came up. I left her standing in the entrance hall. As I was marching briskly down the path to the gates, I half expected to hear shouts behind me—but I got away.

The car was empty. I let myself in and settled into the driver's seat. I'd lasted twenty minutes in the school and had come out with nothing more than the unsurprising information that the police had already covered this lead. If any answers had been obtained, Jen Lassalle knew them and I didn't. I began to wonder about contacting WPC Lassalle and seeing whether she would exchange information. Though what I could offer her that she didn't already know was a problem.

After half an hour I began to wonder whether I should go back and rescue Ernie.

Another twenty uneasy minutes, and his stocky form danced around a corner of the science blocks and bounced toward the car. It wasn't hard to see even at a distance of a hundred yards that he was pleased with himself.

". . . so I sort of leaned against a wall till some kid asked who I am, so I said I was a private detective. I said we was looking for Gina Laszlo. After we chatted, some girls come around, and one of them said somethin' about her being crazy about this guy, and she run away to get away from her mum. Her mum doesn't like her being anywhere near this guy. Some girl laughed and says her mum just wanted the guy for herself."

I broke in, "You mean she really did run away because of a boyfriend? Is she with him?"

Ernie thought about it. "I'd say, No. There's another kid from the sixth form, guy called Natty. Long hair, guitar . . . know what I mean? She's with him."

I shook my head. This was getting obscure.

"She's with him, but she isn't *with* him," Ernie said sharply. "They're mates, OK?"

"She's off with a boy from the school called Natty, but he isn't this boyfriend, just a friend?"

"Right."

"All right," I said, "but where are they? I need to talk to her. Have they told the police where to find her?"

"They been around," Ernie conceded, "but that lot don't wanna say anything to them. They reckon it's Gina's business if she don't wanna come back, see?"

I repressed a moan and pretended that I was on top of all this.

"Any idea where?"

Ernie said, "You hearda Fairwood?"

22

Fairwood

"Of course I've heard of Fairwood," Barnabas snapped. "My memory is still quite reliable, you know, and the newspapers have been full of it for weeks. Fairwood is eighty acres of ancient woodland on the southern outskirts of London, which some bureaucrat has decided to decimate in order to build a bypass. I used the word 'decimate' in its correct sense: they propose to destroy a strip of it for their road. There has been a camp of protesters in operation since September. Trees and tunnels."

"I expect you can tell me exactly where it is," I said humbly, "since I seem to have been too busy to read newspapers for the past few months. Or . . . was it in Surrey?"

"Just off the M25," Barnabas agreed.

"Full of protesters holed up in tree-houses and underground tunnels to keep the construction gangs out?"

"And demonstrations by residents. There is a good deal of local support, I believe."

"It would be a good place for someone like Gina to

hide. Ernie was quite sure she's there. Perhaps," I thought aloud, "Ben and I could drive down there tomorrow and take a look."

Barnabas and I turned mutually to the playpen, where Ben was experimenting with removing the head of a stuffed rabbit from its body.

"He is too young to climb trees," Barnabas announced. "If you *will* go—and in the circumstances I don't disagree—I shall come with you. Ben and I will remain safely and respectably in the car while you rush into danger. I have seen pictures in the papers: it is extremely muddy, and there are unpleasant looking private security guards on site."

The "circumstances" were contained in the collection of newspapers piled on my sideboard. The daily and weekly Oxford papers from Richard formed the basis of the pile; Barnabas had added London newspapers, Saturday and Sunday editions. Clare Templeton Forbes' murder was front-page news in Oxford, naturally, and the papers made all they could of the exciting discovery—and recovery—of a certain world-famous manuscript poem. By Saturday the London broadsheets had picked up the story, and there was actually a background piece in one of the Sundays on the career of Orrin Forbes with a note on the literary importance of *Remember Me* by a professor of American literature at one of the London colleges. The tabloids had found the tale of a dead American poet and his modernist poetry less interesting than the weekend football, but there were several short paragraphs about Clare's murder on inside pages.

One way or another, my name was usually mentioned. The word "alleged" appeared everywhere, which nowadays, as Barnabas says, always suggests black guilt.

Since Saturday my telephone had been so busy with calls from newspapers and business contacts that I'd had the answering machines switched on permanently, forcing my sister Pat to drive in abruptly from St. Albans on Sunday afternoon to ask me why I hadn't phoned back to explain myself.

I wasn't happy. This conversation with Barnabas, on my return from Oxford, was no tea-time chat. So I surrendered.

It wasn't hard to find Fairwood. Somebody had been raising do-it-yourself signposts all the way from the motorway exit. The more publicity the protesters got, the better they liked it. Some enterprising person had been making it easy for the press and the television cameras to reach the camp.

We drove along the edge of the wood itself, past a line of parked vans with the logo of one of the big security firms, and came finally to the raw field serving as a parking lot for a couple of cranes, some earth-moving equipment, a scattering of muddy cars, a couple of prefabricated huts, and an empty police car. A few men were hanging around outside a mobile canteen, but it was the middle of Tuesday morning, and there was nothing happening. I drove past at a stately pace, found an unofficial lay-by just south of the gate, and pulled in.

Barnabas grunted, "It looks peaceful enough. I was expecting something more violent."

"It's a peaceful time of day," I observed. "When they break up one of these camps, they always raid it at dawn. How long has this one been here?"

"More than two months," Barnabas sighed. "Well . . ."

"I'll get on with it," I said, and stepped out of the door

into a patch of mud the consistency of jelly. With a passing regret for my leather ankle boots, I waded onto the pavement and marched back.

One of the huts was the construction company's site office. I picked my way around a collection of rutted puddles to the wooden steps, refused to allow myself to have second thoughts, banged on the door, and opened it without waiting for an answer. Inside, a scattering of tables and chairs offered accommodation for a couple of dozen people; at the moment it accommodated just two men, one in boots and overalls and one in a suit and clipboard.

I had time to remind myself that success depended on my not hesitating now as I watched them take me in, saw a "now-what?" pass across two faces, and said firmly, "Good morning. I hope you can direct me. I'm looking for a runaway minor, a girl from Oxford called Gina Laszlo. She'll be in the camp somewhere. Can you tell me how to get in?"

The suit rose slowly to his feet. "You would be . . . ?"

I still don't know why I said, "DC Jen Lassalle, Oxford CID." My mind must have been running on Mrs. Brown's mistake. "Her grandmother has died," I said quickly. "I'd like to persuade her to go home."

The two men visibly decided that either I wasn't important, or was on their side, or both, and lost interest.

"Follow the track to the right of this hut as you go out," the suit mumbled. "About five hundred yards up, you'll see their sign. You'll find some of them there. You can ask."

I gave a brisk nod and left equally briskly before anyone had time for questions.

The entrance to the camp was a gap in the fence at the

edge of an old coppice. A hand-painted sign on the fence told me that this was the Free Settlement of Fairwood. I stepped past it from the mud onto a carpet of rotting leaves and followed my nose and ears around the edge of the coppice toward a fire with a circle of fallen logs and upturned crates, a kind of gathering place. Beyond it I could glimpse part of a network of treetop ropeways and shelters. A thin trickle of smoke rose slowly and dispersed among the bare branches of old oaks and hornbeams. Four or five booted and anoraked figures raised their faces to me as I walked toward them. Two of them were girls, but neither was Gina.

I said good morning. "My name is Dido. I'm looking for a couple of kids from Oxford: Natty and Gina. Do you know them?" And watched the faces change from welcoming to cautious.

The person who came to meet me was eighteen or nineteen, a thin, tall, long-haired boy—man—whose glasses had been mended with sticky tape. He looked like a cross between a farm laborer and a curate; when he spoke, it was in impeccably upper-class accents.

"Perhaps. What's this about? Can you show us your warrant card?"

I dug into my shoulder bag for my driver's license and handed it over, but he didn't look at it. "You're not from the police?"

I blinked. "No. Why would I be?" He seemed at a loss. I said, "Shall we sit down and talk about this? Were you expecting the police?"

He looked at the others, who sat watching us. Nobody said anything.

I repeated, "Why would I be from the police?"

One of the girls asked suddenly, "Would you like some tea? It's camomile."

I sat myself down on a slatted wooden box and said that I would, which left the tall boy standing alone. He lowered himself onto a section of log and pretended not to watch me while the girl passed me a plastic mug full of something pale brown and hot from a battered kettle. I tasted it cautiously. It was more hot than anything else, but welcome. I repeated: "Why should I be from the police?"

It was the girl who said, "Well, they're always around."

"And you're never sure what they're really up to," I found myself adding a little glumly from my own experience. It was the right thing to say. Somebody laughed. "My name is Dido Hoare. She's met me, she knows I'm not police. Actually, I'm a book seller."

"What do you want from Gina?" the boy with the glasses asked sharply.

I sipped camomile tea and told them about Clare and the funeral. "She should know about the funeral," I said. "It's tomorrow. She might not choose to come to it, though if she does I'll drive her back to London, and she can catch a coach to Oxford, or—well, anyway, phone her mother. She should do that even if she doesn't want to leave here."

The boy interrupted me: "It's up to her to make up her mind what she wants to do."

"I agree. So if you'll take me to her, I'll break the news, and she can decide. I know that she left home because she was quarreling with her mother, but I think this might change things."

The girl said, "But she al—"

"I'll tell her what you say," the boy interrupted. "But

she isn't here now. If you want to leave your number, I'll get her to phone you."

Which is where we stuck. I sat and drank two mugs of camomile tea and argued, but nobody was going to budge. In the end I pulled out one of my business cards, with my office and mobile phone numbers on it. I turned it over and added the number for my flat. "She can get me on the mobile at any time," I said. "I have the answering machine on the other numbers at the moment, so that's probably the best bet. Will you tell her to ring me today?"

They nodded. I stood up and handed the card to the tall boy. Then inspiration struck. "You're her friend, aren't you? Natty?" The self-conscious grin told me my guess was right. "Natty, is it true that she isn't here?"

He hesitated for a second. "Yes . . . yes, it is true, but she's in touch with somebody . . . from home. She was afraid they might send someone to get her. So she's gone to stay with somebody she met, just to keep out of the way for a bit. But I'll tell her what you say."

I blinked at him. "And so she already *knows* about her grandmother's murder?"

He had the grace to look embarrassed. "Yes," he said. "Sorry."

"I need to know who she's in touch with."

He shook his head. "I don't know. A friend in Oxford, somebody. I will tell her about you."

I took a breath. "She must phone me. I want to know she's safe. I don't need to get the police involved in this, but I *must* know, from Gina herself, that she's really all right. There's been a murder, after all. I'm not joking about this: one way or another, I *have* to hear from her today."

The kids looked at one another. It seemed to me that they were frightened. I heard one of them say, "This is a mess."

"You're damned right it is," I snapped, and left them, not very sure who had won the argument, or what it had been about.

I backed into the car and dangled my feet out of the door while I removed my boots with the mud that was attached, and banged them together to get the worst off. By the time I had deposited them recklessly on the carpet in front of the passenger seat, I'd become aware that my back-seat passengers wanted a conversation. Two conversations. I swung Ben over the back of the seat for a cuddle and turned half my attention to his grandfather.

Barnabas said, "Well?"

"She's there, all right. Or not far away. I saw the boy from the school—Natty." I outlined the conversation. When I'd finished, the three of us looked at one another.

"Mick," Ben remarked.

"I happen to have just the stuff," I mumbled, and dug into the bag on the seat beside us for the baby mug. "Barnabas, something is going on."

"Do you think she'll ring you?"

"I haven't the foggiest idea. But I left the number of my mobile, and I gave them a pretty clear threat that I'd contact the police if I didn't hear from her."

Barnabas sighed. "Then we might as well go home."

I handed Ben to Barnabas, backed, turned and started carefully past the array of contractors' vehicles. It felt unsafe, driving shoeless. Drops of rain were spotting the windscreen, and I hoped that Natty and his friends were prepared for the loss of their fire. We made slow progress behind a wallowing contractors' truck toward the main road and had got about five miles when the mobile in my bag bleeped at me. The Citroën was just approaching a lay-by, and I pulled in, switched on, and identified myself.

The voice said without preliminaries, "It's Gina. Natty says you want to talk to me."

I ducked as Barnabas suddenly raised himself out of his seat, reached over me and switched off the ignition. He positioned himself with one ear next to the phone.

"Are you all right?"

There was a slight hesitation. "I have a cold. Nothing much."

Not what I'd meant. "Gina, do you know about Clare?"

"Yes, of course."

"I'm very sorry. I thought maybe, when you didn't come back . . ." The conversation threatened to stick. I hesitated. "There was an inquest."

"Was there?"

"They brought in a verdict of murder."

"I heard."

Oh, you did, did you? "Gina, I really need to see you. I need some information, and I think it would be better if we talked face to face." Easier for me, anyway: I hadn't realized so clearly before how much meaning you take from an adversary's body language. And this was an adversary, clearly, though I couldn't imagine why. "The funeral: you'll be coming to that?"

"Yes. Yes, of course I will." She had answered without hesitation, but I didn't quite believe it. There was a silence. Or nearly a silence. I could hear what sounded like a big church bell in the background.

"Good. Well, I heard this morning that it's . . ."

"Tomorrow at two o'clock in St. Mary Magdalen. I know."

She knew . . . I filed the information. "Will you be staying, afterward? I understand that your mother is living with a cousin just now."

Gina's voice was dull. "That's Fred, I expect."

"Well, will you . . . ?"

"I'm not going back," Gina said suddenly. "Well, if that's all . . ."

"Will you stay and talk to me at the church, afterward?" I persisted. "Just talk, before you leave Oxford again?"

She said, "I don't know what you want, but I don't mind."

"Who did you say you'd been speaking to about . . . ?" I was talking into a dead phone.

"She knew about it," Barnabas observed, settling himself into his seat and contemplating fastening his seat belt again. "She knew about everything. Either the police have been talking to her in the past day or two, or she's rung her mother. She knew about everything and has chosen to stay away and keep quiet."

I started the engine, signaled, and pulled out before I said, "It's odd that she didn't rush home. Do you think she could be frightened?"

"It's interesting," Barnabas corrected me. "I look forward to meeting her. There was a sign which says we turn right at the next roundabout."

"I did notice that," I said.

23

Shadows

I sneezed and dug into my bag for a tissue. Barnabas watched my struggles for a moment and produced an immaculately folded handkerchief, which was big enough to smother any further sneezes. The organ pounded and I blew.

St. Mary Magdalen had turned out to be about as High as the Church of England gets. We had sat through a funeral service in the ritual of the early seventeenth century. I spent most of it looking and sneezing. The interior of the medieval church—stained glass, carved wood, shadows—had filled up with clouds of incense, and the experience on Campion Road seemed to have left me with a sensitivity to smoke of any kind.

I hadn't been too busy scrabbling for tissues to watch Clare's family in the front pews level with our position against the side wall. To Georgina's right sat a smooth-faced, brown-haired man in a black suit, talking to her rapidly in whispers: the cousin, obviously. It wasn't until he turned and spoke to the woman on his other side that I caught sight of the clerical collar and wondered, fleetingly, why Georgina hadn't chosen to have the cousin conduct this service. Not High Church enough? There were a middle-aged man and two teenaged boys further along. Watching them, I assumed they were the second of Fred's sons and children belonging either to him or to the clergyman and the woman with him—the latter, I suspected. Jay Roslin sat at Georgina's left. Georgina's daughter was not there.

I searched the rows of pews systematically with my eyes. It was a fair-sized congregation. Clare had lived in Oxford for a long time, and there were several dozen unfamiliar faces. There were also several I recognized, or thought I did, including Jen Lassalle in a pew near the back, and a blond young man who looked familiar, though it took several minutes before I recognized him as one of the reporters who had been at the inquest. No Gina. I'd half expected her to be lurking somewhere, perhaps with Natty acting as protection, but there was certainly no sign of her. I sat back grimly.

We were exhorted to pray, and most of the congregation knelt on the tapestry hassocks. The church filled with that kind of silence which is so solid you can almost touch it with your hand. If it hadn't been for the muffled noise of buses passing outside the thick stone walls, it could have been three centuries ago.

I meditated on the fact of Gina's absence. When I threw a sideways glance at Barnabas, I found him staring straight ahead. I had the impression that he wasn't doing any praying, either. I hissed, "Gina."

"I see."

"Barnabas . . . are you all right?"

"Just thinking. Shhh."

I considered the fact that he had known Clare a long time ago, and that her death must have affected him. I didn't like the way the lines had deepened around his mouth.

The silence ended, the organ began to play softly, and we stood to let the family leave the church ahead of us. They ambled toward the side door, Georgina between her cousin and his wife and the rest of them following. At closer range, she looked distinctly prosperous, as though the black suit and the little black hat had been bought for the occasion in some expensive boutique. It was the first time I had seen her wear anything that looked as though it cost more than ten pounds, and I suspected that I was seeing some of the proceeds of the Templeton sale. Jay Roslin, walking at the back of the group, noticed me as he drew level with our pew. He threw a quick glance after the others, peeled off, started in our direction, and stopped suddenly.

That was when I realized that someone was at my elbow.

"Miss Hoare?"

I turned to face Jen Lassalle. "Hi!"

"Could we sit here for a minute? I'd like a private word with you, if you don't mind."

I wanted a word with her, too, but I didn't like the look she gave me. Barnabas said that he would go and offer our condolences, and moved slowly along with the rest of the congregants, leaving the two of us in the emptying church. I saw Lassalle look at somebody behind us and followed her glance.

"Isn't that one of the reporters who was at the inquest?"

"It is. He probably wants an interview with you."

"I don't think I want one with him."

"Well, you can just tell him so. That one's all right."
She gave a little smile that suggested she knew him well
enough, and changed the subject. "Gina Laszlo was absent, I see. You don't know anything about that, do you?"

"I certainly don't know why she didn't come," I said.
"In fact . . ." I stopped myself a little too late.

"You were expecting her," Lassalle said.

I gave way to a sinking feeling.

"I hear that I was in Surrey. At a place called Fairwood."

Shit. I asked her how she had heard.

"The police on site phoned us. The site manager mentioned to them that somebody from Oxford CID had been
there, and they phoned to ask whether I'd got what I
wanted. They spoke to the DI, who told them I hadn't
gone anywhere near the place and asked for a description.
He's puzzled, I think; but I guessed it was you. There are
penalties, you know."

I admitted that I did know. "It was just an impulse," I
said. "I was told Gina was there, and I wanted to have a
word with her."

"About . . . ?"

"She must know something about what happened.
She's supposed to be missing. Nobody admits to knowing
where she is. But when I spoke to her on the phone, she'd
already heard about her grandmother's death. At first I
thought she must have seen a newspaper. But she even
knew the time and place of the funeral, and she promised
me she was coming. I arranged to have a talk with her afterward—or I thought I had. The point is, she must have
been in touch with her mother all along, so why does
Georgina claim she doesn't know where Gina is? Is she

protecting her from something? Or does Gina know something? I think she knows something."

Lassalle looked at me. Her eyes were not warm. "I suppose you didn't think of reporting this? Just as a matter of curiosity, how did you find out where she was?"

I said, "I asked. One of her friends told me."

Lassalle pursed her lips and inspected me. I started to wonder what it would be like to be dragged out of a church, handcuffed, on a charge of impersonating a police officer. I wasn't prepared for a sudden laugh. "You were right, of course, and I guess I owe you something for finding her. I think I'd better get down to Fairwood. And I think I want a long talk with you, too. Are you staying in Oxford?"

I explained.

"Then I'll phone you and arrange something. Look, Miss Hoare: you are a suspect. If my boss could work out just what it is that he thinks you did, he'd have arrested you by now. You don't help yourself by rushing around impersonating me and laying yourself open to a charge of intimidating witnesses . . ."

I spluttered.

"All right, but it could be seen that way. You could compromise the case. You may already have done that."

I considered whether I should explain that I suffered from an intolerably large bump of curiosity. She would probably just tell me that curiosity killed the cat, which I didn't need to hear. I said, "Don't you understand that I'm not pleased to be accused of murder, or even of stealing a manuscript? My business is at risk here. Maybe more. Can you *really* think that *I* killed Clare Forbes? *How do you think I did it?* I wasn't alone that night."

She looked at me thoughtfully. "Then perhaps you and Professor Roslin did it together. And what makes you think we aren't finding out what really happened?"

I snapped. "Well, so far you seem to think it was me, whereas I have the advantage that I know it wasn't. And who found Gina?"

Her mouth twitched unexpectedly, and she said, "Don't push it! We'll talk within the next day or so. But please don't make it hard for both of us. This is a new job for me, and I'd like to get it right. I don't want to have to waste my time fighting you."

It was such a . . . *straight* way of speaking that I blinked. "New job?"

"Didn't you realize? I'd put in for a transfer to CID, and they seconded me early because the section is short-handed. I think I'll get an aideship if everything works out all right. But Inspector Ferry . . ." She stopped.

"Inspector Ferry," I remembered aloud, "is a problem. He'll have you making the tea without even realizing what he's doing."

She said, "You said that. I didn't even think it. I'll be in touch."

I came through the old doors just in time to see two of the undertaker's limousines pulling away from the curb, and found Barnabas standing in the watery sunshine under the shelter of the church porch in the company of ten or twelve mourners who hadn't yet wandered off.

He turned his head to look at me when he heard my footsteps. "Your face is a picture of dismay."

"It probably is. I've just been scolded. And I've missed Jay Roslin. I wanted to speak to him."

"Now, there I can help," Barnabas said slowly. "As you were busy, we had a word. Roslin is staying at a small hotel for the rest of his time here—the Southgate, I think he said. I believe he also wants to contact you. Presumably his motives are dishonorable. Today, however, Georgina's family have him firmly in tow." He stopped for a moment, and I knew from experience that he was about to give me the most important news. "And the Forbes Archive has gone to London. An exhibition has been arranged at the Senate House library, with the Canto as its focal point and a good deal of attendant publicity, after which Georgina will send everything to auction in America."

I could only shrug. I would have done the same thing, in her shoes. Georgina would become moderately wealthy, and the designer clothes suggested she was aware of the fact. I couldn't help saying, "Do you think I ought to tell her that it always belonged to her, and not to Clare?"

"She knows," Barnabas said dryly. "Roslin has just explained the matter to me. This is an odd business: I was just beginning to think that Georgina had a falling out with Clare over the material, that she found her mother had been cheating her. I was drawing lurid pictures of matricide."

"And now?"

"Now I can't quite adapt my understanding to the knowledge that Georgina knew the collection was hers all along."

"Perhaps Clare *was* trying to steal something. Perhaps that was why Jay hadn't been allowed to see Canto Eight—Clare had extracted it from the rest at some point, and hidden it. She might have thought that Georgina wouldn't know about it. Of course, it was dedicated to her: maybe she felt it belonged to her, or ought to."

"In short," Barnabas commented, "nothing fits yet."

"And Gina?"

"I asked Georgina whether she hadn't been expecting that her daughter would appear for the funeral. She informed me very clearly that she had heard nothing since Gina's departure and had not been able to contact her and tell her what has happened."

"She *what*?"

"Somebody is lying."

I considered that. It seemed a pretty safe bet.

24

Dealing

I hung up frustrated for the tenth time. I'd phoned Barnabas sporadically all morning without getting a reply; and then ever since lunch time the line had been engaged. I'd even panicked at one point and rung the operator to ask whether the phone was off the hook, but my vision of him lying dead or dying among his books had been erased by the information that it was in use. I played with the notion of my father talking on a chat line. That amusement was interrupted by the thought that I ought to reappear in the front of the shop and circulate helpfully among my customers.

I was open for business once again. Half a dozen old clients, alerted by Barnabas days ago about the new stock, were doing a square dance among the shelves. It was polite but a little competitive, like the opening of a book fair, and I could have used Barnabas' help. As previously arranged, incidentally.

Somebody behind me asked, "How much is this?" My

prices are penciled into the front of the books, so what he really meant was "What discount can I argue you into giving me?" I focused on business, opened with the standard ten percent, and began maneuvering.

By five o'clock I'd decided to put a hard day's selling behind me. It was a little early, but I hadn't been able to close for lunch and enough felt like enough. I said good bye to the last customer, locked the door behind him, and took refuge in the office with a check for ninety pounds. The cash box was pleasantly full. I made a mental note to get to the bank in the morning as soon as it opened, and punched the re-dial button on the phone.

"Professor Barnabas Hoare speaking."

"About time, too. You've been on the phone all day. Is everything all right?"

"Perfectly," my father replied. I could hear that he'd been expecting a different voice. "I am a little tired after yesterday, that's all. I've been resting. Now, you'll have to ring off. I'm expecting a call."

I listened to the sound of a line gone dead. His voice had seemed flat. Perhaps that was tiredness. But what was he doing? *Expecting a call.* Something was wrong. I hung up, reached for my raincoat, and stepped out into the wet evening.

The continuous grumble of the traffic on Upper Street was muffled by the drizzle, and here, around two corners, the street was silent. The street lamp in front of the shop was struggling against the gloom. I calculated six weeks before the days would start getting longer again, and it seemed like a long time. Hunching my shoulders, I splashed toward the parking bay. Rush hour was on, and I needed to move quickly if I was going to see Barnabas and get back by my usual time to receive Ben from Phyl is. I got in, turned the key in the ignition, and listened to the car start up without any fuss.

The lights in the windows of the smart little shops and restaurants along the main road reminded me that I was about ten days late doing essential shopping and that starvation loomed for me and my innocent child. I nearly headed on up the Holloway Road to the supermarkets and left my father to whatever business he was conducting so secretively. However, an unexpected gap in the traffic shot me quickly across the junction, and all the lights were with me as I diverged to the right and headed north.

When I pulled up outside my father's converted flat on Crouch Hill, there was a light in his sitting room. He had drawn the curtains loosely across the window in front of his desk, but I could see him through the gap. It looked as though he was scowling at the reading lamp. Then I saw the telephone receiver at his ear. I trotted up the path, climbed the steps to the front door, rang the bell and let myself in with my emergency keys.

"Barnabas?" He was just hanging up. "What's happened?"

My father raised an eyebrow at me and leaned back in the desk chair. He might have been feeling tired, but his voice was brisk. "A good deal. Quite a bit. Well, I woke up this morning musing on recent events. And on what would happen to my grandchild when you are thrown into a dungeon, as seems increasingly likely. Pat will take him in, presumably. He will become a little Cinderbenjamin in St. Albans while you serve your sentence."

I took the swift decision to ignore this, shrugged off my coat and dropped it in a heap on the carpet, and began the task of finding a place to sit down. The middle of the settee was almost clear of books. I gathered two or three strays, placed them on top of the nearest pile, and inserted myself into the space that I'd freed.

"So," I said when I'd given myself the chance to think, "would you mind telling me what you've done?"

"I telephoned almost every academic I've known during the course of my forty-odd years of respectability. Before my younger daughter took to a life of crime, I mean."

I cleared my throat meanly.

"I thought that perhaps it was time we started to concentrate on Orrin Forbes, and specifically the Forbes typescript. Your 'Missing Canto.' Why must one talk in capital letters about the thing, incidentally? The fashions of the modern firsts market and its associated manuscripts have always been beyond credibility."

I said, "That isn't the point. What have you done?"

"During the morning," Barnabas said slowly, "I drank many cups of tea and rang up friends at one university or another. And friends of friends. And their friends. At approximately ten-thirty, having located an old colleague at Queen's who proved unfortunately to have retired all the way to Cornwall but who was able to make a phone call to introduce me to the Professor of Modern English at the Uni—Well, you asked me. To make a long story short, then, I took a taxi down to University College where I lunched with one of the lecturers, who incidentally was kind enough to admire my *Tudor Love Poems*. He is in charge of the Orrin Forbes exhibition which will open in the University library in about a week."

I blinked. "You nobbled him?"

Barnabas smiled brilliantly. "I am to meet him tomorrow morning, and he will take me into the library where I shall be able to inspect the materials. He assures me that the Canto is with the rest."

I said, "Isn't that odd?"

We looked at each other speculatively.

"It does seem that Mrs. Laszlo will not be pressing charges. If she were, the typescript would be impounded as evidence. It would be in police custody in Oxford, not in London."

"Jay said she wouldn't."

"I wonder why not?"

"I beg your pardon?"

Barnabas smiled at me benignly. "You so clearly stole it. There it was in your car, you've even admitted it. The police found it in your possession. Or, actually, in my hand, though they don't appear to have . . . But Georgina is not pressing charges?"

"I think the police weren't willing to go ahead," I suggested. "When Jay told them he'd been with me all night, they could hardly go on. I can't help feeling relieved."

"So it has been dropped," Barnabas commented. "They are to forget about it, although they haven't gone so far as to tell you so, presumably because they prefer to keep you on your toes." He looked at me severely. "Why has it been dropped?"

I indicated that I awaited enlightenment.

"Oh, I don't have the answer! There is a whole list of possibilities: they believe it was an honest mistake, they don't think they have enough evidence, they know you didn't take it, they know who did take it, they . . ."

I asked, "Are you getting anywhere?"

Barnabas closed his eyes and leaned back. "Sometimes," he said irrelevantly, "I wish that I still smoked. A pipe would just . . ."

I coughed.

"Alternatively, of course, she has a simple commercial

motive. I spoke to Allen Ferrars at Quaritch. He is very clear in his own mind that the inclusion of the typescript more than doubles the value of the Forbes archive."

"Georgina was wearing some very smart clothes at the church," I told him. "She may be building up a credit card bill—they looked expensive."

"Too expensive for a dental nurse?" Barnabas asked rhetorically. "Well then. It would delay things, and presumably cause practical problems, if the item were being kept by the police as evidence in some trial to be held in six months' time."

I said, "She's a dental nurse?"

"It was mentioned in passing during my conversation with Clare during that dreadful meal. It might argue that she is not in the mood to wait for her fortune. And then there are other possibilities."

"What?"

Barnabas looked at me sharply. "I've been able to gather the information that I am not the only scholar being given access to the Forbes materials. Professor Roslin is involved in setting up the exhibition. My informant sounded as though he felt that he would have been able to manage without assistance; I got the impression that Mrs. Laszlo insisted."

"Well then," I said, "Jay's got what he wanted. I'm glad it's turning out all right for him after all."

Barnabas said "Ye-e-es" very slowly.

"What is it?"

"I haven't explained what else I've been doing today, though I may well need financial assistance with my next telephone bill. I have been on the line to several American institutions, including Macklin College. Extensively."

My moment of cheerfulness vanished.

"I was, as it were, taking up Professor Roslin's references."

"Barnabas, what's wrong?"

"I don't know. I spoke to his head of department. I gleaned the information that your friend is on leave in England, researching into the life of the poet Orrin Forbes."

I stared at him. "Well? That's what he told me. Us."

"Indeed. But something is certainly wrong. I have no idea what: I am talking about her tone of voice."

"Her?"

"Professor Giselle Vicario. Head of Department. She was the model of discretion. Fortunately, when somebody is trying to be a model of discretion, it shows. I shall have to speak to her again."

I scowled at my father. "You're saying there's something wrong with Jay because of what you think was the funny tone of voice of an American lady to whom you spoke on a long-distance phone line and who has never met you?"

"It does seem rather ridiculous," Barnabas agreed. His voice was amicable, but he was frowning. "Well, I don't see that I can get much further. Indeed I only got so far because a research student of mine took up a post at the University of Southern California some five years ago, and I was able to speak to him . . ."

I was staring. "It's a spider's web."

My father mumbled something about the usual academic networks. I stopped listening.

"I'd better get home. Phyllis and Ben will be waiting for me."

"I'd invite you to dinner," Barnabas said, "but I think I shall go to bed instead. It has been a tiring day, and I'm afraid tomorrow will be as bad."

I asked him whether he was really all right, and he said that he was. Though there was something in his own tone of voice that made me wonder whether he was also being a model of discretion.

When I got home, Phyllis and Ben were waiting, and it was a couple of hours before I had a chance to inspect my answering machine and deal with the messages.

The first was from Jay. He was sorry to have missed me, but he was going to be in London on Thursday, and could we have dinner?

The second voice belonged to Jen Lassalle. She had been at Fairwood and returned to Oxford without having found Gina. The word was that she hadn't been there for days. And Lassalle would be coming to London in the morning to have a word with me.

25

Reprise

Standing in the street outside the shop, I watched the little blue car pause at the top of the road and turn left. We'd been drinking coffee and having what Lassalle insisted on calling "our chat" in the chaos of my sitting room for the past hour.

I looked in through the shop window, past the display of illustrated books from Campion Road. Ernie was shop-keeping this morning while Barnabas and I were out of action. In theory he was putting my Templeton purchases into the stock list in the computer. In practice, I'd left him on his own when Jen Lassalle arrived at ten o'clock. As I watched, I saw him speak cheerfully to the one customer in the place, a tall man I didn't recognize, and give a nod. His eyes slid toward the window, and he gave me a furtive thumbs-up sign. Under control. I returned a wave and shot back through the door to the stairs. At least I could clear the cups away and turn off the coffee machine. I could also grab a few private minutes to digest the discussion I'd just had. I could even start speculating about why we'd had it.

On her arrival, Lassalle had produced a photocopy of my original statement, and her notebook. "Think back . . ." she'd kept saying. "Mrs. Forbes put the document down on her bedside table?"

"Under the lamp. Yes." I was picturing the envelope sitting in a pool of light.

What else had been on the table?

Cigarettes. Ashtray. Lighter. I couldn't remember.

She'd asked me to pass her the pills. They had been on top of the chest beside the door. Clare took the bottle, sat on the edge of the bed, swallowed the tablets with a mouthful of water.

I had left. I heard the key grate in the lock.

I was getting bored with this and said so. "Why don't you tell me what you want to know and I'll tell you whether I know it?"

She'd hesitated. And laughed. "I might even do that if I was sure. Look, Ferry has me running around doing most of the legwork on this. While I've been traveling I've been doing a lot of thinking."

"You can do a lot of thinking, driving through the road works on the M40," I agreed with feeling.

"Right. So I'm simply banging around trying to make sense of what happened. The locked door is bothering me. Did you actually see the key, by any chance?"

If I had, I hadn't thought anything of it. "Why?"

I thought she hesitated again. "Well—what we found was a new key. Brand new, all shiny. The marks of the cutting wheel were still sharp. But after the fire, they discovered the original in the ruins of the bedside table. The forensic report mentioned it, but nobody else seems to think it's odd. Ferry just shrugged."

I had no desire to shrug. It *was* odd. "But she might have lost one and found it again, and thought she needed a spare? I don't suppose it means anything."

"No," she'd said hesitantly, "I don't suppose so. I just can't quite put it out of my mind." She shook her head in irritation. "Now . . ."

Lassalle had been forthcoming about her trip to Fairwood. Maybe oddly forthcoming? It sounded as though she had more or less followed in my tracks. She seemed to accept that Gina was not on the site, and she had not found Natty, either. When she asked for him the protesters had merely pointed out that people came and went as they wished.

At the end, she frowned at me. "You'd gone about five miles when she phoned your mobile? How long would you say that took you?"

I told her I hadn't been hurrying, but it couldn't have been more than twenty minutes after I'd left the camp fire.

"So she might have been at the site, despite what they told you?"

I'd thought about that too. "She could have been there or close; but Natty could have phoned her, too. Somebody in the camp must have a mobile phone. Only I heard a church bell in the background, which probably means she was somewhere else." Looking back on it, I'd had the feeling that the people I'd spoken to were being evasive. Well, Gina could have been sitting on the branch of a tree over my head for all I knew. I didn't see any reason to say so.

I half-changed the subject. "She told me that she wouldn't go back. She was quite positive. But we did arrange to talk at the funeral, and it sounded as though she meant to be there."

"Perhaps," Lassalle had said slowly, "she didn't want to risk talking to you, or perhaps she just couldn't face her mother after all."

We'd left it at that. She had an appointment and I had work to do. I still wished I knew why she'd come when there had been nothing in our conversation that couldn't have been covered in a telephone call. Perhaps she was trying to impress DI Ferry with her activity? Perhaps she was just trying to keep out of his reach?

The telephone was ringing in the sitting room when I got to the top of the stairs, so I picked up speed through the door of the flat, turned right, danced sideways to avoid Mr. Spock, and got to the receiver just as the answering machine picked up the call.

"I'm here. Wait a second." I switched the machine off and listened to Barnabas' voice rise out of the sound of my own recorded message.

"Dido?"

"Yes, I'm here."

"Are you alone?"

"She's gone," I said. "How are you getting on? Is everything all right? Where are you now?"

Barnabas' voice was faint. "I'm using the public telephone in the entrance to the library. I just wanted to make sure you will be there in about one hour's time, because I want to talk to you."

"What's wrong?"

"What's wrong?" he echoed. "What isn't? Specifically . . ."

I waited.

"Specifically, I fear we are back at square one."

26

Ink

"There is an anomaly," Barnabas said, "which I should have seen earlier. Look at this."

I watched him dig into his briefcase and extract a sheaf of photocopies, which he dealt out along my kitchen table like a pack of over-sized playing cards.

"They let you take photocopies?"

Barnabas raised his nose. "I still have some reputation in academic circles, you know. I have promised they will go no further."

The nine sheets of the "Missing Canto" stretched along the table's edge; above them he had placed seven or eight pages copied apparently at random from other documents in the archive. I nodded to indicate recognition, but Barnabas wanted more.

"Look at them," he said sharply.

I looked without understanding. "They're all the same. It's the same typewriter—the same type face: I checked that. You think there's something wrong?"

"It's the training," Barnabas was saying to nobody except perhaps Mr. Spock, crouching with the obvious intention of jumping up onto the table and sitting down on these interesting papers. He put out an arm and persuaded my cat to change his mind. "You modernists have never been taught to focus on the tangible detail. And yet we have remarked on this before, and it is perfectly clear in these photocopies. Look at the typing on the first page of your Canto, and compare it with that on page five. Now consider, let us say, *this* page from the middle of the typescript of *After the Fire*. Admittedly they are a couple of years apart, but the physical nature of the two is quite similar."

Barnabas had moved into his didactic mode, but I wasn't in the mood. I said, moderately, "Just tell me."

My father insisted, "You look for yourself. The typing of the first page of the Canto script is faint."

"I noticed that. I thought that the typescript had been left in the light, maybe the sun, at some time and the ink has faded."

Barnabas nodded. "Now look at the second page."

I mustered my patience and did as I was told. And felt my heart drop into my stomach. "The first couple of lines are still faint; then it begins to darken. At the bottom of the page it's darker still." I shuffled the sheets. "It happens gradually, not all at once. Then it stays that way until . . . No, it doesn't. Does it? Is it getting fainter again by the last page? Or is it just the photocopier?"

"It is not the photocopier," Barnabas said, "though that does exaggerate the contrast a little. It happens, as you say, gradually and not suddenly as it would have done had the typist merely changed a worn-out ribbon."

"This is a fake."

"I am *thinking* that this is a forgery," he corrected me, "and possibly recent work. I'm not saying it. Not yet."

"Barnabas, it's a *fake*! Even though the typing is right."

"The machine is right," he conceded. "I wonder whether an expert examination would confirm that the *typing* is 'right.' Forbes' own machine was used. But when? And by whom? It's no guarantee that the typist wasn't wrong."

I said, "I don't . . ."

"I would have thought," Barnabas said patiently, "that a typist must have personal habits in the way he—or she—strikes the keys. Some letters will be struck harder, some lighter, depending on the strength in the fingers, the typist's unconscious habits. I am speculating that detailed examination might indicate the pattern of pressures was dissimilar to that on other documents which we know Forbes typed. My primary concern, however, is that as it would be necessary in creating a forgery to use the original typewriter, it would also be essential to use the original ribbon. As far as I can recall, I've not seen this old-fashioned dark blue typewriter ink in years. It was quite common before the war, and for a little time after. The point is that this example would obviously have to match all the rest of the *original* typescript, which I am assured is in an academic collection in Texas. Anything else would arouse instant suspicion. Not to say derision."

We looked at each other. I said, "How do you explain it?"

Barnabas shrugged. "Somebody had the machine, its old ribbon and an unused stock of the old paper. The ink would have dried out with the passage of time, but as they wound the ribbon on they would have found a length in the middle of the reel which had been protected from the air. Assuming that some forty years had passed, it might not have been a great length, but it sufficed.

"I'm not inventing this: I have been in touch with Professor Soutter of Yale University. Indeed, I read portions of the poem to him over the telephone, having explained that there is a problem about faxing him a copy as he requested, and he feels that the work is authentic in terms of style, versification and vocabulary; but he still wishes to see a copy of it (quite properly), before he ventures an opinion as to whether Orrin Forbes is the author. Apparently Forbes' page layout is unique. However, if it was not Forbes, the author was certainly at ease with his style. I wonder whether we are dealing with an actual textual forgery, or simply a modern copy of a genuine text which has somehow been lost. Do you follow me?"

I did. I might even be ahead of him. An authentic-seeming "poem in the style of Forbes" would be the work of a man who was a lifelong student of the poet and steeped in his style; whereas for a cheeky copy of an existing poem, I would put my money on the tricksy abandoned lover. I could easily see Clare setting up a small production line to make copies of valuable Forbes typescripts. If Jeff's warning and my instincts were right, it was just her style.

Barnabas cleared his throat. "Dido?"

"What can we do?"

"I shall tell my contact at University College, Doctor Govett, that there is a question of authenticity; I shall be allowed to send Soutter a copy—no academic likes to be made to look a fool so very publicly. In the meantime, there is apparently a little collection of Forbes typescripts in the Beinecke Library, and Soutter has offered to air-express some photographs for comparison. We should have them by the middle of the week."

"It was Clare! She tried to con me!"

"It is most likely to have been Clare," Barnabas agreed, "if this was done recently. It is not impossible that we have stumbled across an older crime, and that Clare herself genuinely believed in the article. I wonder whether the typescript will stand up to the kind of textual analysis that an experienced Forbes scholar would give it?"

"If they gave it a textual analysis," I said dully. Manuscript and typescript forgeries have been known to pass through the hands of even the most eminent auction houses and dealers. All book sellers know some stories. I amplified: "The provenance is so unquestionable. It came from Orrin Forbes' own collection, in the possession of his former lover and his daughter!"

"And Dido Hoare, the rising young London bookseller, was so certain of its value that she even attempted to steal it from the naïve owner, thus guaranteeing the discovery a certain notoriety. Why would anyone imagine that there was anything wrong with the item? Why should people look at it critically?"

"I'm not laughing," I snarled.

The phone rang in the sitting room. I nearly left it unanswered, except that I was suddenly sick of the sight of those pages. Ernie's voice said, "Dido, there's a guy here who wants to know if we got a *Temples of Candy*. Is it in the cookbooks?"

I blinked and took a moment to work out what he meant. We did have a copy of *The Temples of Kandy*, because I'd been looking at the pictures while I waited in the Templetons' stuffy sitting room. I reminded myself that it was a busy Friday and that my computer programmer was not really a book seller. Also that I still needed to make a living while I awaited arrest on charges of stealing a forged manuscript. I said I was on my way.

And I spent the next hours trying with limited success to make myself concentrate. Ernie, who is sharp enough, noticed that there was a problem. He took advantage of a quiet moment to sidle up and ask in a hoarse whisper, "Dido? Whassup?"

I said flippantly, "I keep worrying about being arrested for stealing—you know. And to top it all, Barnabas says it's a fake."

Ernie grinned slowly. "A fake? 'S good."

"Good?" My voice had risen and the two of us caught a couple of curious glances from the browsers.

Ernie was unabashed. "Well," he whispered confidently, "if it ain't worth anything, they won't do you, will they?"

I struggled toward comprehension.

"Look," he said in the patient tones of a kindergarten teacher, "supposing I fake some fifty pound notes, and somebody pinches them. Am I gonna get that guy arrested? Nope! Cause Plod will come along and say to me, 'Hey, mate, where'd you get that rubbish? That stuff you're handing around at the pub, that's bogus, that is. You're coming in.' And they say to the guy who pinched it, 'Let's do a deal: you come an' testify,' and he says, 'Yeah,' and they say, 'Thanks, mate, you done a public service.' "

I picked up my lower jaw and said, "Ernie, I've been really, really stupid, haven't I?"

Ernie grinned reassuringly. "You just ain't bent enough, thas-sall."

But I was just working out the implications. Or, rather, I was finally asking the questions.

Assuming Barnabas was right about this, was the forgery connected with Clare's death? And who was the forger? I'd jumped to Clare at once because I hadn't trusted her. I had no proof. How can you find out about a crime which could have happened any time in the last forty years?

Well, in this case, Dido, you'd better try to find the typewriter.

I thought about it. Forbes had used the same machine all his life. He had taken it to Italy, so it must have been there when he died. The forgery, if Barnabas was right, could have been made any time since his death.

The machine was the key.

If Barnabas was right, there was only one place where the typewriter could be, assuming that it was not forty feet deep in some Italian rubbish dump. Or buried under the leaf mold in Fairwood, of course. . . .

27

Warpath

I walked out of the police station and stood on the pavement trying to collect my temper. I'd dropped in to ask Lassalle about Gina and been shunted onto Dave Ferry instead. Not being entirely asleep, I'd changed my question and listened to Ferry's refusal to give me Georgina Laszlo's current address. Then he had given me kind advice about going home and minding my own business.

The trip had been an impulse, or as much of an impulse as you can afford when there's a baby to organize. I'd handed Ben over early at the flat belonging to a sleepy Phyllis Digby and her invisible husband, shot across London in the wintry, pre-dawn darkness, and was driving over the ridge of the Chilterns as the gray light grew to reveal the misty flat lands of the flood plain with Oxford a smudge in the distance.

I'd left the Citroën on the double yellow lines in front of the police station, and had even got back to it before it had picked up a ticket. And was wondering whether that was going to be my first and last piece of luck for the day.

One of many worries fought its way to the surface as I sat at the wheel of the car and waited for a chance to pull out into the stream of traffic: Barnabas. He had spent most of Sunday either in bed or at his desk. He'd claimed he was thinking. I turned off my indicator, punched a button on my mobile, and listened to his phone ring for a while before I gave up. Presumably he was off somewhere again talking to people about his photocopies. Presumably he was all right.

However, thinking about him suggested my next destination. I took advantage of a red light somewhere down the road, pulled out into a gap, and drove toward the Randolph, beating a cruising BMW into an empty parking bay. Almost overcome with self-satisfaction, I made my way into the lobby of the hotel, found a free armchair in the corner, and ordered a pot of coffee and a copy of the Oxford telephone directory. If I couldn't get any help from the police, there was always the alternative of doing it the hard way.

I turned to the list of dentists in the *Yellow Pages*, poured myself a coffee, added milk from the little jug, and dialed the first number on my mobile.

It was the fifth or sixth call that hit the target. "But she left nearly two weeks ago," a man's voice told me. "Her mother died."

"And she's not coming back?"

"No. If you'll excuse me, I have to get back to my patient. My temp hasn't turned up this morning, and I'm pretty pushed."

"One thing," I said quickly. "My name is Dido Hoare. I'm an old neighbor from Campion Road. Their house is closed up, but I noticed some water running out of a pipe on the side wall." I quickly crossed my fingers. "I wanted to phone Georgina and tell her she'd better get a plumber in before there's any more damage."

The voice said rapidly, "Oh. Ah . . ." I imagined a patient writhing in the chair and kept my fingers crossed. "She's staying with relatives. She sent me a note . . . Wait a second. Here it is . . . Twelve Willow Road, Summertown. Telephone number . . . no number."

I let out my breath. "Don't worry, it must be in the phone book under her cousin's name. Thanks *very* much." I switched off to leaf rapidly through the residential pages and found the Rev. Colin A. Templeton. Dialed. Found myself explaining to a woman's voice that I was wanting to contact Gina Laszlo, and wondered whether her mother could give me her phone number.

The pause told me it wasn't going to work. "What did you say your name was?"

"Dido Hoare."

"Miss Hoare." The level tone told me that the name was familiar to the voice. "I'm sorry, Georgina isn't here just now. She is very busy sorting out her marriage arrangements."

I opened my mouth and managed to close it again without squealing *She's what?* I opened my mouth again and said that I hadn't realized. Then I pulled myself together and said, "About Gina . . ."

"I'm afraid nobody knows anything about Gina. If you'd like to leave your number, I'll ask Georgina to ring you. When I see her."

I left the number of my mobile and switched off without much hope. The coffee was cold. I waved at the waiter and recklessly ordered a second pot.

"I'll go there," I mumbled. "I'll ring the bell and get her to talk to me, and if I have to, I'll sit outside the door until she does."

"Excuse me?"

"Nothing," I said. "Could you bring me a bun?" Once I'd declared my presence, I might have a long wait. I thought I'd better fortify myself: breakfast now, and stock up with mineral water and chocolate before I reached the side streets of the suburb. I wasn't going to give up.

I had my legitimate errand to do on the way. It had been one excuse for this expedition: the fact that I'd forgotten to post Richard the book I'd promised him, and really ought to deliver it and maybe even see whether there was something I wanted to buy from him. The shop that he and his partner run is close to the Randolph in a little side street full of antique shops and eating places just beside my old college. The car could sit illegally on another of those yellow lines for a minute or so. Yet, when I turned into the narrow road that was my goal, I found a parking place just in front of the shop. This was beginning to be scary.

Normally I would have stopped to look at the books in the window display; I decided I wasn't in the mood. I knew suddenly that if I did try to buy anything it would probably turn out to be a disaster. The shop bell jangled as I shut the door behind me. The place was empty, and for a moment I just stood and smelled the dust of old books and attended to the feeling of my stomach churning. Maybe the bun hadn't been such a good idea. Then Richard popped out of the back. He saw me, and I watched his face freeze.

I said, "Hi! I brought you the Warren Hastings. I'm

sorry I never got around to posting it—I've been run off my feet."

I thrust it toward him, and he took it gingerly and stood without looking at it. "Thanks. I'll, uh, send you the check."

I thought of saying, "It's absolutely genuine, you know. I didn't steal this one from anybody, and I'm not here to steal from you either;" but it wasn't Richard I was angry at. I said, "Cheers. That's fine." And went away.

Summertown next. I stopped opposite the post office, and the second person I asked knew Willow Road. I made a couple of right turns and found myself in a cul-de-sac of twenties semi-detached houses. Number 12 was at the end, beside a small suburban church built of the same brick as the houses; a sign on the gate confirmed that I had found the vicarage. I turned the car around, parked it across the driveway, and went to ring the doorbell.

A curtain shook in the window beside the door.

When nothing else happened I rang again and Georgina opened the door as though she had been standing behind it all along.

We looked at one another. She said, "I'm sorry I wasn't here when you rang. Thank you for coming to the funeral. I can't ask you in, I'm just going out myself."

"Would you like a lift somewhere?" I suggested.

She shook her head. "Maddy said you were asking after Gina. I'm sorry, but I still haven't heard from her."

"Did you know she was at Fairwood?"

I watched her deciding to say, "The police told me. They say she isn't there anymore."

I couldn't stop myself asking, "Why did she run away from Campion Road?"

Georgina fixed her pale blue eyes on me and told me that it was none of my business. "Now you can go away," she said. "I don't know what you think you're going to gain by bothering us."

I'd been going to congratulate her on her engagement, but she was so quick at shutting the door that it happened before I could open my mouth again. I raised my hand to the bell and brought it away. Then I went and sat in the car and watched until the door reopened and Georgina appeared, wheeling a bicycle. She rode it down the driveway and around the front of the Citroën without looking at me. I started the engine and followed. At the main road she turned left, and the traffic was too heavy for me to be able to match my speed to hers. I overtook her outside the post office and carried on for a couple of blocks before I could pull over. When I looked back, there was no sign of the bicycle or the smart black coat.

And then after all, heading down the Banbury Road toward the city, the Citroën turned left almost without any decision by me. I pulled into a space on the east side of Campion Road and found myself once more staring at the smug, crumbling, silent face of number 42. The tape across the gate had broken and was lying on the ground. Nothing moved. I wasn't even aware that I'd made a decision until I got out of the car, locked it, and started across the empty road. It felt as though I was crossing some kind of bridge. I still didn't know what I was going to do. But I did know I was angry.

28

Temporary Insanity

It occurred to me just as I stepped over the fallen tape that I mustn't be seen, especially by the kind neighbors who had taken us all in on the night of the fire. I was wearing jeans and my old navy jacket, as I had been then, and they would certainly remember me. There had been nobody in sight when I'd crossed the road, but I dodged quickly around the rusting Ford.

The face of the house looked back at me. I could have sworn that it was crumbling in front of my eyes, and in fact I was standing on fresh crumbs of brick that had fallen from somewhere above. There were voices in the street. I slipped into the area between the side of the house and the hedge. In that shelter I could stop to think about what I was doing.

I was looking for the typewriter. Naturally. Even if I got into the house it was pretty unlikely that I was going to find it, but at least I could look, since nobody else was going to.

If I were seen, I didn't care. I'd just plead temporary insanity.

I drifted toward the back garden and found myself remembering something else. I'd grown up in a house just down the street which had been built at the same time as this one and, I realized, roughly to the same plan. In the old days when I'd come home from school I used to let myself in at the side. I almost stumbled into the little sunken area with its brick steps leading down to the kitchen door. The treads were overgrown with grass that had seeded itself on them. A couple of old flowerpots held dry brown plants that had flowered there a couple of years past; the door obviously hadn't been used in a long time. I climbed down cautiously and tried the handle. For a moment I thought the door shifted, but that was wishful thinking.

There were bars fixed over the glass. I pressed my face against them and found myself looking into a deserted kitchen. I could see an ancient gas cooker against the back wall and an antique refrigerator with rounded corners. There was a little plastic-topped table holding a dirty teacup. The furniture was pretty basic, but there were some wall cupboards and I needed to look into them. A doubt tried to surface: if I was going to search every cupboard in this house, it could take hours.

Better get on with it, then.

I picked my way to the back between encroaching brambles and peered around the corner. The garden was overgrown. What had once been a lawn had become a patch of wild grasses and weeds with self-seeded bushes and dock struggling toward the middle. Japanese knotweed had invaded from the next garden and formed a sheltering hedge with its dried wintry stems. I crept in beside it.

It didn't take more than a glance to see that the rear face of the house was hopeless for my purposes. The two basement windows which let a bit of light into the kitchen were defended by iron bars, and somebody had nailed great sheets of ply over the lower three-quarters of the tall sitting room windows. Unless I could find a ladder, climb conspicuously to a height of about eighteen feet, smash a windowpane and let myself fall head-first over the top of the barrier onto the floor below, I wasn't going to get in at the back. I dug my driving gloves out of my pocket in a sudden anxiety about fingerprints and put them on before I shook the basement bars. They held firm.

Then I fled back to the knotweed. All right, it had to be a door. A door needs a key. Maybe . . . ?

I climbed down into the area by the kitchen again and picked up the flower pots, one by one. The key was underneath the third one. It had been hidden there for so long that it had sunk into the muddy slime that coated the bricks. I picked it up, rubbed it clean with the fingers of my gloved hand, and tried it in the lock. The mechanism stuck, shifted, and turned, and I jerked the door open and let myself in.

The stench was so strong that I gagged and nearly ran for it . . . something had died here. *No. Calm down!* I flicked the switch and checked that the electricity had been turned off. The smell was coming from the fridge.

All right, get this over with.

I raced around the room opening doors: wall cupboard, broom cupboard, sideboard; tins, plates, tumblers . . . Beneath the sink I found buckets, detergents, rags, and the smell of wet rot. I slammed the door and was turning away when the sight of something nudged a memory.

The plug was in the drainhole, and the sink was still half filled with water in which sat four mugs and a milk pan. They were the things Georgina had used to make hot chocolate on the night of the fire. Somebody had carried them downstairs and left them soaking. Georgina? I thought she'd gone upstairs. Jay? He had been the last person in the sitting room.

Whoever had done it hadn't bothered with the dinner dishes—just these.

I lifted a mug and emptied out the water. It was clean. I had to file this puzzle, there was work to do.

Either the air in the passageway was a little more breathable, or else I was getting used to the smell. The room at the front of the basement was a large bed-sitter, and it had been inhabited recently. It was scantly furnished with a narrow, unmade bed, an old oak chest, a wooden chair and table under the window, and an armchair with frayed green upholstery. A wardrobe door swung open, revealing a tangle of wire coat hangers. There was a hand basin in one corner with a wastepaper basket underneath. I picked it up and looked inside but found nothing except a cheap ballpoint pen and an empty toothpaste tube. When I straightened that out, I found I was holding a brand that I knew, but the design on the tube was unfamiliar. I turned it over. *Made in Trenton, NJ.* I was in the room that Clare had rented to Jay. It felt dank, and I wondered for a moment whether a white middle-class American wouldn't have found Clare's life style a shock. The drawers had been cleared and a second wastepaper basket under the table was empty. I closed the door carefully behind me and headed for the stairs.

Near the front entrance I stopped again, thinking that I'd heard something, and stood still until I was sure I'd been wrong. It was probably mice. Maybe rats. I shivered and calculated: the longer I was in the house, the better chance of my being discovered. Therefore the best idea would be to start at the top and come down, getting closer to my escape route as I worked. I ran up to the top floor.

The smell of the smoke still lingered everywhere. I made myself ignore it.

Four bedrooms, two in use. The spare rooms seemed possible hiding places, and I turned to them first. More of the old oak furniture, crammed to the top with *things*: clothes, household linens, ornaments—things put away long ago, hoarded. Some of the clothes were a man's, and probably dated from before the death of Clare's father. I checked my watch. I had about four hours before it got dark. However, a typewriter was big enough to be noticeable. Abandoning my scruples, I adopted the quick and simple method of sweeping the contents of shelves and cupboards onto the floor. It would be instantly clear to the quickest glance that somebody had searched the house. I didn't care.

The uninhabited rooms took me fifteen minutes and held nothing of any interest, barring the knowledge that Clare could have stocked a dozen charity shops when she finally moved out. I passed into the third bedroom, the large room at the front above the one which had been Clare's. Neat: Georgina, then. When I opened the wardrobe I made out that it was half empty. The drawer in the bedside table was open and empty too, and the contents of the chest of drawers seemed meager. The police must have allowed her back in to get some clothes. I checked the wardrobe and a cupboard, saw nothing like a portable typewriter, and fled.

Gina's next, at the back of the house . . . The walls were plastered with posters of pop groups (Gina favored Orbital, and also Left Field, the poster with shark's jaws swimming in what looked like a sea of apple sauce). The room was a chaos of clothes, CDs, school books and papers, ballpoint pens, magazines. A fair mixture of all of these were tangled in the bedclothes. Anybody who had never been a teenager would probably assume that an intruder had already searched it, but I decided that I was seeing the results of a sudden departure. I didn't expect to find the typewriter here, but I went through the motions.

I turned to the desk last. If Gina had been thoughtful enough to leave a diary . . . But if she had one, she'd taken it away with her. In the bottom drawer, however, I found a cheap organizer with a flowered plastic cover. I turned to the diary section and checked that the dates were this year's. The page I examined had notes of homework assignments, exam dates, and some first names and times. No pourings out of her girlish heart, but a record of appointments was better than nothing. There could be something that would help me to find out where she was hiding. I slid it into my jacket pocket.

Beneath the organizer was a layer of sweaters. I ran my hand along the front of the drawer, felt something, and hooked it out: an unbelievable black negligee, trimmed with wide bands of lace, dangled from my hand. Real silk. Very nice. I wouldn't have minded owning this myself. The label carried the name of Oxford's smartest shop. I caught myself shaking the thing, as though an answer might drop out of a pocket. It didn't. Maybe Gina had shoplifted the thing, it was so unlike anything else she owned. I stuffed it back.

Out in the hallway, a cupboard door remained. Likely. Very likely! I flung it open hopefully and found myself staring at a hot water tank. I reached in to a shelf and pulled out the piles of old sheets and frayed towels, dumping them onto the floor. Nothing interesting.

The next floor down contained the bathroom, an uninhabited room beside it, the little spare bedroom where Jay and I had slept, and the room where Clare had died. That was the point where I began to realize there was a part of this project I didn't want to face. I dealt with the other rooms and then avoided the moment by running back to the ground floor and sticking my head through the sitting room door. I checked to be sure that it was as empty as it had been when I was last there. I went into the dining room with more hope, because I remembered what that had been like: every drawer and shelf crammed to bursting.

The clocks had stopped. I glanced at my watch. Nearly three. I didn't have much more time. At a pinch, I could go back to the car and get my emergency torch; but it would be a dead giveaway if anybody passing in the street noticed a light moving around. I ought to finish before dark.

So I settled to it, keeping away from the windows. Wardrobe, roll-top desk . . . The desk was a temptation. I pulled out handfuls of old letters, old forms and bills, broken pens, old newspapers and dust. I could swear that none of it had been touched for decades, and certainly none of it was a typewriter; but I couldn't get rid of the feeling that I might find something—a document, letter, a little reel of typewriter ribbon, something—that would suddenly tell me everything I had to know. The police really ought to take the whole lot away for examination. I saw nothing that mentioned Orrin Forbes, but there wasn't time to look closely.

Finally I checked the cupboards beside the fire. The record files had gone to London, of course. So had the Orrin Forbes photograph, presumably: the pale rectangle on the wallpaper overhead was empty. I looked into the bottom of the cupboard.

There was a difference. I reached into the cardboard box and pulled out the newspaper-wrapped soup bowl that I'd looked at once before. It was the same one, or identical, but the last time I'd been there it had been sitting at the top of the box full of wrapped china. Today the box was half empty. I slid a hand down the side and felt to the bottom. More wrapped crockery. Something was missing. I could guess what it had been, and my heart lurched.

I sat for a moment in Clare's own chair and surveyed the table top. The takeaway containers and dirty plates and cutlery were where we had left them on the night of her death. The smears of sauce had dried, and despite the cold were starting to smell. I was trying to put off the moment when I went back upstairs.

I don't believe in ghosts.

When I looked out, the sky had darkened and it was starting to drizzle again. There wasn't much time, and I couldn't come back. *Just do it. Don't sit there wittering.* I listened to the silence and ran out of the dining room, up the stairs, past the broken window, to the damaged bedroom door.

It was unlocked. The curtains had been left open, and it was still light enough inside to see the tumbled, charred mound which had been Clare's bed, the blackened bedside table and the streaks of black which ran across the rug.

The walls and ceiling were smoke-darkened, and everything in the room sat under a layer of greasy soot.

My imagination wanted to see Clare on the bed, a large body blackened and still. I turned away.

All right. I'd keep away from the bed itself, be careful not to disturb anything which might be evidence: though from the tracks in the mess on the floor, it was clear that the firemen and ambulance staff hadn't been so careful, and the forensic investigators had come and taken their photos and samples, and gone away. I sidled around the edges of the room, opening the doors and drawers. I wouldn't actually disturb anything if I could avoid it, not even with my safely gloved hands. I didn't really even want to touch the greasy soot. I knew I'd be throwing my driving gloves away when I left the house. *Pull yourself together, Dido.*

I was so busy being careful that I almost forgot to look on top of the wardrobe. I climbed onto a chair because of some memory that people keep suitcases on top of wardrobes. At first I thought I'd found a little vanity case. Then I moved the chair, climbed back up, and saw the name "Underwood" on the black leatherette. There was a catch on the front of the case that opened by squeezing. I reached over and pushed the lid up.

It was an old-fashioned portable typewriter, sturdily built. I heard myself let out a shout of triumph and stood motionless until the sound died. After a while I reminded myself that there was nobody to hear.

The thing is, I'd seen it before. It had been sitting on the dining table, that very first evening when I'd come from the book fair: and I'd *seen* it, I'd actually *seen it then*! I pulled back sharply. I had almost *caught* Clare preparing her little scam. I stopped myself pulling it down. All I needed, what I had to have and couldn't risk leaving behind, was the ribbon—if it hadn't already gone. On that ribbon we might still be able to see the impressions left by typing out the words of Canto Eight. I found one of the reels by touch. It seemed to be locked in place. And the other. I pressed myself against the wardrobe forgetting everything except my determination, stretched up and fumbled, and almost decided to get the case down. Then my finger shifted a small catch, and something sprang loose. I felt for a catch on the other reel. And almost fell off the chair, panting, clutching the ribbon in both hands.

Part of me knew that it would be better to leave it in place. The other part argued that I'd done the damage already just by being in the house. And somebody might know that the evidence was here and might come back for it. I balanced on the chair and worked it out.

Clare set up the con trick. She'd had the typewriter, she'd set up the sale. Somebody had killed her. That had to do with the Forbes archive. Obviously. And the murderer probably knew about the typewriter.

Georgina? She was the one with knowledge, opportunity, motive; and she was the only one of us in the house that night without an alibi. If I were Georgina, I'd come back as soon as I thought it was safe and destroy the evidence. If I couldn't remove the typewriter, I'd certainly take the ribbon. That was much too dangerous to be left. If I were her I'd get myself in, police seal or no police seal. They might even allow her to come back to get more of her things, and she would have worked out that this room was where Clare must have hidden the machine. She would get herself in here somehow. If I left the reel, it would vanish. Anyway, I'd left the typewriter in place, and the grimy deposits around it would show that it had been there since before the fire.

I'd left the lid open. I took a tissue, wrapped the reels in it, and pushed them down into my pocket behind Gina's organizer. Then I closed the case and ran. Somewhere down toward St. Giles I could hear a church bell. The old house creaked and settled. *I don't believe in ghosts.*

It was as dark as night in the basement. If I hadn't grown up in a house like this one I might have had a problem, but I felt my way to the door, got out into the fresh air, locked it again, and left the key in its place under the flower pot, wondering whether anybody still alive knew it was there.

The Citroën was at the city boundary when I woke up.

I could have used the mobile. I could have phoned Oxford CID and told them what I'd found and gone back to sit on the stairs outside the door of Clare's bedroom waiting for them to arrive.

I pulled the car into a lay-by too fast and had to stand on the brakes to stop before I ran out of road. Then I opened my window and sat and thought for a long time.

29

Truth and Memory

Dribbling the last drops of the milk into my coffee, I recognized that the result looked exactly like milk heavily diluted with hot water in which something brown had, very briefly, sat.

Ben, sitting beside me in his chair, made a remark.

"You mean," I said, "something has to be done."

I thought I could remember an old jar of instant coffee on the shelf over the fridge. When I found it, the powder at the bottom had congealed into a crust. I tapped at it with the spoon, picked out a lump, and tried to get it to dissolve. It tasted just the way you'd expect.

Mr. Spock, wearing the smug air of a cat who has dealt with his own breakfast in the normal way, stood at the window and indicated that he would take a stroll now. In the time that it took me to open it for him, I admitted that what was in my cup was undrinkable. "We'll go to the supermarket. Maybe when we get back Barnabas will be speaking to me again."

I'd phoned my father the night before from halfway down the motorway and explained. I wasn't expecting to be congratulated. The conversation had been short. Almost icy. And this morning I had heard him arrive and let himself into the shop without following his usual custom of ringing my bell and saying good morning. I'd been sticking it out upstairs, giving him a little time.

He was supposed to be writing catalogue entries. I hoped that by now he had stumbled across another Templeton gem and forgotten his anger. Perhaps not.

Barnabas' idea was that I was about to be arrested. Looking at the situation in the cold light of a November morning, I thought he was probably right.

When I stepped into the street a few minutes later with Ben and his stroller, it wasn't quite raining but the sky was black and the air felt like water. I could see a light in the office. The door between it and the shop was ajar, and Barnabas was leaning over the desk turning the leaves of a book. Good. We crept off toward the car before he noticed us.

Ninety minutes later, or thereabouts, I finished staggering up and down the stairs with the shopping. The smell of fresh coffee filled my kitchen. So did a supply of food. I'd overdone it: either I was reacting against the bare cupboards of my recent life, or I was subconsciously expecting a police siege. Ben was in his cot, sleeping off the excitements of the supermarket. I set the baby alarm, poured two mugs of fresh coffee, and headed toward my delayed encounter with my father, preparing a speech that began, "You don't have to tell me, because I know I shouldn't have."

I edged around the office door. Barnabas was scribbling on a filing card. I opened my mouth. He said, "So you're sorted? Well, where is it?"

"Actually, it's in the bottom drawer on the left."

"Here? Ah!"

I'd abandoned the typewriter ribbon there in its tissue wrap when I'd arrived back the night before. Now Barnabas retrieved it, laying the little parcel on a sheet of my letterhead paper and unwrapping it delicately.

"Did you touch this?"

"A little," I confessed, "but not with my bare hands."

"So there might still be some chance of useful fingerprints," my father concluded acidly. "Never mind that. Do you happen to own any ordinary pencils?"

"Top left," I said.

I watched him poke two of my wooden pencils into the central holes of the reels and lift the ribbon gingerly to a position under the reading lamp. He established the correct amount of tension and began slowly to roll the ribbon from one reel to the other, examining it closely. I held my tongue and listened to the tap dripping in the sink.

"You're right."

"What?"

"The typing is legible. This ribbon must have been almost new when it was left in the machine. Fortunately. There is a small amount of over-striking, but I can see letters quite clearly. I wish I could show Doctor Govett."

I struggled and remembered that was the name of the man who was in charge of the Forbes exhibition. "Why don't you?"

"Because I shan't have the opportunity. Never mind, he will certainly postpone the exhibition, if not cancel it, when I tell him about this; and as presumably the police will arrange to make some kind of record of these images, the evidence will be available. I wonder whether the real Canto still exists, and if so, where? If this thing is a copy, no doubt the original will turn up in response to the publicity of the trial."

"Trial of . . ."

"Of Clare's murderer."

"I was thinking," I said, "that Clare made the typescript."

Barnabas made an equivocal sound in his nose which indicated that he awaited my evidence.

"I saw the machine, you know," I said. "The first time I visited her, after the book fair, it was on the dining room table."

"A shame you didn't remember that before," Barnabas remarked.

I understood his annoyance, but said I'd had a lot of things on my mind lately, and anybody who could remember any one item from Clare's rubbish tip was probably obsessive.

"Nevertheless . . . Well, as you say, she probably did. And her motives were certainly financial."

"It doesn't help much," I said. "I mean, I don't yet see the link between the Canto and the murder."

Barnabas frowned. "At this rate, we'll probably discover that you saw that too . . . and forgot it, like the typewriter."

I snorted feebly. The trouble was, I halfbelieved he was right.

"What are you going to do now?"

I said slowly, "I'm going to have to give this to the police and tell them what it is and how I got it. I'm not looking forward to it, but I don't see anything else to do."

"Neither do I. I can't *imagine* . . ." He stopped himself with a visible effort.

"So I'd better phone Oxford."

"I am afraid so."

I reached for the phone and stopped when Barnabas said, "Are you packed?"

"What?"

"They will arrest you. It might be like going into hospital: you'll need an overnight bag."

I snapped. "They won't arrest me—I'm cooperating!"

"Also we had better phone Phyllis, even though it's not one of her usual days. You must try not to frighten Ben."

"I'll make sure I'm handcuffed and dragged away screaming from somewhere out of sight," I snapped. Still, warning Phyllis might not be a bad idea. Also getting up to date with the messages on the answering machine, opening the mail and looking for checks to be deposited, and reading through any postal catalogues. After that, the business could run, or not run, for a while by itself. I told Barnabas that no doubt he would want to contact Ernie and sign him on as a partner for the duration of my sentence.

"It is not a joke," Barnabas said firmly.

"Not entirely," I agreed.

"And as it happens Ernie is due here at any minute."

"Ernie? It's a college day."

"Nevertheless. I asked him to do some shopping."

I blinked.

"I've decided that he's right. We need to go on the Internet."

"I'm not thinking about starting up a web site catalogue right now!"

"Indeed, no. Though Ernie assures me that it is the medium of the future. However, I understand that the Internet is a source of information of all kinds, and Doctor Govett concurs. Therefore I gave Ernie a hundred pounds in cash yesterday, and this morning he is to appear with various telephone leads and an appropriate computer modem. By the time you have finished with the Oxford CID, we shall be On Line."

"And informed?" I asked.

"Informed."

"About . . . ?"

Barnabas looked at me. "About Orrin Forbes. And other people."

We both heard the rattling at the door. I slid quickly out of the line of sight before I realized I meant to move. Barnabas looked sardonic. The newcomer was Ernie, looking bright and carrying a bag with the logo of one of the computer shops on Tottenham Court Road. I let him in and took myself upstairs, carrying the last two days' collection of letters and catalogues, to put my affairs in order and phone Jen Lassalle. I'd done most of the first, and was pulling myself together to do the second, when the door bell rang and I went downstairs to answer it, still composing a speech that began, "I am phoning you to report."

I didn't need it. Dave Ferry was blocking my doorway. He said, "Dido Hoare, I am arresting you on suspicion of breaking and entering premises at number forty-two, Campion Road, Oxford. There may be other charges. You do not have to . . ." He made a long speech: I'd heard bits of it before—on television—so I had the time to wonder what Jen Lassalle, standing beside him with an absolutely expressionless face, was thinking. Barnabas arrived out of the door of the shop and took the whole picture in with one glance.

I said, "I'll have to get . . ."

"You won't need anything," Ferry said.

I said, "You don't understand."

"Perhaps you should get your coat," Lassalle suggested. "That's all you'll need."

Barnabas cleared his throat. "I shall telephone the family solicitor and ask him to meet you in Oxford. I am advising my daughter to say nothing until he has arrived." He looked at me significantly and said, "I'll make sure Stockton brings what you need."

I understood. "In the meantime," I said, "don't get surfing so hard that you forget Ben. And can you feed Mr. Spock?"

Barnabas frowned and said, " 'Surfing'?"

30

Caution

I shifted furtively on my chair and wondered whether Leonard Stockton, who had been sitting beside me for the past two hours and still managed to appear both alert and at ease, could possibly feel as comfortable as he looked. Perhaps a legal training immunizes people from both boredom and numb buttocks. As for me, I knew that both my legs had gone to sleep and if I tried to stand up I would probably fall over.

A gust of wind blew the rain against the window over our heads. Across the table in the dank interview room, Dave Ferry and Jen Lassalle exchanged looks and then turned back, as a team, to contemplating what was sitting on the table between us: a clear plastic bag holding the typewriter ribbon I had rescued from Campion Road. Stockton had arrived with it, as Barnabas had promised. Explanations had followed. And been repeated several times. I found myself taking a childish pleasure in pointing out that I had *tried* to tell them about it back in London. This attitude clearly annoyed Ferry, and we'd spent a certain amount of time at cross purposes until Stockton suggested acidly that perhaps we might make progress if we tried harder. I thought for a moment that Ferry was going to give way to the temptation to arrest my lawyer too, possibly on a charge of impudence. Instead, he had stuck his head out of the door and sent somebody for tea.

Then he turned back and flung a sideways glance at Lassalle. "Take that thing and give it to Horton. Tell him I want it fingerprinted. Anything he can find. It doesn't look very hopeful, but he might get partials. And I want photographs of the whole length of the ribbon. Tell him I want to try to get an image of the key strikes. They're there, all right. I can see them myself. I want a record. Tell him to send it to Scotland Yard. I want this thing photographed, fed into a computer, enlarged, digitalized, enhanced—the whole lot." He cast a look at the clock ticking on the wall behind my head. "Interview suspended at three-twelve." He flicked the switch that turned off the video camera over our heads, and Lassalle gathered up the plastic bag and left.

It seemed the time to ask, "What happens next?"

"Specifically," my solicitor said in a neutral tone of voice, "are you proposing to charge my client?"

Ferry shot Stockton a look of pure dislike. "Specifically," he mimicked, "I haven't made up my mind yet." His voice was level. "Let's just go through the story one more time, and maybe I'll be able to decide."

He went through the business of putting his head out of the door, calling, and returning with a male detective I hadn't seen before, who had apparently been loitering outside. The two of them settled shoulder to shoulder across the table. Ferry flicked his button again and said, "Interview with Miss Hoare recommencing at three-fifteen p.m. November fourteenth. Now, Miss Hoare, will you tell me again what made you decide to go to number forty-two Campion Road on Monday, November the thirteenth?"

I caught his eye. I said sweetly, "To tell you the whole truth, the reason I went there was because when I came to this station to ask for help locating Georgina Laszlo and her daughter, whom I believe have information about the murder of Clare Forbes and the forgery of what is supposed to be a valuable document which I was accused of stealing, you told me to go home and mind my own business." I stopped for breath and noticed Stockton wince. "Your attitude made me angry. I went to Campion Road without any special plan, though I did think that I might be able to find some evidence that would establish my innocence. I was looking for Orrin Forbes' typewriter."

Ferry threw me a hard look. "You aren't helping yourself."

That was probably true.

"Very well, will you tell me again when and where you obtained a key to the house? Did you have that key on the night of the murder?"

I crossed my ankles under the table and set about repeating the story of my raid. At the end of it, Ferry terminated the interview.

"You can stay here," he said abruptly. "I'll have sandwiches sent in. Unless you have anything else to tell me: there are a couple of things I'm going to check." He seemed to think that was a threat.

I made myself consider my abandoned infant and cat, and kept my mouth shut.

When the door had closed, Stockton said, "I warned you I'm not a criminal lawyer."

I seemed to be getting warnings from all directions. I put an elbow on the table in front of me and leaned. "And I'm not a criminal. Sorry. You must be really pissed off at having to rescue me again. I hope you weren't busy today."

"I wasn't due in court," Stockton said. We both noticed that this was only a partial answer. We went on waiting. The plate of sandwiches, when it arrived, looked like yesterday's rejects from an obscure railway buffet, but there was a whole pot of tea. We amused ourselves with this for an hour. When I tried to talk to Stockton, he shook his head in a silent warning. For a moment I didn't understand. Then I did.

"You think they're recording . . . ?"

"Not impossible. I believe they do, sometimes. Let's talk about . . . Professor Hoare. How is he?"

"Not thrilled at what's happening," I admitted. "I think he feels that I ought to be leading a more respectable life." I remembered. "He got a new toy today. He sent Ernie out to buy a modem and he's probably sitting in the shop right now learning how to use the Internet. We're going to start issuing On-Line catalogues."

"I believe the Internet is a good research tool," Stockton commented. The remark seemed a bit pointed. After a second I started to suspect he meant it would be better for me to stick to a keyboard than break into the scene of a crime. I thought of defending myself and stopped. The idea of a hidden microphone was inhibiting. We wound up talking about old Hollywood movies, which he knew a lot more about than I did.

It was nearly five when the door opened again abruptly and I jumped. Ferry and Lassalle filed in and sat down.

"We've checked. The key was where you told us."

I was carefully silent.

Stockton said, "Can we assume that you also found the typewriter where Ms. Hoare told you? And that you know that it has been in the place she described since before the fire?"

"We found it," Ferry said shortly.

"Then can I ask you whether my client can leave? As you're aware, there is no possibility of her absconding."

Absconding . . . I would love to abscond.

Ferry growled, "We're prepared to bail Ms. Hoare to return here in two weeks, but with a condition: if she is found within half a mile of Campion Road during this period, we'll assume that she is trying to tamper with evidence, and I'll cancel the bail and remand her in custody. Is your client prepared to accept the condition?"

Stockton said that I was, and Ferry appeared to take his word for it. Nobody asked me.

"I'll make the arrangements," Jen Lassalle offered. Which she did, with efficiency and a reasonable speed. Nevertheless it was nearly six o'clock before the three of us were making our way toward the main entrance.

"Just as a matter of curiosity," I found myself saying, "how did you find out I'd been at the house?"

"We had a phone call from one of the neighbors. They said they'd seen a prowler. I went to have a look, and as soon as I let myself in I could see that the place had been turned over. I asked next door. One of the girls who lives there said there was a flashy blue car parked out front all day, and she'd seen it before. I knew it was you."

"Next time I'll come by train," I said grimly.

"I have a question, too," she said suddenly. "Why did you want to find the Laszlo women? And did you?"

"Only Georgina. She still claims she doesn't know where Gina is, but I don't believe her."

"For any special reason? I mean, apart from what we discussed in London."

I said that I thought that was a perfectly good reason, and then I told her about my odd visit to Summertown. It occurred to me that possibly Lassalle could tell me one thing. I asked her whether she knew that Georgina Laszlo was engaged. When she didn't answer for a moment, I looked and caught an odd glance.

"Where did you hear that?"

"Her cousin's wife mentioned it. I started to wonder whether this was a recent thing. Do you know who she's engaged to?"

I could have sworn it was embarrassment on the woman's face. That made sense when she said abruptly, "I thought you might have heard. I understand she's marrying the American. Professor Roslin."

This news was so absorbing that I stopped looking where I was going and fell off the step onto the pavement. I looked at the constable, who was watching me.

"Are you all right?"

"That's . . . odd," I said with considerable self-discipline. "I saw no sign of . . . Are you certain?"

"That's what I heard." She was buttoning her raincoat against the first drops of another rain shower. "I'm going off duty. I'll be seeing you."

I said to Leonard Stockton, "I don't believe it."

He hesitated. "Bad news?"

I didn't understand for a minute. When I did, I laughed. "Not that kind of bad. I'm gobsmacked, though."

Stockton raised an enquiring eyebrow.

"I can't explain. I just . . . didn't see that at all."

He hesitated again. "Look, when I was up here at Balliol, I spent a lot of time in the Bird and Baby. I wouldn't mind a visit, for old times' sake. Could you use a drink? I don't think it's within half a mile of Campion Road."

I knew the place he meant, though he was using the student nickname, not the one that appeared on the inn sign. I'd spent hours there myself as an undergraduate. I told him that it sounded good, and five minutes later he slid the Saab into a parking space in St. Giles, and we were taking refuge from the drizzle and the darkness in one of the minute, wood-paneled cubby-holes just inside the front door of the old pub. I sat on the bench seat at one of its two blackened tables and watched him weave among the students to the bar. He was a neat, prosperous man of forty in an expensive gray suit. He no longer belonged in this kind of studenty, scruffy place. Not as I still did. Maybe in another five or six years I'd just be a tourist, too. I was focusing on that idea when he came back with the drinks.

"Are they going to prosecute me?" I asked him.

"No. Well, don't count on that, but I imagine they'll only caution you. If it came to the worst, you wouldn't get more than a suspended sentence. I don't think they'll bother."

I suddenly wanted to laugh. "My criminal career is pretty pathetic."

"I'm sure Professor Hoare would prefer you not to have one."

As there was nothing to be said about that, I told him again that I was sorry I'd wasted his day.

He shrugged and focused on his glass. "It's years since I did anything like this. When I was just starting out, I did my tour as an idealistic duty solicitor at Tottenham Court Road, would you believe it? Nowadays I spend my time on paper work, and the occasional visit to the civil courts."

He looked at me suddenly. His narrow face was flushed, and the pale gray eyes smiled. "Actually, I'm not sure this isn't more fun."

I decided that this was the moment to broach a suggestion I'd been mulling over for the last ten minutes. I said carefully, "While we're in the area, would you mind if we went and had a look at the Templeton house?"

He stared. "You obviously know it would break the condition of your bail."

"It's dark and wet, and this isn't my own car. I just want to drive past. Who'll notice? There is just one thing I want to look at. It will only take a second, and save me coming back on my own. But if you can't, I'll say goodbye now and come back to London by train, and then you won't have to know what I've done."

Stockton looked at me. His expression was unreadable. He said, "You would, too."

We finished our drinks and ran back to the car through driving rain. He required no directions to Campion Road—more memories of his student years, I imagined. He pulled up not far from the spot where I'd left my flashy blue car far too long yesterday, and we stared at what could be seen in the uncertain light from the street lamp.

I opened my door, slid out into the rain, and circled around the car. Behind my back I heard the Saab's engine die, and his door slam.

"What are you doing?"

"I want to look at one thing."

He kept pace with me across the road and onto the gravel and repeated, "What?"

"The tree. I thought of it when we were in the interview room, but it doesn't work. I suddenly wondered if you could climb from its branches to Clare's bedroom windowsill."

I craned and received a splash of water from the branches full in the face. It reminded me of being kissed there by the man who had surprised me by being Georgina Laszlo's fiancé. The old, bare tree I remembered was rooted in the middle of the front garden, close to the house, but the ends of the branches within reach of the front wall were just twigs. Nothing heavier than a squirrel could have got from them to the window. I said so.

"Then we should go."

"In a minute," I said.

"What made you think of it?"

"Logic," I said. "Clare locked her door and it was still locked when we reached it."

I heard Stockton's feet shuffle uneasily on the gravel. After a moment he said, "She was murdered in her bedroom, and there was a rather amateurish attempt to hide the crime by setting a fire. But the murderer had to enter through either the door or the window."

I nodded. It was too dark for him to see it. "The door was locked when the firemen found the body, and they said at the inquest that they found a key on the inside: the door was locked from inside the room. Either Clare let the murderer in, and he or she relocked the door and climbed out through the window; or the murderer both entered and left through the window. There should have been some signs of that, except that the firemen climbed in afterward. I just wanted to see whether it's possible to reach the window from that tree."

"But it isn't. Shall we go now?"

Stockton's voice was uneasy, and I couldn't push my

luck. I asked him to give me just a second, and strained to look up through the moving shadows that the branches of the tree threw on the bricks. Faint, confusing shadows in the light of the street lamp. Only a squirrel . . .

I became aware of Stockton repeating, "What is it? You must come away."

I only vaguely heard what he was saying, because I was looking again at the front of the house. The double window of Clare's bedroom was on a level with the window of the spare bedroom where Jay Roslin and I had spent the first few hours of that confusing night. Both windows had ledges of yellowish stone. It was the first time I'd noticed that the builder had emphasized the line of the sills by running a row of dark brown ornamental bricks across the fifteen or sixteen feet that separated the windows. They stood out a little—not more than an inch, I'd guess—from the yellow bricks. The decoration ran a few feet above the top of the landing window. It wasn't nearly deep enough to allow anybody to walk along it, of course. Even if someone (say Georgina for the sake of argument) had climbed out of the landing window and reached up to the brown bricks, it would be physically impossible for her to pull herself up onto such a narrow ledge, much less inch along it.

"I hadn't noticed that ledge before," I explained.

Stockton frowned. "It isn't really a ledge, is it?"

"Not really," I agreed. "Though if you *could* stand on it somehow, the tree would hide you from the road. I know it's impossible. I was just thinking that at night, you probably wouldn't be seen from the street."

"Especially," Stockton laughed, "if you were only a *very small* squirrel. Look, I think . . ."

I suddenly wondered what Ben was doing, and whether Barnabas had found what he was researching. The house would still be here when I came back for another look. If I ever did.

31

The Matter

I knew I'd missed something, so I went back. I parked the
car across the mouth of the Templeton driveway and made
myself walk between the gate posts. The night was so still
that I heard nothing but the noise my feet made on the
gravel. It was dark under the tree, and I saw that the street
lamp was broken. I strained through the darkness to make
sure that what Leonard Stockton had said was true: that
the branches of the tree didn't reach the house. But he'd
been wrong. Why hadn't he noticed how they were growing fast toward the window of the room where Clare had
died? They were scraping against the wall. Something big
was moving among them like a flapping blanket. It drifted
through the tree to the house and seemed to blow against
the window, and I heard the thud of a fist beating against
the glass . . .

"Dido?"

I opened one eye. A smear of sunshine was gleaming

uncertainly through the eastward-facing windows of my
sitting room, and Phyllis Digby was hovering over my
sleeping bag with a mug in her hand.

"Your father asked me to make you a cup of tea and tell
you it's ten o'clock. There's something he wants to show
you downstairs. I'm sorry, you look as though you need
the sleep, but you know what he's like."

I did. I struggled to a sitting position and reached for
the mug. "Thanks. Ben . . . ?"

"Perfectly happy. Don't worry. Ben and I can manage.
Dido? What's happened? Your father says you got arrested
yesterday."

I sipped the tea, which was strong and hot enough to
burn my tongue. "I broke into the Templeton house."

Phyllis plonked herself down in the armchair. "Is it serious?" she asked hesitantly. "I mean . . . well, you know
I'll always see that Ben's all right, don't you?"

I found myself smiling at her. She is a sharp, fiftyish,
Australian nurse with sandy-colored short hair, blue eyes,
a big nose, and a wanderlust that sent her working her way
around the world, until she met and married a retiring,
semi-invalid Englishman, and settled in a flat about ten
minutes' walk from mine. While I'd only known her for
the eight or nine months since she'd turned up in answer
to my advertisement for baby-sitting, I'd come to trust her.
Even with Ben! He loves her. In fact, she is the closest
thing to a grandmother that he knows. And yes: she would
always see that Ben was all right. I told her I hoped it
wouldn't be necessary, and recounted the story of yesterday's involuntary trip to Oxford.

At the end of it she snorted, "They're trying to scare
you."

"They might have managed if Barnabas hadn't sent Leonard Stockton after me. I suppose I'd better go down and see what he wants. Is Ernie there?"

Phyllis told me that Ernie had been there when she arrived but had rushed off almost at once saying he was late for classes. Apparently Barnabas had been having a computer lesson and wanted me to join him. "I'll make toast and coffee while you're getting dressed," she added.

I agreed. The idea of a long, hot bath seemed infinitely preferable to making a start on the day's business, but it would have to wait. Barnabas (like my overdraft) wouldn't.

The church bell was ringing eleven o'clock by the time that I got into the office, but Barnabas gave the impression that he hadn't noticed the delay. He had pushed the books he was supposed to be working on to one side and focused fiercely on the computer screen, pointing and clicking the mouse with an air of command.

I leaned on the door jamb to ask how he was and what he was doing.

"Excellent," he mumbled in a deeply absorbed voice. "Look at this. Now we are really getting there. Ernie found this."

I pulled the visitor's chair around and sat beside him. The screen was an interesting jumble of text and images. At the top of it was the picture of sunlit grounds and a long, two-story brick building with columns and a central tower topped by a steeple.

"What is it?"

"This," Barnabas said, "is an Internet site. You type in a name, whatever you want, and the system matches it, and you click on something underlined . . . That's the main campus building at Macklin College. 'Founded in 1928,

Macklin College is a liberal arts institution in Macklin, Ohio. It has a student body of eight thousand seven hundred and twenty-eight . . . ' You see?"

Suddenly I did.

"There is a bar at the left of the screen," Barnabas continued the lecture, "where you can click on anything that interests you. For example . . ." He clicked and the computer produced a screen headed "Courses and Tuition Fees."

"Staff?"

Barnabas clicked back with clumsy care, and clicked again on the bar entitled "Academic Staff." A list of names began to scroll up the screen. "For example," Barnabas orated, "there is Professor Vicario, to whom I was speaking the other day." He clicked on a name, and a photograph of a self-conscious-looking middle-aged woman appeared. I skimmed the text: "Dr. Vicario, Associate Professor of Comparative Literature, Head of the Department of English and Comparative Literature from last September for two years."

"They must rotate their head-of-department appointments," Barnabas was saying. "It appears to be largely an administrative post, and they take turns."

I continued to skim her academic qualifications, a list of publications, a biographical paragraph which said that she had been born in Chicago, was married with one daughter, and hobbies were painting and needlework. Finally, "Professor Vicario can be found in Room 3424 of the Arts Wing, office hours from nine to eleven daily."

"There is not much more one could wish to know. Now you try," Barnabas said. He clicked on an arrow, and the list of names reappeared.

I said, "Why are you being coy? It doesn't suit you." I scrolled up to Jay Roslin's name and clicked.

The camera had caught him in the middle of blinking, and his eyes were hooded, so that he looked almost blind. "Dr. Jay Roslin, Assistant Professor of American Literature, appointment for three years from last year . . ."

Beside me, Barnabas' voice said, "I think that means he doesn't have tenure."

I nodded. "That's why the Forbes papers are so important to him. If he publishes his book, he'll get onto the permanent staff." I scrolled down . . . "a B.A. from the University of Massachusetts, a Ph.D. from the State University of New York, publications the Forbes *Selected Letters* and various articles, hobbies hiking and mountain climbing, divorced, one son . . ." and dropped the mouse, so that the pointer jumped wildly. There was one final line. Jay had been on "Indefinite leave of absence" since last April.

I'd said, "That's odd," before I knew what I was thinking.

Barnabas narrowed his eyes at his thoughts. "Very generous of them to give a three-year appointee indefinite leave to pursue his research, especially starting just before the exam period. Professor Vicario gave no hint of this when I spoke to her. In fact, I thought she implied that he would be returning for the second semester."

I offered the opinion that it was a mistake.

"Very possibly," Barnabas agreed. "I wonder how one finds out?"

"Probably," I suggested meanly, "one phones Professor Vicario again and says, Hey, toots, what is it about this Roslin guy?"

Barnabas scowled. "Perhaps you might, but I'm not sure I could maintain the character. Now, will you tell me exactly what happened yesterday? You claimed to be too sleepy to go through it all, but I should really like to know whether you are only here because of a daring jail-break."

I said, "In a minute. I just want to see what else is here. Could you possibly . . . ?"

I'd heard the shop door open, setting the bell tinkling; the newcomer was a book runner we'd done some business with before. Barnabas went to deal with it.

I clicked back to the index page and looked down the list of topics: Courses and Fees, Sports Facilities, Environs . . . I didn't know what I was looking for until I found the last item of the list—Student Information. I clicked on it and found a list of topics of interest to undergraduates on campus. One of them said "Chat." Feeling clever, I clicked on it and found yet another long list of topics, and the names of people who had contributed comments. It looked like a discussion site, and it seemed to cover gossip about courses, fraternities and other clubs, student accommodation, sports teams . . . The names of contributors were attached to various comments and additions. I didn't find what I wanted, but I was in the right kind of area. I clicked tentatively on a box that said "Post," and a new section popped into being at the bottom of the screen with a blank box for my text . . . Feeling distinctly clever, I positioned the cursor and typed slowly.

Hey, guys, does anybody know when Jay Roslin's coming back? I met him last year, and I'd really like to see him again. Is it true he's not married anymore? Wow!

Being in a nasty mood, I signed myself *Georgina*.

Then I disconnected, feeling as if I'd invented the Internet myself. Ernie wouldn't believe it when I told him. In the meantime, I went out to look at the quarto of illustrated fairy tales that Barnabas was haggling over. It was open at a picture of Little Red Riding Hood. She was lost in a wintry wood full of trees like the one in my dream.

I got through the rest of the day without actually forgetting to ask any buyers to pay for their books. At one o'clock Barnabas departed for the university and a conference with Dr. Govett. At five o'clock I locked the door of the shop and turned the computer on.

I'd found a sheet of instructions on the desk in my father's precise hand, obviously written to Ernie's dictation. "*Step 1 turn on computer . . .*" I could do that. I pressed the switch and looked at step 2. With the guide-sheet, I found myself successfully calling up the Macklin College site and navigating my way cautiously to where I had left my message.

A comment had appeared. It said, *Georgina, do you really mean Roofie Roslin? You gotta be kidding!* It was signed *Kyle* and had a *PS—Dont you know really?*

I stared at it for a while without feeling enlightened. It didn't seem likely that even Ernie could help with this. I clicked "Post" again and typed, *Kyle, "Roofie?" I don't get it. xxx Georgina.*

That seemed to cover the situation.

32

Organizing

It was eight o'clock before Ben started to feel sleepy and I could attend to other things. Like food for myself, for instance. I'd bought a tray of chicken breasts at the supermarket, and I set one of them to cook in butter while I sliced some mushrooms. In the comfortable mindlessness of cooking, I had a chance to remember the organizer sitting downstairs in the desk. I ought to have given it to Ferry, but I'd honestly forgotten it. I turned the gas to a low flame, clattered down to the shop to retrieve it, and sat with it and a glass of Chardonnay at the kitchen table while the chicken simmered.

Gina's organizer was a small loose-leaf volume, thick with insertions and frayed with long use. The cover was a cracking plastic picture of old roses defaced by stickers advertising Pulp and *Pocahontas*. I turned to the diary section and opened it at September.

Her notations might as well have been written in code. Half of them were just doodles. The beginning of the school term was heavily annotated, and one of the things at the front was a timetable which made it clear that Gina was doing History, Geography and Sociology. Most of the entries in the diary section said things like "+R +Ev Forum 8:30," which I identified as notes to herself about meeting people and going places. I noticed with interest that "N" appeared in these entries fairly often, especially at weekends. Natty? But other initials were also repeated. I flipped the pages with sinking expectations. Gina was a busy girl, but she had spread herself around a wide group of friends. If any of them were especially important to her, this wasn't going to tell me. I scanned her notes all the way through to Christmas without getting anything significant.

A faint smell of scorching butter brought me to my senses. I splashed half of my wine into the pan and looked at the clock over the fridge. It was nearly eight-thirty, and I could hear my stomach rumbling. Ben, who had been talking to himself in the bedroom, was silent.

Mr. Spock, profiting from my inattention, came and sat down on the little book. His way of making sure he was the center of attention. I slid the contents of the pan onto a plate, grabbed a slice of fresh seeded bread and another glass of wine, returned to the table, said, "Scram!" and settled to eat and see whether I could find anything useful.

The addresses were at the back. Apparently Gina didn't believe in organizing her friends, because the names had been written in without reference to alphabetical order. I slid the tines of the fork down entries on the first couple of pages while I was chewing mushrooms. Natty and his telephone number appeared near the beginning. She must have known him for a while. I skipped to the last page, but the telephone numbers added most recently belonged to people called "Sam" and "Gaby" and "new dentist." I played with the idea of phoning one after the other (not the dentist) and accusing them of knowing Gina Laszlo's whereabouts. Probably Jen Lassalle would arrest me for harassment; and theft, of course. I threw the organizer down and decided to eat my food before it congealed. Then I picked it up again and found Natty's phone number, went into the sitting room to phone, and asked an absentminded female voice speaking against the backing of a television programme, whether Natty was in. She said that he was, and called out. I crossed my fingers: he had come home, all right.

". . . Hello . . . ?"

"Hello, Natty. It's Dido Hoare. We met at Fairwood—I came looking for Gina Laszlo, and I talked to you and your friends, remember?"

For a moment I thought he was going to hang up on me, but then he said quickly, "I think I'd better take this upstairs. They're watching television in here. I'm hanging up. Will you hold the line?"

I waited through the click and the silence until another click told me he was back. "Are you there?"

I said that I was. "Look, I was a friend of Gina's grandmother. The one who was killed. Gina hasn't turned up. Do you know where she is?"

"No. I don't." The voice was firm. I was afraid I was hearing the truth.

"Have the police spoken to you?"

There was another pause. Then he said, "Yes."

"Look: everybody's starting to wonder whether she's safe. Her grandmother was murdered. I think she's likely to be in danger too."

"I don't think so."

I struggled to hold on to my friendly coolness. "I'd

rather hear that from her! Can you tell me which day she left Fairwood?"

"The day before you turned up." It had been an easy question: I could hear his relief.

"And you phoned her to pass on my message. Thanks for that, by the way: she rang me almost right away. So can you give me her current phone number?"

"No. Sorry, but I don't remember it. She said to tear it up if the police came around asking, and they did. There was a woman detective. I threw it on the fire when she arrived."

I snarled silently at the telephone. "Do you *really* not remember?"

"No."

I had an inspiration. "Do you remember the area code? London?"

"Oh, Oxford," he said quickly. I wasn't sure I believed him; and then I remembered the bell that I'd heard in the background when she had phoned me. Oxford is full of bells. Well, she could have gone to stay with friends, but it seemed hard of her not to go to Clare's funeral.

"I heard," I said slowly, "that she was quarreling with her mother about some man. That isn't you?"

Again, it sounded as though I'd asked an easy question when he said, "No, of course not! I'm into music. Mostly techno. Some of us do pub gigs at weekends when we can get them, and Gina's interested. She comes around with us in my old van. She sings a bit, sometimes, just for fun. She isn't really good enough."

"Do you know who the man is? Can she be with him?"

"She could be." That answer was guarded.

"Did she talk about him sometimes?"

"No. It's a bit weird, because you'd expect, you know, something. But . . ."

"But what?"

"We got the idea it was somebody older. She said something once that made me think he's an undergraduate. And she said about her mother thinking he was too old for her."

"So she ran away because her mother didn't like the boyfriend?"

The voice hesitated, "No. She said . . . I'm pretty sure she said her mother had kicked her out. Told her to get out and not come back. She wanted to go to Fairwood, so I said I'd drive down in the van at half term and take her. I thought she was going to stay after we left."

"And you came back at the end of the school break."

"I have A levels this year," he said simply.

I said I could remember what that was like. I was making conversation and trying to think at the same time. I said, "Is there anything at all you know that could help me find her? Wait a minute: how did she leave Fairwood? Did she get a lift? Catch a bus? What?"

"Somebody came for her."

"What?"

"Sorry, I should have said. A man came for her. In a car."

"You mean it was arranged?"

"I know she made a phone call from the box up the road, and somebody turned up the next day in a car."

I said hopefully, "The boyfriend? What did he look like?"

"I can't help you. It might have been a mini cab from the village, even. He stayed in the car and she went out to the road. I walked her past the construction people and the security, but I didn't get a look at him. This was just after dark."

"And you don't remember the car's number or anything?"

"Too dark," Natty's voice said simply. "It was just an ordinary car, a Ford or Vauxhall or something. Not very big. A dark color. I didn't try to see the plate. Look, I ought . . ."

"That's fine!" I said quickly. "I'll phone you again if anything comes up. Meantime, good luck with the exams."

He thanked me, and hung up. I went back to the kitchen. The last scrap of my chicken had vanished. Mr. Spock was sitting on the draining board washing his face, and it served me right for not concentrating. I snarled, "I hope that cats can digest mushrooms." I was lying: I wasn't very hopeful. I unwrapped a new roll of kitchen paper in anticipation.

33

Roofies

I woke to a room where the only light came from the street lamp outside the shop bouncing off the white ceiling, and looked at the little alarm clock on the end table. Just after six. That worried me. I sat up to listen for whatever sound had woken me and discovered an edge of excitement that made me feel queasy. Where it came from I had no idea, but it was pretty certain that I wasn't going to drop off to sleep again.

It was cold. The central heating timer wasn't due to switch on for another half-hour. I unzipped the sleeping bag, slid out onto the chilly carpet, and fumbled for my terry robe. Then I padded down the hallway to the bedroom door, open a crack. By the glimmer of the night light I could see Ben in his cot, asleep on his back, pursing his lips rhythmically.

I had no inclination at all to do the same, so I pulled the door to and continued on my way to the kitchen. The tiles underfoot were icy. I hopped over to the boiler, flipped the timer a notch and listened to the rumble of the gas. The little orange light on the coffee maker called to me. I poured a cup of last night's coffee and, moving softly, splashed in a bit of milk. The coffee was revolting, but it would do for the moment. My first task wasn't to make a fresh pot: it was to try to work out what had roused me so thoroughly and why. My brain had been operating busily in my sleep and had obviously woken me with an alarm call because it had come to some kind of conclusion.

It took me a moment to work out what that was. I had to get downstairs.

Yesterday's clothes were in a heap on the armchair. I finished my coffee as I was dragging them on. In the bathroom I wiped a cloth over my face and pulled the brush once or twice through my hair. There were still no waking sounds from Ben. I grabbed the keyring from the hook by the door and tiptoed down the stairs.

The office behind the shop was even colder than the flat, with little bursts of an icy draft entering around the door to the yard. Mental note: buy some draft-proofing and *really get around to putting it on this time*. I flicked the lights and stirred among the papers on the desk (past time for a tidy) until I found the sheet of paper I was looking for. *Step 1: Switch on . . .* I followed the Ernie route, clicked on my browser, and watched the picture of what looked like the expanding universe pop onto my screen. Still following the guide like a recipe, I clicked on "Search," watched pictures of mountain ranges grow, and scrolled down to the bottom of the page where there was a nice little box for me to type in ROOFIES. I hit "Submit," and watched the screen changing.

This Internet stuff isn't so difficult, after all.

My new screen offered nearly two thousand items. I

didn't need more than half a dozen, and I didn't even try to go to any of the sites it was offering me because the index told me all I needed to know.

Alpha Xi Delta: Roofies *A drug posing a sexual assault threat.*

news. roofies *Abundance of new drug concerns officials. An illegal sedative drug labeled as the "date rape" drug has recently . . .*

FLUNITRAZEPAM (ROOFIES) *Rohypnol, commonly known as "Roofies" Drug information for Officers, Teachers, Students . . .*

"ROOFIES" FACTS ABOUT THE DATE RAPE DRUG *Published by the University at Albany . . .*

ROOFIES What is it? Rohypnol is a colorless, odorless drug with slightly bitter taste, which dissolves quickly in drinks . . .

I sat for a moment, not looking at the screen. *Which dissolves quickly in drinks*, for example in strong hot chocolate that has been made really sweet to hide any *slightly bitter taste* and which is then drunk by two people, only two of the four, Clare Templeton Forbes and Dido Hoare, before their mugs are carefully, carefully washed up to destroy the evidence.

I looked again. Flunitrazepam. A name you heard and either forgot immediately or tucked away as an oddity in a corner of your memory. I wondered when I'd done the latter and came up with an answer: at the inquest, and afterward when Barnabas had repeated the word.

That was when I began to wonder whether I was really

the only person who had this information, this new information I'd just found.

Ernie's step 8 said "If you want to keep information shown on the screen, First . . ."

Yes, I wanted to keep the information on the screen. In fact, I wanted to have it there permanently for other people to see. Barnabas, in the first place. I did as I was directed. I was just about to switch off when I remembered little "Georgina" Hoare. I moved back and back to the browser and went again to the Macklin College Chat Room, and silly "Georgina" and her hots for the glamorous Professor Roslin.

Somebody else had been there. The second message said, *Georgina, come to WSSG, urgent, check Roslin link.*

It meant something: I would have loved to know what. I arrowed my way back to the main Macklin page, started at the top, and looked at everything, watching my phone bill mount up. I'd gone all the way from "Arts" to "Students" before I found it: *Women Students Support Group.* I clicked. And then I read the warning that somebody called Dana Martin had left for "Georgina." When I knew what had happened at Macklin, and why the previous Head of Department, a man named Charles Heising, had sent Jay Roslin on indefinite leave of absence, I switched the computer off feeling sick.

The street outside was beginning to be visible in the light. Ben had been on his own for too long. And I almost knew what I was going to do, even though I hadn't worked out all the details.

The first thing was to phone Phyllis with an SOS. Then I'd phone Barnabas and tell him he was on his own in the shop for the day, and first of all to start up the computer and look at the file that I'd left for him. No—I wouldn't risk it until I was ready to leave for Oxford. In fact, to be on the safe side I'd phone him when I was on the road.

I would, I promised myself, avoid going anywhere near Campion Road and being arrested. But that probably wasn't going to be necessary any more after today. I was really looking forward to never seeing the Templeton house again, or anybody who had ever lived there.

34

Telling the Truth

I was waiting my chance to turn onto the big roundabout at the eastern outskirts of Oxford when the car radio announced that it was eight-thirty-one. A quick trip. The traffic coming into London had been three lanes deep and moving at a crawl; but going west, I'd had a clear road.

I'd phoned Barnabas nearly an hour ago from the Westway. It had taken him a while to answer his phone, but his voice wasn't sleepy.

"I was taking a bath, and I am quite all right, thank you. To what do I owe the pleasure of this unusually early communication? Are you up to mischief?"

I said that to be frank I was. "There are some things I want you to do for me," I said. "It's urgent. Do you have a pen?"

My father reminded me tetchily that the telephone was on his desk, which was amply supplied.

"First of all," I said, "I'm not at home. I'm going to Oxford. I . . ."

"Had you forgotten," he said, "that you were dining with Professor Roslin tonight?"

"I wasn't thinking about it," I lied. "But it doesn't matter, because I'm not. I don't think he'll turn up. If he does by any chance phone, don't say anything. No—you can tell him I've gone to Oxford to talk to the CID."

"And have you?"

Not if I see them before they see me. "Actually I've gone to find Georgina and make her talk to me. I think that something nasty may have happened to Gina. I've got to find out."

Barnabas demanded to know the details at once. I told him that I was driving one-handed and couldn't go through it all now. "But I've left something for you in the computer. So will you go to the shop, please, and stay there until I speak to you again? I need to know where I can find you quickly if I need help."

Barnabas said, "You are going to break into something!"

I assured him that this was the last thing I had in mind. "But while you're there, you can read a web site that I found. I've down-loaded it. There's a note stuck to the screen to tell you where the file is so that you can read it as soon as you get there. You'll understand. Don't delete the file, because I want to print out a copy for the police. Barnabas, it all fits together if you know."

"Is Ben with you?"

"No, of course not, he's with Phyllis."

"So you really are doing something you shouldn't be," Barnabas concluded. "When will you be back?"

"This afternoon. Some time. I don't know."

Barnabas exploded, "Will you for goodness sake be careful!"

"I certainly will," I said. "Barnabas . . ."

"What?"

"I probably ought to make sure you understand that even though I said he was with me I was wrong, and Jay Roslin may have killed Clare."

"Well of course he did!" Barnabas exploded in my ear. "Dido . . ."

"Roundabout," I said hastily. "Got to switch off."

This time I avoided the route through the center of Oxford, driving around the bypass and coming down to Summertown. When I arrived outside the Reverend Templeton's house and turned the car around at the end of the cul de sac, the open door of the garage showed me that the car was out. Hopefully, Mrs. Templeton was out on the school run with those boys. Hopefully, the Reverend Templeton was out on church business. I needed to talk to Georgina and I preferred not to have any interference. I crawled out of the car, activated the locking system, took a couple of deep breaths, and told myself not to hang about. If Georgina would just believe what I had to say, I'd be on my way home in an hour or so. Because I was so sure she knew how I could find Gina. I rang the bell; as I listened to the sound of footsteps on the other side I glanced at my wrist-watch. The minute hand was a hair's breadth off the hour. Georgina opened the door. I pretended not to notice the expression on her face.

I said, "I want to talk to you. I can get the police here, if you'd rather talk to them."

Then she said, "Come in." When I didn't move, she said impatiently, "What's wrong now?"

I shook my head casually. "I'm waiting for the church bell to ring. I was wondering what it sounds like." As a matter of fact, I'd just about made up my mind that this was the bell I'd heard when Gina had phoned me, and I'd solved the problem of her hideaway.

My suspicions were rudely disappointed when Georgina laughed shortly. "You'll wait for a while, then. There isn't a bell. There's an amplified sound system that's switched on before Sunday service. Go straight through into the dining room. My cousins are out, we can talk in there until they get back."

In the dining room, we sat at opposite sides of a table from which the breakfast dishes had already been cleared, the crumbs had been wiped. The room was cold. I watched Georgina. She sat quietly, very straight in the chair opposite me, and she was watching me just as I was watching her.

I said, "I want Gina. She's here in Oxford."

I hadn't been prepared for her to shrug and laugh shortly. "You can believe what you want. I don't know where she is."

I shrugged and laughed in my turn. "She left Fairwood last week. Even before the funeral. She gave Natty an Oxford phone number, and he spoke to her here last week."

I was thrown off balance by the startled look Georgina threw me. "Left?"

I repeated what I'd said. "So she is in Oxford. Is she here? In this house, I mean? I presume she's hiding for some reason, probably with you, and I want to talk to her. Now."

The woman's face was breaking into an expression I couldn't read; but I was almost sure that bewilderment was a dominant part of it. And anger?

"She isn't here. She's never . . . You can look, if you want to. She told me she was going to Fairwood with friends. I let her . . . If she's in Oxford, she must be staying with a friend from school, but I don't . . . I didn't . . . she isn't staying with that boy Natty, is she?"

"No. He was still there when I visited the site, and he says he didn't leave until the end of half term. I haven't checked with his parents, but he said he doesn't know where Gina is, and I believe him."

Georgina was silent, and now she was certainly alarmed. She licked her lips. "Then where is she?"

"What do the police say? They're supposed to be looking."

"They say that . . . that they're watching for her. I don't think . . ."

"What did you quarrel about?" I snapped. "Gina told everybody that you were fighting, and that you threw her out of the house. What was the problem?"

"I don't think that's any of your business!"

"I can still call the police," I said.

"You saw what it was like," Georgina snarled. "For the past year she's been . . . been . . . like a savage. Her school work has been rotten, she runs around day and night no matter what I say."

"And then there was the man," I said. "Not Natty. The other one. I heard the two of you arguing one day, and you were obviously fighting about him then. I heard you laying down the law to her, and then she slammed out. Natty knows about it." *Though not enough.* "Who is he?"

She looked at me silently for a very long time. "Somebody unsuitable," she said quietly. "Somebody very unsuitable. I won't let her. Where has she gone?"

Now I saw where Gina was. Probably Georgina did too, because her expression changed. Something was going to happen. I tried to lean back and look comfortable. What I wanted to do was jump to my feet and pace up and down yelling, but we were playing a different game. I tried another casual shrug and twisted the knife. "She's with him, I presume. Going to Fairwood was just a chance to get you off her case. Perhaps she even goaded you into telling her to go? Anyway, it doesn't matter now. I still want to talk to her. I still believe you have an idea where she is, and I want you to tell me."

Georgina sat straighter in response to my easy slump. "You can think that if you want."

"I do think that. You'd better think about it too. Think about the consequences of all this lying. The police are just about to clear up Clare's death. Or didn't you know that? Because they are. I happen to know that they'll be making an arrest today. I found out this morning."

Georgina was opening and shutting her mouth, but nothing came out. In the silence, I heard soft footsteps upstairs that seemed to be crossing the room above us. I looked at the ceiling and I looked at Georgina, sitting with a white face. Maybe my first idea had been right after all.

I told her, "There's something else you ought to hear. Do you know why Professor Roslin has been able to take so much time off to stay over here? He's actually on indefinite leave because two of his students accused him of raping them. They say that he drugged them with a kind of tranquilizer. The authorities are trying to counsel the girls and decide whether there's enough evidence to go to court. Some of the students are pretty bitter about the way the complaints are being handled, but everybody there knows about it. They won't have him back, you know. The Womens' Students Support Group says that they aren't going to let him off the hook, whatever anybody thinks. It's only that the two girls are the kind of kids who are reluctant to go through a court case. You know. It can't be easy for a nice eighteen-year-old."

Now she flushed. "I don't believe you. That's a lie. I don't know whether those girls are lying or you are, but it isn't true."

I said, "Talking about lying, can't we stop this?"

Upstairs, something fell to the floor. I stood up. "I'll take you up on the offer. I think I will look for Gina."

It was becoming unbearable to sit there watching her face, and seemed only decent to give her a minute to herself. If it had been me, I would have been screaming. It was time to go upstairs and tell Gina she could stop hiding. When I ran into the hallway, I was feeling pretty pleased with myself. I'd done it. Another five minutes, and I could warn Gina, and it would be finished. I could go home and talk to Ben and then go downstairs and sell some books, which is my real business.

I ran up the stairs, paused for a second in the hall to orient myself, and headed toward the room above the dining room where the footsteps had been and jerked open the door without knocking.

In the bed, a boy with a flushed face turned and looked at me blearily and said, "Hi! Who are you?"

I found enough breath to say that I was Dido Hoare, and I'd seen him briefly at Clare's funeral, and that I was sorry to burst in on him like that but I'd assumed he was at school and I thought I'd caught a burglar. He croaked a laugh and followed it by a cough.

I said, "You're ill?"

He nodded and grinned. "Flu. Missing the English test, too."

"Are you all right? Do you need anything before I go back downstairs to Georgina?"

He shook his head. "I'm just sleepy," he said. His eyes were heavy.

I said I'd let him get some rest and wished him better and shut the door.

Somewhere downstairs there was an echo of the sound. I hurtled into the dining room, but it was empty. Then I ran down the drive just in time to see Georgina's back as, mounted on the bicycle, she turned out of the end of the street into the main road.

35

A Cold Wind

I remembered my last attempt to follow Georgina's bike and shot into the main road just in front of a delivery van, earning a roar from its horn. I could see her thirty yards ahead, and I wondered about falling back but didn't dare. Anyway, she had her head down and was pedaling hard toward the city center. After a few minutes we were level with the first of the turnings for Campion Road. I was certainly breaking my bail conditions now, and I wondered what I'd do if she was going to the house. I needn't have worried: she shot past both turnings without slowing and continued toward St. Giles through heavier traffic. That was when I realized that a bicycle might have the advantage over the car here. *Damn it!*

The lights at the junction turned green just as we arrived, allowing us both to carry on. Traffic in St. Giles was bad, but Georgina was slowing. The racing pace must be beginning to tell on her. I fell back a little, but I daren't risk losing much ground.

Halfway down I began to wonder what would happen if she rode into the pedestrianized area in the center. I'd just decided I would keep on going and pretend to be a bus when her bicycle slipped recklessly between two cars. She was turning into Beaumont Street. I honked and pulled out myself. She slid across on the amber. I gritted my teeth and accelerated through on the beginning of the red light. I heard a yell, but we were passing the Randolph and the Playhouse, heading toward Gloucester Green.

At which point my doubts flared up again. She wasn't going to the police, was she? But after a couple of minutes I knew she wasn't. She made a right turn into Hythe Bridge Street, riding against the one-way traffic. I gritted my teeth, shot across the intersection and jammed on the brakes. When I'd set my hazard lights flashing I fell out, locked the car, and rushed back just in time to see her execute a sharp right turn into a road I didn't even know existed. I dodged in front of a bus to reach the safety of the pavement on the bridge over the canal, and peered over the iron railings.

To my right, the dark water was splashing over a small ornamental weir with a little park above it. To my left, across the side road, a row of old brick cottages faced the canal. Three or four of them had been refurbished, with fresh paint and window boxes, and from this angle I could just read the discreet green-and-gold painted sign which told me that they had been converted into the New Southgate Private Hotel.

I could almost feel my thoughts shift and rearrange themselves. It was the name that had misled me. We were nowhere near the southern edge, or gate, of the medieval city. But this was where Jay Roslin had gone after the fire. She was running to Jay. I had a nasty feeling that she was going to confront him with what I'd said. It wasn't what I'd meant to happen, I'd just wanted her to lead me to Gina. Ironically, there was a lull in the traffic at that moment and from behind me, borne on the easterly wind, I heard the sound of the big bell at Christ Church ringing the hour. I recognized it. I'd heard it when Gina had phoned me. I reached for my mobile, but there was no time to use it.

She had flung her bike against the front of the little hotel, and I plunged past it and through the main door. And stopped. Something had happened: I heard shouting. When I passed through the inner door, I found the receptionist in a tiny lobby with her back to me, peering up the empty staircase. She turned uncertainly.

"Excuse me. Somebody just . . . Can I help you?"

"I'm looking for Professor Jay Roslin."

"That's Room 102, but he's out."

I followed her glance at the key rack. There was no key hanging on the hook marked 102. I said, "Are you sure? The key's not there."

She was distracted and said, "Oh, the professor's gone out, but his wife always stays in."

I still couldn't make out what was happening, but I decided to find out for myself. I was five steps up when the receptionist started to call, "Excuse me? *Excuse me!*"

She was just behind me, catching up. I stopped and turned and said, "*That* woman is Professor Roslin's wife—the one you just saw running upstairs, not the one who was here already. Now, I am going up there to stop anything happening. You should phone the police. Tell them to send Inspector Ferry or Constable Lassalle, because they are looking for that girl you've had staying here."

I could see from her face that she didn't understand, but there was no time to impress her with the power of my personality, or even with the truth. She said, "I'm going to call the manager," and turned back. In her place I might have done the same, but I didn't have that luxury. Presumably I had at least a few minutes to . . . what?

I skidded to a halt at the top of the stairs. A sign on the wall told me that Rooms 101 to 106 were to my left. The corridor was empty. I could hear Georgina's voice, but I couldn't make out the words until I was closer to the room, only the outrage. Underneath it at first, but rising, was another voice I recognized. I had found Gina Laszlo.

I crept toward the door and heard Georgina say in a monotone, "You don't know what you're doing. You just don't understand."

"No, you don't understand!" Gina. "Jay and I are flying to America tomorrow. So this is my last day in England. We're going to be married in New York, and he's going to write his book and look for a job at another university where they don't know anything about the divorce, or how he was treated, or anything like that, and I'm going to take courses there and get my degree. I know you thought that he was going to marry you, because you're going to sell all those manuscripts and be stinking rich, but he's not. He never wanted your money, he just wanted you to let him use the things for his book. He doesn't need you now. He's got the poem, and you can't say anything to the police or you won't get a penny for it. And there's nothing you can do about it, because I was eighteen last month and I got that passport last summer, so I'm all ready."

"I'll have him arrested first."

"What for?" Gina cried. I could hear the hysteria in her voice. "Making a fool of you?"

"For killing your grandmother."

There was a second's silence, then, "Well, he says that was your idea, *you* did it, and you made him help you."

There was another silence inside the room. A long silence, before I heard Georgina speak.

"You knew?"

"What, that my mother and my boyfriend are murderers? You're the one who got him into this, you blackmailed him. You always wanted to get back at her. She was an old cow, but you're no better! And I love Jay. If you really want to know, he's great in bed."

Ouch.

It occurred to me that the very best thing to do would be to return to the lobby, or preferably right back to the car, and phone the police. Dave Ferry was the man to handle this. He was paid to do the dirty work, I wasn't. I retreated toward the stairs and was nearly there when a voice in the lobby, just beyond my angle of sight, said, "Professor Roslin? Professor, there are some ladies upstairs. Two of them just arrived. I don't know them, but they went up to your room. Shall I . . . ?"

The nearest door was marked "Bathroom." I shot through and pushed it to. Through the crack I saw Jay Roslin come leaping up the stairs. For a moment his eyes lingered in my direction. Then he vanished. I gave him a second and stuck my head out just in time to watch him go through the door of 102. It slammed.

I hooked my mobile out of a pocket and hesitated. I couldn't hear a sound. Something in the silence made me think of corpses. I switched on and poised a finger to ring 999. Then I imagined trying to explain. We were less than half a mile from the police station, but I needed help now, not arguments. I listened again. Nothing, but at any minute I would hear shouts, screams . . .

I fell down the stairs into the lobby. The receptionist was behind the desk, speaking into her telephone with a fretful air that wasn't what was needed at all.

She looked at me. "I'm talking to the manager. I warn you . . ."

I screamed, "Never mind that! Phone the police. NOW! They have to get here before something happens!"

She smiled at me calmly. "We don't want a disturbance here. The manager will be down in a minute, and he'll deal with it."

There was a lovely big vase full of yellow chrysanthemums on the desk. I picked it up and threw it at the wall. The vase exploded with a satisfactory crash, showering the lobby with water and flowers and slivers of glass. Her mouth fell open.

I yelled. *"NOW phone the police!"* and turned and ran back upstairs.

When I reached the door, they were talking. I couldn't imagine what they had to say to each other, but something in the sound made me cringe. *Idiot! Nothing's going to happen, not here, not here in the middle of the day.* But I knew that it was, and that it was partly my fault. The room opposite was empty, its door open, waiting for the cleaner. I backed inside and glued my eyes to the door opposite. Someone started to sob, a quiet, wrenching sound that made me want to scream. It was drowned out by a crash. You could say that they all deserved whatever was going to happen to them. You could say that nobody did.

I'd flung the door open before I realized I was moving. Three faces turned toward me as I walked in. I stepped on something. The room key with its big plastic tag was on the floor under my foot, where somebody had dropped or thrown it, and that was when I saw what to do. I scooped it up, slammed the door behind me, and locked it. Jay opened his mouth in a silent howl and lunged, but I got the bed between us, found myself beside a window that was open an inch, and stuffed the key through the crack. I thought I heard it land on the path outside, but it was something else. Time froze. A car door slamming. Voices. Then voices inside the building, and a thundering knock on the door. I think I called, "It's locked." A key grated. When the door opened, Dave Ferry was pulling the receptionist aside. Jen Lassalle was behind him, and there were two uniformed men with her.

I held up my hand. I said very softly, "If you give her a chance, Georgina Laszlo will tell you just exactly what they did to Clare Forbes. In fact, they'll probably fight each other about who's going to tell you first." I could still hear the anger and pain in those voices as I pushed past them all and headed toward the stairs.

36

Hungry People

I sat with my elbows propped on the table at the back of Rocca's Restaurant in Holborn. Barnabas' favorite. "As your previous dinner partner is engaged elsewhere," he had announced firmly on my return, "you are eating with me. Frankly, I need both refreshment and information. The table is booked for seven. Afterward, I shall deliver you by taxi to the door, pick up Mrs. Digby and deliver her in turn to her home, then continue onto Crouch Hill; and you are to go to bed."

I'd decided to excuse the masterful tone just for once. I too needed a change of scene. I'd discovered that I didn't much want to eat, but I watched my father negotiating a chicken *cacciatore* while I pushed a fork through my salad. What I needed was to wind down so I could get to sleep. I appreciated Barnabas' intentions.

"Are you all right?"

"Of course I am. In what way?"

My father hesitated in a thoroughly uncharacteristic fashion, and I waited.

"You were . . . taken with him."

I said, "He has bedroom eyes," before I could stop myself.

Barnabas looked cynical. "I was afraid that you might be feeling—"

"I am," I interrupted carefully. "I'll get over it. I was lucky. It's safe to say there's no harm done."

"But you—" Barnabas started. He stopped. I knew he was thinking of the night of Clare's death. So was I, though not in quite the way he might have feared. I set about telling him so without speaking too frankly. Barnabas' generation does not talk easily about sexual matters.

My father sipped his Pinot Grigio and tried not to look too relieved at being able to change the subject. "Well, then?"

I said, "Jen Lassalle said one or two things before I left, but I'd worked most of it out for myself. It must have been Clare's plan to use the old typewriter to produce Forbes fakes. She'd wanted to sell the archive, but it really belonged to Georgina, and I don't think that Georgina had any intention of sharing."

Barnabas shrugged delicately. "The atmosphere . . ." he said, and stopped.

I said, "Don't. Anyway, the typewriter must have been one of the things that was sent from Italy when Forbes died, and Clare worked out how she could use it. With one or two really good forgeries, there'd have been enough money for both her and Georgina to take their cut."

"And then Roslin turned up," Barnabas said. "Somebody so steeped in Forbes' prosody that he could write a brand new 'unpublished' poem. Clare presumably couldn't believe her luck. It would be even more valuable—provided of course it was well enough done to be acceptable—and without the disadvantage that the original might pop up and cause trouble."

"Considering it was going to be announced that Clare Forbes had owned it all along, she could count on people not looking that closely," I said. "I don't know why she hatched the scheme to plant it on me."

Barnabas was remembering. For a moment, he almost looked amused. "She never could leave well enough alone, that girl. I suspect she concluded that if the thing was found in your possession, you would be forced to pay handsomely for it just to keep the matter quiet, or at least they could have recruited you to help them sell it in the trade. Clare probably regarded the plan to embarrass you as an insurance policy. And Roslin was hungry."

"Hungry?" But when I remembered what Jay had said to me in the pub, I'd known all about that, too. Jobless. Without a marriage or a reputation. With a trial pending that would ruin him, whether he was found guilty or not. He'd had no choice: either find something so remarkable that he might hope to recover the life he had planned, or give it up and—what? Drive taxis?

"Clare always enjoyed manipulating people," Barnabas said softly, still remembering. "Fred, myself, Georgina, Roslin . . ."

"Roslin?" I exploded. "Mr. Manipulator himself? Honestly, Barnabas! He probably made love to her," I said. "Well, flirted. She liked that kind of thing." I was thinking of her behavior with my father. "As he did to Georgina, and afterward to Gina, I suppose. Georgina was going to have lots of money and the rights to the archive. He needed her. But Gina . . ."

"Speaking objectively," Barnabas said, "more attractive than her mother, especially to a man with a taste for teenagers."

I let that pass.

"If you've finished torturing that bit of tomato," Barnabas remarked, "perhaps you'd like a dessert? Something with soothing chocolate? Or a cognac with me?"

I chose the second, and spent the time, while Barnabas waved at the proprietor and gave his order, by marshalling my own ideas. There was no point thinking I could get to bed until Barnabas knew everything and had commented.

"So they were all ready and eager for a confidence trick," Barnabas urged me on.

"I don't know whether Gina knew anything. But she had a crush on Jay. From what I heard this morning, Georgina was outraged. She couldn't bear it when Jay made a play for her daughter. I don't know whether it was jealousy that made her tell Gina to get out, as Gina believed, or an attempt to keep her out of trouble. Or both. Whatever, it didn't work because Gina already had an understanding with Jay. She got Natty to give her a lift down to Fairwood in his van; she must have phoned Jay from there, and he came down as soon as he could and picked her up. She's been hiding at the New Southgate ever since. Of course she couldn't go out, somebody might have seen her. I suppose she stayed there and read magazines and dreamed about getting married and going off to a glamorous new life with the sexiest man she'd ever known."

"What is happening to her?" Barnabas asked thoughtfully.

"Jen Lassalle told me that unless she's implicated, she'll be able to go and stay with the reverend cousin for a while. She'll be all right, eventually, because if Georgina

is convicted she won't be allowed to inherit my money . . .
Clare's money. That will go to Gina. Tough. In the mean-
time, I don't think Gina will find it a glamorous life in
Summertown, and the boys are too young for her."

"Tough," Barnabas agreed calmly. "It is the contempo-
rary equivalent of being sent off to a convent to repent. So
Roslin and Georgina . . ."

"Have been charged with murder and conspiracy to
murder. Georgina was screaming out the whole story from
the moment Ferry appeared until she vanished from sight
at the police station. She was trying to persuade them that
Jay had played the major part, and he was trying . . ." I
stopped. I could hear my own voice getting loud, and
there was no need for it.

"About Clare's bedroom door . . ." Barnabas said
hastily.

"There were two locked doors," I reminded him, "and
neither of them was really locked. Clare's plan was that she
would show me the typescript and then give it to Roslin to
hide in my car. When I found it, I was supposed to be overwhelmed with confusion and guilt, and, ready to be blackmailed, help out in any way I was asked. He fixed my car.
You were quite right that he disabled the lock. I didn't explain: we found one of the boxes in the hallway after
Richard and his mate had left. I assumed they'd forgotten it.
When Jay put it into the car for me, he must have fixed that
rear door. All he had to do was creep out afterward, pull the
catch for the bonnet from inside the car, and do something—detach the battery leads, take off the distributor cap:
I don't know. So when I tried to leave, it wouldn't start.
Probably it was Clare who phoned the AA, said she was
me, and canceled the call so I'd be there until she could produce the manuscript and Roslin had the chance to plant it

and then remove the putty or whatever it was from the lock."

"I wonder whether we would have been able to prove it was a forgery if they hadn't all been swept away by Clare's mad scheme?"

"Like you said, they were hungry." All of them: Jay, all three women . . .

"That extra key to the bedroom," Barnabas said suddenly. "He must have had the spare made as an insurance policy. She was supposed to unlock the door when he knocked, and give him the poem; but he had to drug her—he couldn't risk a noisy struggle—and being an intelligent man he had allowed for her to be unconscious by the time he arrived."

"And he'd judged it correctly: she must have put the key on her bedside table and fallen asleep. He got in with his own key. Then he found it was too dark to see the original and he had to use his spare to leave the door locked. With the key on the inside and me for an alibi, he must have thought he was safe. He didn't need the key anymore because he'd set up another way to leave. Jen Lassalle says he'd driven pitons into the brickwork above Clare's window and the window of the spare bedroom, where she'd put me, and he must have fixed a rope between them beforehand."

"Evidence of premeditation," Barnabas said sharply.

"The rope gave him a handhold so he could sidle along the brick coping from her window to the spare room. That's why it was absolutely essential that I didn't notice him either leaving the spare room or climbing back in."

"A dreadful risk," Barnabas remarked. "You could so easily have discovered what he was doing."

"No," I said. I would have preferred to leave it at that,

but Barnabas looked at me sharply. "It's true I'd been drugged too. Not as much as Clare, because she'd added a couple of her sleeping tablets to the stuff that she and I both had in that hot chocolate. Roofies—the stuff that the pathologist found in her blood. The stuff Roslin used at Macklin. I was so relaxed that there wasn't any chance I'd notice he had gone, or catch him coming back. Even at the end, when the fire had caught hold, he had trouble waking me. I suppose I ought to be glad he didn't just leave me there."

Our drinks arrived. Barnabas lifted his glass to me silently, and I returned the favor.

Then I fixed my eyes on the cognac. "He went in, re-locked her door, put a pillow over her face . . . He must have sprinkled the rest of his bourbon around and lit it with her lighter. He thought her death would be put down to an accident. Smoking in bed. He left through the window. I still don't know why he carried out Clare's plan for Canto Eight, when she was already dead."

"Perhaps," Barnabas suggested quietly, "because he saw it would give him a hold over you, too. Your freedom depended on the alibi he gave you, but his depended on your testimony, though you weren't supposed to notice that fact. And it might have prevented you asking too many questions in the event that you had wakened enough to see something."

I thought about that. It made sense. So did my new per-ception of Roslin as a man who had to control the women around him. Shame about the eyes.

"The funny thing . . ." I said.

Barnabas looked attentive.

"The funny thing is that the police had noticed the

spikes, but they didn't know what they were. Ferry assumed they'd been installed by some builder, or the telephone company. He's not a mountaineer."

"Good lord," Barnabas breathed. "Roslin . . . his potted biography said, 'mountain climbing.' "

So it had. "I suppose he doubled the rope so he could untie it and pull it through when he was back inside? Lassalle says they'll look for it in the house."

"Clare of course would have thought she was paying him off with glory. But he had decided he wanted Georgina's money as well," Barnabas said. I watched his lip curl and remembered that he too was an academic. Though not Jay Roslin's kind.

"He was screwing us all, one way or the other," I said. "He wanted everything."

A hungry man, as Barnabas had mentioned. But they were all hungry, weren't they? You had to remember that.

I realized that my father had been watching my face closely when he suddenly waved an imperious hand, and one of the Rocca family appeared at our table. "We have changed our minds," Barnabas announced. "My daughter will have an order of your chocolate cheesecake with double fudge sauce."

"If you think it will make me feel better . . ." I said.

Barnabas patted my hand. "It will," he said confidently. It did, a bit.

The Joanna Brady Mysteries by
New York Times Bestselling Author

An assassin's bullet shattered Joanna Brady's world, leaving her policeman husband to die in the Arizona desert. But the young widow fought back the only way she knew how: by bringing the killers to justice . . . and winning herself a job as Cochise County Sheriff.

DESERT HEAT
0-380-76545-4/$6.99 US/$9.99 Can

TOMBSTONE COURAGE
0-380-76546-2/$6.99 US/$9.99 Can

SHOOT/DON'T SHOOT
0-380-76548-9/$6.50 US/$8.50 Can

DEAD TO RIGHTS
0-380-72432-4/$6.99 US/$8.99 Can

SKELETON CANYON
0-380-72433-2/$6.99 US/$8.99 Can

RATTLESNAKE CROSSING
0-380-79247-8/$6.99 US/$8.99 Can

OUTLAW MOUNTAIN
0-380-79248-6/$6.99 US/$9.99 Can

DEVIL'S CLAW
0-380-79249-4/$7.50 US/$9.99 Can